This Time a Better Earth

This Time a Better Earth

—

A novel by
TED ALLAN

A Critical Edition
Edited and with an Introduction by
BART VAUTOUR

University of Ottawa Press | OTTAWA

The University of Ottawa Press gratefully acknowledges the support extended to its publishing list by Heritage Canada through the Canada Book Fund, by the Canada Council for the Arts, by the Federation for the Humanities and Social Sciences through the Awards to Scholarly Publications Program and by the University of Ottawa. The University of Ottawa Press also gratefully acknowledges the financial support provided by Editing Modernism in Canada.

Copy editing: Lisa Hannaford-Wong
Proofreading: Joanne Muzak
Typesetting: CS
Cover design: Lisa Marie Smith
Cover image: 1938 Topps Horrors of War Trading Card ≠89.

Topps Horrors of War Card used courtesy of The Topps Company, Inc. For more information about The Topps Company, please see our website at www.topps.com.

Library and Archives Canada Cataloguing in Publication

Allan, Ted, author
    This time a better earth / by Ted Allan; edited and with an introduction by Bart Vautour. -- A critical edition.

Includes bibliographical references.
Issued in print and electronic formats.
ISBN 978-0-7766-2163-0 (pbk.).--ISBN 978-0-7766-2165-4 (pdf).--
ISBN 978-0-7766-2164-7 (epub)

    1. Spain--History--Civil War, 1936-1939--Fiction. I. Vautour, Bart, 1981-, editor II. Title.

PS8515.E75T5 2015   C813'.54   C2015-900302-4
                                 C2015-900303-2

© University of Ottawa Press, 2015
Printed in Canada by Gauvin Press

To the men and women who fought against fascism.

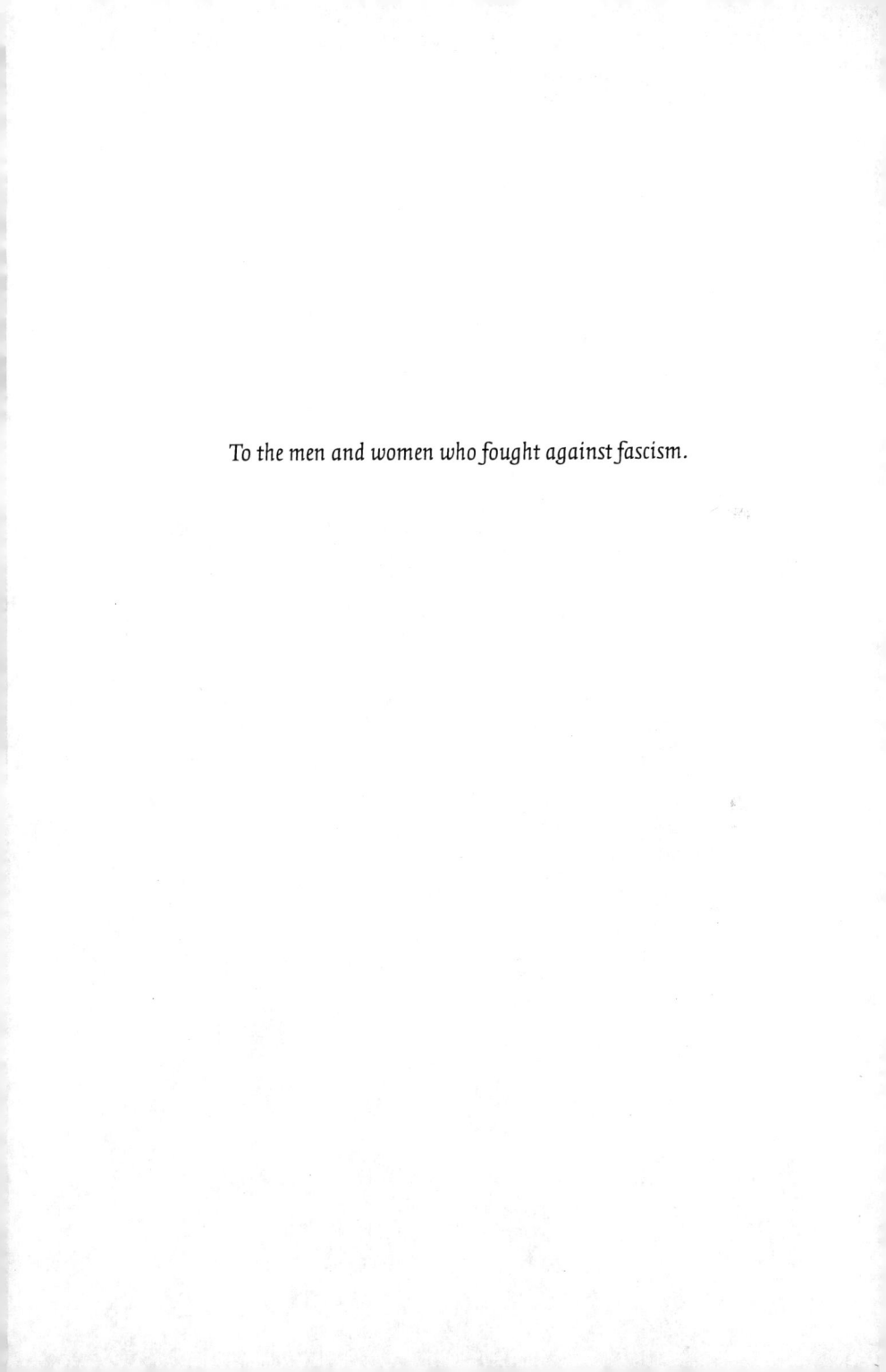

Contents

ACKNOWLEDGEMENTS xi

INTRODUCTION xiii

I. Ted Allan and The Spanish Civil War xv
II. Gerda Taro xx
III. Textual History and Reception xxiv
Bibliography xxix

·

THIS TIME A BETTER EARTH 1

·

EXPLANATORY NOTES 163

TEXTUAL NOTES 183

Introducing
Canada and the Spanish Civil War

This *Time a Better Earth* marks the first publication in a sub-series of the University of Ottawa Press's Canadian Literature Collection. The sub-series is comprised of Canadian texts in which the Spanish Civil War features prominently. These print publications emerge out of a larger scholarly and public project dedicated to the exploration of Canadian involvement in the Spanish Civil War. For more information, visit: spanishcivilwar.ca

BART VAUTOUR and EMILY ROBINS SHARPE
Co-directors of *Canada and the Spanish Civil War*

Acknowledgements

Working on this edition of *This Time a Better Earth* has been a long and rewarding process. Part of that process has brought me into contact with some very generous and helpful people. While some have invited long and rewarding conversations about the Spanish Civil War, others have visited archives and libraries on my behalf. In particular, I'd like to thank Emily Robins Sharpe, Dean Irvine, Kim Johnson, Vanessa Lent, Jennifer Logue, Cary Nelson, Deanne Fitzpatrick, and Erin Wunker. I'd like to thank Karen Smith at Dalhousie University Special Collections, the staff at Library and Archives Canada, the staff at the Marx Memorial Library in London, UK, and the staff at the J. F. K. Presidential Library and Museum for access to their Hemingway Collection. My colleagues in the Editing Modernism in Canada project deserve thanks for their collective support of the recovery of under-represented texts of Canadian literature. I would also like to acknowledge the Social Sciences and Humanities Research Council of Canada for their support of my doctoral studies, during which the bulk of the work on this edition was accomplished.

Extra thanks go out to Emily Robins Sharpe, whose many energetic conversations with me prompted our initiation of a larger project devoted to the recovery of Canadian cultural materials on the Spanish Civil War: spanishcivilwar.ca.

Introduction

When the Spanish Civil War erupted in 1936 it enlivened the hopes and fears of many people outside the borders of Spain. Indeed, for a few short years Spain became the epicentre of the clash between Western political ideals. In many ways, the conflict marked the beginnings of what would escalate into the Second World War. The Spanish Civil War, and the antifascist cause in particular, became a focal point for those writers interested in politics as well as culture. The conflict was central to the work of many transnationally well-known authors such as W. H. Auden, Martha Gellhorn, Ernest Hemingway, Josephine Herbst, Langston Hughes, André Malraux, Pablo Neruda, George Orwell, Stephen Spender, among many others. The literary works that took up the challenge of representing the Spanish Civil War continue to garner critical attention in many different national and transnational contexts. The Canadian literary contributions to the antifascist cause have not enjoyed the same sustained critical dialogue. Ted Allan's first novel, *This Time a Better Earth*, has been a casualty of this omission.

Originally published in 1939, the novel has not been reprinted until now. Few copies are available in libraries, and even fewer copies are available for purchase. This scarcity is disproportionate to the novel's significance both as an historical document and as an innovation in the history of the novel in Canada. Allan's novel evocatively depicts a model of transnational solidarity while sustaining candid and brutal descriptions of the horrors of war. While the maturity of its conception should not be underestimated, it is also a youthful novel—one written by Allan while in his early twenties—rife with the anxieties and fervour of coming into adulthood in the midst of large-scale political and social turmoil. This critical edition, published more than seventy years after the novel's initial publication, reacquaints readers with a poignant moment in world history while giving a sense of the Canadian involvement in that history.

My hope is that this new edition marks the initial stage in the recovery of the novel. It is my belief that the process of recovering cultural works that have been left out of canons and critical considerations begins with a reinsertion of the text into the cultural field without overcompensating for its absence with disproportionate critical reading. There are certainly instances in which literary texts have not been wholly neglected since their initial publication, and in those cases I think a detailed critical assessment is warranted in an editorial context. Irene Baird's *Waste Heritage* (1939), which also appears in the *Canadian Literature Collection*, is a good example of a literary text that maintained some circulation and critical attention (for example, the novel was republished in 1973). In that context, an editorial introduction should take stock of the critical history and help invigorate further critical conversations.

In the case of *This Time a Better Earth* (which has not had a significant readership since it was first published in 1939), I have aimed to present an editorially sound text with explanatory notes that provide historical context, geographical information and linguistic translation, as well as textual notes that give full attention to the ways in which different versions of a text can provide possible variant readings. While I can anticipate many critical frameworks through which the novel can be read, many contemporaneous texts with which the novel can be productively compared, and many ways the novel can help us rethink our current understanding of Canadian and transnational modes of citizenship, I would not like my editorial voice to determine the direction of what should be larger conversations involving students, teachers and interested readers. This introduction does not dwell on narrative techniques, styles or figurations. In short, I would like to see critical conversations emerge out of the text's recirculation. Ideally, the mode of editorial intervention practiced here allows room for wide scholarly and public engagement with the book in both cafés and classrooms. For me, the raison d'être of the literary-critical recovery of such a neglected text is to get others to do the talking.

While not wanting to dictate the terms upon which twenty-first-century readers take up this text, I would be remiss in not providing some basic contextual information. *This Time a Better Earth* is a work of fiction inspired by the Spanish Civil War and, as such, some knowledge of the conflict is required for an appreciation of the text. While few Canadian readers in 1939 would have been unacquainted with the events in Spain, it is no longer an assumption that can be taken for granted. I begin, therefore, with a short outline of the Spanish Civil War alongside a review of Ted Allan's part in the conflict. In addition to this short history on the Spanish Civil War, I include a brief section on a woman upon whom the narrative hinges: Gerda Taro. Finally, I provide a review of the novel's textual history and initial reception.

I. TED ALLAN AND THE SPANISH CIVIL WAR

What began as an attempted coup d'état in July of 1936 turned into a full-scale conflict lasting until the spring of 1939. The attempted coup began when a collection of Spanish Army generals conspired against the democratically elected government of the Second Spanish Republic, which had been elected just a few months previously. The rebellion was, in part, a response by the political right in Spain to the long-term reform policies upon which the Republic was founded in 1931. The military uprising began soon after the 1936 elections produced a coalition government of parties on the left—the Popular Front. The uprising was led by rebel Nationalists and supported by landowners, monarchists, Carlists, conservative Catholics and the fascist Flange. The ruling Republicans were supported by workers, moderates, the educated middle class, socialists and communists, as well as Catalan and Basque regionalists and anarchists. The socialist premiers Francisco Largo Caballero, Juan Negrín, and the liberal president Manuel Azaña y Días led the Republican government. The Republicans (also called Loyalists) were sent support from the Soviet Union and were also joined by a volunteer force, the International Brigades, in their defence of democracy. The Nationalists received troops, tanks and planes from Nazi Germany and Fascist Italy, which used Spain as a testing ground for new methods of tank and air warfare. France and Great Britain alleged they were attempting to prevent a general European conflict when they supported a non-intervention pact, which was signed in August 1936 by twenty-seven nations (Germany, Italy and the USSR included). The right-wing Spanish General Francisco Franco commanded a professional army in Spanish Morocco, also know as the Army of Africa, which was blockaded by Republican warships until Hitler and Mussolini provided him with transport aircraft to get his troops into Spain. It was the arrival of Franco and his army that turned the failing coup into a longer conflict. Franco consolidated power and became the leader of the Nationalist cause during the course of the war.

The Nationalists' initial campaign seized much of northwest Spain and parts of the southwest. In the autumn of 1936 Franco's troops advanced on Madrid, but the initial assault failed and they were met with defeat in their subsequent attempts to encircle the city—at Boadilla in December 1936, Jarama in February 1937 and Guadalajara in March 1937. In April 1937 the indiscriminate bombing of the town of Guernica by German planes, famously commemorated by Pablo Picasso, became well known across the globe and helped gain the Republicans widespread popular support. However, this popular support for the Loyalists did not transform into governmental or military support from the Western democracies.

Gradually, the Nationalists—with the continued support of Hitler and Mussolini—wore down the Republicans. Late in 1938 the International Brigades were disbanded. Franco eventually launched an offensive that advanced to the Mediterranean, separating Catalonia from the rest of the Republic. Barcelona fell in January 1939, and Madrid fell in the last days of March 1939. The Republic, which had given great hope of a more just future to a whole generation who had either suffered or inherited the trauma of the First World War and the Great Depression, was defeated. The onslaught of the Second World War quickly grabbed the world's immediate attention, but Spain remained in the hearts and minds of those who had experienced the hope of the cause—those who were certain that the antifascist fight would usher in a better, more just world.

Much of the history of the Spanish Civil War has been written from outside of Spain. This is, in part, because Franco's regime lasted until his death in 1975. During his lengthy dictatorship, writing that shed negative light on the nationalist cause was forbidden. Michael Petrou suggests in *Renegades* that, as a result, histories of the Spanish conflict tend to have more of an international focus than they would had they been written by Spaniards, and non-Spanish historians have been criticized for highlighting the international elements of the war. Petrou acknowledges the criticism—that the conflict had deep roots in Spain's class and regional divides—but only "to a point" because "the conflict was also played out on the international stage" (5). Apart from official intergovernmental affairs, such as Hitler's assisting the Nationalists with his Condor Legion (Air Force) and France and Britain's participation in the Non-Intervention Committee (to name only a few instances), there was much transnational involvement from around the globe at the level of non-governmental organization. The formation of the International Brigades was an example of the global character of the conflict. Coming from many different countries, men and women volunteered to fight alongside Spanish antifascists in defence of the democratically elected government. According to Hugh Thomas, approximately forty thousand internationals fought for the Republic, and a solid portion of those volunteers travelled from Canada (982).

While there have been previous histories of the Canadian participation in Spain by Victor Hoar, William Beeching, and Mark Zuehlke (all of which merit reading), the most recent and comprehensive is Michael Petrou's *Renegades: Canadians in the Spanish Civil War* (2008). By way of introduction, Petrou asks an important question:

Canadians in the 1930s had little obvious reason to feel as if their own lives and fates were entwined with those of Spaniards. Spain was, after all, far away. Its inhabitants spoke a different language. Few Canadians could trace their origins to Spain or had any relatives there. The two nations might as well have belonged to different worlds. And yet, between 1936 and 1939, almost seventeen hundred Canadians chose to fight in the Spanish Civil War, of whom more than four hundred were killed. Why? (3)

Though the answer is complex and larger in scope than can be covered in these introductory remarks, the question remains vitally compelling. Why did so many Canadians risk life and limb to go to Spain? In part, the motivation to go to Spain came out of a growing animosity toward the emergence of far-right politics both at home and abroad. The conditions that brought about this understanding and attitude in the Canadian context were a mixture of economic, political, ecological, class, xenophobic and colonial circumstances. The world was in the midst of the Great Depression, and Canada was hit particularly hard: Canadian agricultural workers suffered because of ecological disaster; the Conservative government of R. B. Bennett had done little to relieve the most blatant effects of mass unemployment; recent immigrants to Canada were subject to the racist anxieties of the dominant cultures; and, more and more people became aware of the rise of barely latent fascism in Canada, especially the support given to fascism by the Catholic Church (which had greater repercussions in Quebec). Many of the volunteers were unemployed men. Others were recent immigrants who were fearful of the rise of fascism in their European homelands. Still others were dedicated communists who thought that Spain would be a springboard for global revolution. Although the reasons for volunteering were often diverse, the vast majority of the volunteers were united in their potent antifascist beliefs. Whatever the particular motivation, the fact remains that almost seventeen hundred Canadians were compelled enough by the plight of the Spanish Republic to make their way to the Iberian Peninsula to fight fascism.

When the Canadian volunteers started arriving in Spain they joined the International Brigades, with most of the English-speaking Canadians joining the Abraham Lincoln Battalion as part of the XV International Brigade. Non-English-speaking Canadians were often placed in battalions of the International Brigades organized by mother tongue. A separate battalion was formed for the Canadian volunteers early in the summer of 1937: the Mackenzie-Papineau Battalion. The battalion, which also housed many American volunteers, was named after William Lyon Mackenzie and Louis-Joseph Papineau, who were leaders of the 1837 pro-democracy rebellions in Upper Canada (Ontario) and Lower Canada (Quebec).

The volunteers—the men and women who actually made their way to Spain—were not the only Canadians who took notice of the events shaking Europe.

Spain became an obsession for many in Canada. Committees were formed in support of the Republic, speaking tours were organized, rallies were held, and money was raised. More than ever, Spain saturated the news. With the concurrent rise of news agencies, photo agencies and transnational networks of mass communication, accounts of what was happening in Spain were making their way around the globe in quick succession. The Spanish Civil War became part of the Canadian public imaginary. The artistic community adopted Spain as one of the most rigorously represented subjects of the time. Indeed, the anti-fascist cause in Spain helped to reorganize some of the prevailing aesthetic principles circulating throughout Canada. In the midst of the conflict, for example, Spain acted as a catalyst for the meta-poetic expression of modernism in some Canadian poetry. Even a *partial* record of poets who have written on the events surrounding the Spanish Civil War reads like an anthology of modernist poetry in Canada even though many of these Canadian poets aren't recognized troubadours of the Spanish Civil War: Patrick Anderson, Louis Dudek, Ralph Gustafson, Irving Layton, Leo Kennedy, A. M. Klein, Kenneth Leslie, Dorothy Livesay, P. K. Page, E. J. Pratt, Sir Charles G. D. Roberts, F. R. Scott, Raymond Souster, A. M. Stephen, Miriam Waddington, Patrick Waddington, Joe Wallace and George Woodcock, among others. Canadian fiction was also to feel the reverberations of Spain for quite some time. In retrospective novels Spain is often treated as a sort of character in itself, or an ideal of (often masculine) social expression, or the catalyst for a character's action, or (ironically) a socialist utopia. Spain plays a major part in Malcolm Lowry's *Under the Volcano* (1947), Hugh Garner's *Cabbagetown* (1950/1968), Hugh MacLennan's *The Watch That Ends the Night* (1959), Mordecai Richler's *Joshua Then and Now* (1980), which was dedicated to Ted Allan, Mark Frutkin's *Slow Lightning* (2001), Denis Bock's *The Communist's Daughter* (2006), June Hutton's *Underground* (2009) and, most recently, Stephen Collis's *The Red Album* (2013). During the conflict itself, two novels with strong Canadian connections were published (though not in Canadian editions) that deal directly with the events in Spain: Charles Yale Harrison's *Meet Me on the Barricades* in 1938 and Ted Allan's *This Time a Better Earth* in 1939. Unlike much of the fiction listed above, these two novels have all but disappeared from the Canadian literary imaginary.

Ted Allan was one of those Canadians who, for one reason or another, decided to go to Spain. Born Alan Herman in Montreal in 1916, Ted grew up in Montreal's working-class Jewish neighbourhood. He began writing at a young age and, like so many other writers of his generation, adopted a pseudonym. The moniker stuck. He was known as Ted Allan both in print and in person for the rest of his life. The change in name was concurrent with his growing involvement with leftist politics in Montreal. He later penned a self-portrait of this time in *Love is a Long Shot*, which won the Stephen Leacock Medal for Humour in 1985. He joined and wrote journalism for the Communist Party of Canada, and it was in that capacity, at the age of twenty, that he was sent to Spain, along with Jean Watts of Toronto, to cover the conflict for the *Daily Clarion* and the monthly magazine *New Frontier*. While in Spain he joined an acquaintance from Montreal, Dr. Norman Bethune, and acted as Political Commissar for Bethune's Blood Transfusion Unit. When Allan returned to Canada in August 1937, after eight months in Spain, he set about writing *This Time a Better Earth*, wherein he fictionalized his experiences of the conflict. Shortly after his return from Spain, Allan moved to New York where he met and married Kate Lenthier (née Schwartz), the widow of a comrade who had fallen in Spain and with whom he would have two children: Julie Allan and Norman Bethune Allan. Before moving to England in 1954, Ted spent time living in New York, Mexico and Los Angeles. Toward the end of his life, Allan returned to Canada and settled in Toronto, where he remained until his death in June 1995. Allan lived a full and storied life. As *This Time a Better Earth* was his first book, written when he was very young, the comprehensive details of his very full life lie somewhat outside the purview of this edition. As this introduction is being written, his son, Norman Allan, is preparing a biography of his father.[1]

Allan became prolific in multiple genres. He worked for years in the theatre, he wrote children's stories, radio dramas, journalism, short stories, screenplays, and he continued to write novels. He was perhaps best known for *Lies My Father Told Me*, his screenplay about the Montreal Jewish community of the 1920s, for which he earned an Academy Award nomination in 1975 for the writing of an original screenplay. *Lies My Father Told Me* won a Golden Globe for best foreign film in 1976. At the same time, "[t]o many Canadians, to the Chinese, and to the Left of all countries," Terry Goldie suggests, "he is known for his collaborative biography of the Canadian socialist physician Norman Bethune" (4). The biography, *The Scalpel, the Sword: The Story of Dr. Norman Bethune* (1952), was co-authored with Sydney Gordon. It has been reprinted many times over, revised in 1971, and translated into many languages. Though Bethune died while Allan was still very young, Allan was involved with representing Bethune for the rest of his life. In addition to the biography, he wrote an obituary for Bethune, multiple newspaper articles, and a screenplay (*Bethune: The Making of a Hero*, starring Donald Sutherland and Helen Mirren).[2] While Bethune became a lasting spectral figure for Allan, the famous communist doctor does not play a significant role in *This Time a Better Earth*. The doctor introduced in Chapter 10—Doc Woods—may be loosely based on Bethune. While Bethune seems largely absent from *This Time* a *Better Earth*, another historical figure who played a substantial role in Spain pervades the novel: Gerda Taro. Taro was a figure who was recognized as a vital representative in the antifascist cause—a martyr even—yet she too disappeared from public memory.

II. GERDA TARO

This Time a Better Earth, much like Allan's own life, is haunted by the figure of Gerda Taro. Born Gerta Pohorylle in Stuttgart in 1910 (she is often incorrectly said to be born in 1911), she was a woman who would have profound influence on the history of photography and who Allan fictionalized as Lisa Kammerer in *This Time a Better Earth*. Just prior to her birth, Taro's parents arrived in Stuttgart from eastern Galicia. She was educated in Stuttgart, but spent a year in a Swiss boarding school before returning to Stuttgart to attend a college of business (Schaber, "The Eye" 12). In the early 1930s, the Pohorylle family moved to Leipzig amidst the rise of the Hitler-led National Socialists. Taro, along with her two brothers, became politicized and maintained loose affiliation with the Sozialistische Arbeiterpartei Deutschlands (Socialist Workers' Party [SAPD]). The Nazis arrested her in March 1933. Upon her release, it was obvious that she must leave Germany.

Taro left for Paris in the autumn of 1933, and after a year in the city she met the Hungarian-born Endre Ernö Friedmann, who called himself André while in Paris. Schaber suggests that it was after a two-month holiday on the island of Sainte-Marguerite with André in the summer of 1935 that Taro began taking photographs. "Out of this leisurely, untroubled holiday," Schaber writes, "there developed a relationship based on mutual assistance that would have a profound impact on the history of photography and the history of the Spanish Civil War" (14). André began to instruct Taro in photography and she, in turn, became a sort of manager for his photojournalism career. By October of 1935, André's friend Maria Eisner—the founder of Alliance Photo—hired Taro as an assistant, and within six months she received her first press card from the Amsterdam-based ABC Press Service. Just prior to the attempted coup in Spain, André and Taro came up with an ingenious idea that would have far-reaching effects: they invented the persona of Robert Capa, a famous and successful American photographer. They created a backstory for their character and began collaborating under that moniker. Taro eventually invented "Gerda Taro" for herself. Schaber writes that their "pseudonyms and their self-penned legend, which resonated with the success of the international stars of the time—Frank Capra and Greta Garbo—created a projection screen on which they intended to be the protagonists" (17). Apart from the anti-Semitism of Nazi Germany, their adoption of new names was doubtless a reaction to the growing resentment directed towards refugees in France.

While they created new names for themselves, the attribution of the actual photojournalistic work is more complex. They created separate personae, but the creation of Robert Capa was, according to Schaber, "their joint photographic project, as Gerda also published her photographs under the concept 'Capa'" (16). Taro and Capa also published under the photo byline REPORTAGE CAPA & TARO. Subsequently, Taro also used the red-stamped signature PHOTO TARO for her own, independent projects (18). Some photographs bear more than one accreditation. Given all the different options, it has often been difficult to come up with a definitive attribution.[3] Capa went on to reach substantial fame while the recognition of Taro's role receded. Schaber provides some explanation: "While Capa's photos were absorbed into the historiography of the Spanish Civil War, the partnership with Taro slowly transmuted into a love story central to his biography. The question became ever more unclear—and even less important—as to whether Gerda Taro has herself been a photographer" (34). Let there be no mistake: Taro was an exceptional and meticulous photographer. Throughout 1936 and 1937 Capa and Taro went back and forth between Paris and Spain. In Madrid, they became part of the expatriate community that included Ted Allan. They were on the set of Joris Ivens's film shoot of *The Spanish Earth*, which was scripted by Ernest Hemingway. They shot photos of workers at a munitions factory in Madrid. They were at the offensive of the Navacerrada Pass (immortalized in Hemingway's *For Whom the Bell Tolls*). They covered the Second International Congress of Writers for the Defence of Culture in Madrid and Valencia. In short, they documented all aspects of life related to the conflict in Spain. In early July they took a short leave in Paris, where they celebrated Bastille Day. Taro returned to Spain alone, with Capa staying on in Paris.

On 25 July 1937 Taro and Allan travelled together to the Brunete front. Despite being ordered away from the fighting, Taro, with Allan in tow, rushed toward the fighting to take photographs. After enduring aerial bombardment for several hours and having run out of film for her camera, Taro and Allan began their retreat. They jumped on the running board of a car that was taking the injured to a field hospital. The fascist planes returned and caused large-scale confusion on the road. A tank struck the car. Gerda died in hospital the morning of 26 July. Allan survived and returned to Canada after a period of convalescence in Paris.

Taro's death propelled her into a type of martyrdom. After being laid out in Madrid and Valencia, her body was taken to Paris. Allan also went to Paris, where he wrote a short narrative about Taro's death in *Ce Soir*. According to Schaber, once her body was in Paris, "the French Communist Party organized a memorial service verging on a state funeral, intended to generate political effects that would resonate far beyond personal sorrow" (31). Further, she suggests that

> [f]ollowing the calls from unions, political parties, and Spanish solidarity committees, on August 1, 1937, tens of thousands gathered for the funeral cortège, their number including many prominent literary and political figures. The funeral was a spectacular manifestation of international solidarity with the Spanish Republic. (31)

For a period of time Taro remained a popular figure of solidarity. In mid-August, *Life* magazine published an article entitled "The Spanish Civil War Kills Its First Woman Photographer." One of the more baffling representations of Taro appeared in 1938 in the United States. The Gum, Inc. company of Philadelphia portrayed her death on a trading card in their *True Stories of Modern Warfare* series. Presumably marketed to young people, the colour illustration on the front of the card depicts Taro—she is prone on the ground, having just dropped a camera—surrounded by explosions and retreating soldiers. A very cartoon-like tank is already upon her. On the back of the card is the following account of her death:

> Probably the first woman photographer ever killed in action, pretty Gerda Taro covering the Spanish Civil War for the Paris "Ce Soir," was crushed by a Loyalist tank during the great battle of Brunete on July 26, 1937. The Loyalists had taken Brunete, lost it, taken it again, and then lost it. Gerda Taro had left Brunete once in the retreat, and then decided to join the Loyalist rear guard in the city. For almost an hour she had crouched with a remaining battalion under Rebel bombardment. Finally she hopped on the running board of a press car. Suddenly, as part of the Loyalist counter attack, a tank, cruising blind, careened into view. With an unexpected swerve the creeping, shell-spitting monster bumped the daring young woman from her perch and crushed her beneath the revolving lugs! She died the following morning in the Escorial Hospital[,] her husband-photographer, Robert Capa, at her side. (n. pag.)

For a series that advertises itself as *True Stories of Modern Warfare*, there are certainly some glaring errors: the accident was on 25 July; the car was carrying wounded soldiers as well as Taro's cameras; and Capa was neither her husband nor was he at her side, since he was in Paris at the time. Perhaps the "horrors of war" were enough without highlighting what the card's audience may have deemed to be the impropriety of a "pretty" unmarried woman amongst thousands of male soldiers.

Capa, along with fellow Hungarian André Kertész, put together *Death in the Making*, a volume of photos taken by both Capa and Taro while they were in Spain. It was published in New York in 1938 with a preface written by the American journalist Jay Allen. The preface tells his story about first seeing Gerda—in the Hotel Grand Via in Madrid—and being too intimidated to speak to her because she had already gained the status of a legend:

> Legends? There is no knowing how they come into being. From out of the million acts of heroism preformed by humble people every day, they do arise and it is usually when there are men there to write and sing the deed. For love sometimes. I may be wrong but I feel that Gerda Taro, already legend in that last of the world capitals, Madrid, will grow. Much will be written and much more unwritten until later. (n. pag.)

Jay Allen's foresight is eerie. *Death in the Making*—Capa's homage—is dedicated to Gerda Taro, "who spent one year at the Spanish Front, and who stayed on" (n. pag.). True to the spirit of their collaboration, the photos are not attributed to either Capa or Taro. In a way, this has played a role in the large-scale disappearance of Taro from public memory. After the initial public recognition, Taro's legendary status began to wane in the face of the urgency of the Second World War and the rising fear of leftist politics that accompanied the onset of the Cold War. It is only now, seven decades after her death, that the life and work of Taro is regaining ground in the public imagination. This edition of *This Time a Better Earth* means to contribute to resuscitating that public memory of Taro.

Aside from Schaber's comprehensive biography, François Maspero has written the memoir *Out of the Shadows: A Life of Gerda Taro*. Maspero's memoir was written and published in French by Éditions du Seuil in 2006, with an English translation appearing in 2008. Multiple gifts of substantial archival material to the International Center of Photography (ICP) from Cornell and Edith Capa (Robert's brother and sister-in-law) have enabled the ICP to mount an exhibition of Taro's work from September 2007 through January 2008 in New York. The exhibition has catapulted the figure of Taro into a full cultural renaissance. The exhibition—*Gerda Taro*—became one of the ICP's "Travelling Exhibitions," visiting the United Kingdom, Italy, Spain, the Netherlands and Germany.[4] More recently, the ICP has received what they have called the "Mexican Suitcase," which contains a collection of previously undocumented film negatives from Capa, Taro and David Seymour (known as "Chim"). Among this collection of Spanish

Civil War photos are three previously undocumented film rolls from Taro's final days of shooting the Battle of Brunete just before her death.[5]

Toward the end of his life, Ted Allan revisited Gerda's death. In an unpublished typescript held in his archives, Allan interweaves his own prose from his short story "Lisa" and *This Time a Better Earth* with a reflection on how Gerda's death shaped his life. At the outset of the typescript—a twenty-two-page prose narrative entitled "That Day in Spain"—Allan tells the story of how Hemingway, having read some of his short stories in Spain, suggested that it is always a good idea to put stories away "for ten years and then go back to them" (3). He ends "That Day in Spain" with the following reflection: "As for Hemingway's advice to the young writer, I have taken it ten times over. He told me to put a story away a mere ten years before reworking it. I've waited almost fifty years with this one and I don't think its [sic] all that better than the first version I wrote in 1937" (22). It has now been over seventy years since Allan's novel of Spain was published, and we now have the chance to reread an early version of the story. Moreover, the republication of Allan's novel also provides us with an opportunity to think about why this particular story has been forgotten.

III. TEXTUAL HISTORY AND RECEPTION

As is often the case, Allan's novel is the culmination of many different pieces of writing. He went to Spain as a journalist and wrote many short pieces for the *Clarion*. He wrote three pieces for the Toronto-based journal *New Frontier* that reveal the wide-ranging scope of his involvement in the Spanish Civil War. In "Blood for Spanish Democracy" (February 1937) he gives an exposé on the Servicio Canadiense de Transfussion de Sancre (Canadian Blood Transfusion Service), which was directed by Bethune. The two-page report on the transfusion service ends with a call for Canadians to give financial support to the Canadian Medical Mission to Spain. Allan's second piece for *New Frontier*, "Bombardment at Albacete" (May 1937), is a signature example of narrative reportage. "Full moons are nice to watch when they don't act as a spotlight for bombing planes" (16), he opens in a pointed manner of expression typical of the genre. Throughout the short narrative Allan gives an indication of the style he later employed when writing about aerial bombardment in *This Time a Better Earth*. Allan's third instalment for the magazine, "An Interview with Ernest Hemingway" (July–August 1937), uses the famous author's credentials to put forth an argument for literature as a tool for witnessing atrocity. According to Hemingway's suggestion that it was absolutely necessary for writers to see Spain, it follows that the fate of literature depended upon bearing witness to atrocities in much the same way as the fate of global democracy relied upon defeating Franco.

Allan also wrote the introduction to a pamphlet issued by the Friends of the Mackenzie-Papineau Battalion called *Hello Canada! Canada's Mackenzie Papineau Battalion* (1937). The pamphlet is dominated by A. E. Smith's narrative of his visit to Spain, but also includes excerpts from letters of the Canadian volunteers in Spain. Allan writes in the introduction about talking to the Canadian volunteers and their wish for him not to exaggerate their experiences: "They used to tell me to make sure that when I wrote I would not depict them as heroes, that I would make sure to show the horror of war, what it did to people, how insane it was, and they wanted me to tell the people back home why they came here and why even mountains could not stop them" (4). He stays true to their wish. Much of the three-page introduction does not frame the volunteers as heroes but rather as resolute Canadians following in the footsteps of those who have fought for democracy in Canada (Louis Papineau and William Lyon Mackenzie) as well as those Canadians who demonstrated determination and prowess when fighting in other conflicts. He suggests that "we Canadians must never forget that on the battlefields of Spain, Canada has once again made a name for herself in shaping the history of the world" (5). Allan draws on a rhetoric that would frame Canadian participation in the Spanish Civil War as a continuation of the nation-building project. Yet, in a culture that repeatedly tells itself through official war discourse that the Canadian "nation" came to maturity through sacrifice at war in Europe, contemporary Canadian commemorations all too conveniently forget about this socialist, antifascist cause.

Allan began publishing in the United States upon his return to North America. He had two pieces published in *New Masses*, a leftist journal based in New York. Allan's first piece for *New Masses*, "A Gun is Watered" (January 1938), is a short story made up of dialogue between two International Brigade volunteers—Butterley and Durnor—out of which he develops *This Time a Better Earth*'s Milton "Milty" Schwartz. The story sets the scene for the way in which Milty—of "the Brooklyn Schwartzes"—becomes increasingly attached to his machine gun, which he names "Mother Bloor." Allan's second piece for *New Masses*, "Canada's Fascists: Duplessis Lets Them in the Back Door" (June 1938), does not focus on Spain. Rather, it is an intricate three-page report on the rise of fascism in Canada in which he gives a damning portrait of Premier Hepburn of Ontario, Premier Duplessis of Quebec, and Adrien Arcand, the leader of the fascist National Social Christian Party. In July 1938 Allan published in *Harper's Magazine* "Lisa: A Story," an early version of the penultimate chapter of *This Time a Better Earth*.

Although these short pieces give a sense of Allan's writing leading up to the novel, there is no known surviving manuscript. There are only two apparent choices of text to use for the basis of this edition of *This Time a Better Earth*.

The British edition of *This Time a Better Earth*, published in London by William Heinemann in 1939, serves as the copy text for this critical edition. William Morrow published the American edition of Allan's novel in New York in early 1939. The British edition was published a few months after the American edition. This sequence of publication presents the possibility that Allan might have had the opportunity to make changes to the text of the British edition after the publication of the American edition. This edition takes that possibility seriously and favours an editorial rationale that privileges the latest published version that appeared during the author's lifetime.

There is a very remote possibility that McClelland & Stewart published a Canadian edition of *This Time a Better Earth* in 1939. Reviews of the novel appeared in the *Winnipeg Free Press* and *Saturday Night* that signal McClelland & Stewart as the publisher. A thorough search has yielded no editions or imprints bearing the name of McClelland & Stewart. George Parker's history of the publisher indicates the possibility of a McClelland & Stewart imprint. Carl Spadoni and Judy Donnelly include *This Time a Better Earth* in their bibliography of McClelland & Stewart imprints in a list of those titles they were unable to locate (762). In a 1939 issue of *Quill & Quire*, a list of Canadian representatives for international publishing houses includes McClelland & Stewart as the Canadian representative for William Morrow. From this we know that there was a formal agreement between the two publishers. A search of other novels published by Morrow in 1939 signalled the existence of *Ordeal: A Novel* by Nevil Shute. In the case of Shute's novel, a separately printed leaf has been tipped in that indicates its publication as a McClelland & Stewart imprint. A wide-ranging search yielded no physical evidence of a McClelland & Stewart imprint or edition of *This Time a Better Earth*, but that does not conclusively rule out the possibility that one existed. There may have been a McClelland & Stewart edition: possibly a small print run—perhaps one hundred copies—issued to secure copyright and to distribute to reviewers. In all probability the Canadian imprint or edition, if it existed, would be from sheets of the American edition or sheets from rented or borrowed plates. Even so, the possibility that *This Time a Better Earth* made it to the point of being a McClelland & Stewart imprint is remote. It is more likely that McClelland & Stewart acted as the Canadian agent or publicist on behalf of William Morrow. If this is the case, two of the Canadian reviewers did not look to the title page for publication information. Instead, the reviewers or the publishers of the *Winnipeg Free Press* and *Saturday Night* presumed that the distributor, McClelland & Stewart, was also the publisher.

Whatever uncertainty may have existed among reviewers about McClelland & Stewart's role in the publication process, the novel was well received in Canada. The reviewers understood that the conflict in Spain was not just about Spain.

Indeed, Edward Dix, in his review in *Saturday Night*, goes as far as to suggest that *This Time a Better Earth* is "not just another novel about Spain as we may begin to number novels about Spain, but a justification in the eyes of people other than Spanish that what has happened in Spain, and what is still happening there, in not primarily the concern of Spanish people" (20). While many reviewers focus on the action within the novel, it is notable that the Canadian reviews, as if judging his performance of Canadian character, focus on the character and affiliations of the author to a greater extent than do the British or American reviews. For example, J. R. MacGillivray, in the 1939 "Letters in Canada" section of the *University of Toronto Quarterly*, focuses on the relationship between Allan's political affiliation and literary skill—as if the two are normally mutually exclusive—when he writes that "Mr. Allan, like several of his characters, is probably a Marxist, but at no point does he allow political enthusiasm to vitiate the clarity and integrity of his impression of the Spanish war" (295). The review in the *Winnipeg Free Press*, which suggests Allan's prose "bites clean and swift, like the hand grenades the International soldiers could not have," rhetorically calls Allan's reliability into question: "He says that the names of his characters are fictitious. But their actions, their courage, their clear-sightedness and their wounds and their deaths have a terrible reality" (Ted Allan Fonds [TAF], box 4, file 22).[6]

This Time a Better Earth was also widely reviewed in the United States. Unlike many of the Canadian reviews, the novel's American reviews tend toward comparison and discussion of the book's status. The reviewer for the *San Francisco Chronicle* writes that *This Time a Better Earth* "is an exciting picture of an exciting time. May the other novels that are sure to be written against the same background be as good" (TAF, box 32, file 37). John T. Appleby, in the *Washington Post*, claims that Allan has written "the best story to appear in English about the recent Spanish war since [Elliot Paul's 1937] 'Life and Death in a Spanish Town'" [sic] (TAF, box 4, file 22). Howard Rushmore, in *People's World* of San Francisco, speculates that many more writers will take up the subject of the North American contribution to the fight against fascism in Spain and surmises that there is "room and plenty of it for such fiction but until it is written Mr. Allan's book stands out as a pioneer work of more than average stature and significance" (TAF, box 4, file 22). Leland Stowe, winner of a Pulitzer Prize in 1930, gives the book praise in a review for the *New York Herald Tribune*. Stowe focuses on the respect *This Time a Better Earth* pays to the volunteers when he suggests that the novel has not "smirched these unsung heroes with propagandistic oratory or sloppy emotionalism" (TAF, box 4, file 22). "Rather," he continues, the novel "has achieved a remarkably honest and accurate portrait, yet one which will appeal for its narrative value alone. . . . One reason for this, I think, is that Ted Allan is a good reporter" (TAF, Box 4, file 22).

British reviewers were supportive, to be sure, but perhaps slightly less enthusiastic in their support than were their American and Canadian counterparts. This lukewarm support may be a result of the novel's focus on the American and Canadian volunteers and not the British contingent of antifascists who travelled to Spain. The British reviews tend to fixate on the novel's descriptions of bombardments and warfare in general. The reviewer for the *Perthshire Constitutional* focuses on the many scenes of bombardment, calling *This Time a Better Earth* a "breathless and immeasurably stirring account of six young volunteers who go to the aid of Republican Spain" (TAF, box 4, file 22). The review in the *Yorkshire Post* also makes much of the novel's description of modern war and praises the novel for not romanticizing war and presenting heroes who are often afraid. The review in the London-based *Daily Worker* asks: "Have you ever felt like a balloon that has just been deflated; as though you had been all tense and then suddenly relaxed[?] That is just how you will feel after reading Ted Allan's description of an air raid. Everybody should read this book if only for that section alone" (TAF, box 4, file 22). Contrasted with a concern for the novel's political affiliations, romantic plot, or portrayal of transnational camaraderie, the British fixation on Allan's descriptions of modern warfare—especially aerial bombardment—uncannily anticipates the Blitz, which shook Britain starting in early September of 1940.

Since the initial flurry of reviews in 1939 and 1940 that gave the book general approval, critical treatment of the novel has been very sparse. The only scholar to date who has given more than passing reference to the novel is James Doyle. In his landmark survey of Communist literature in Canada, *Progressive Heritage: The Evolution of a Politically Radical Literary Tradition in Canada*, he suggests that *This Time a Better Earth* is the only Canadian novel of the 1930s that "rigorously follows the formulas of socialist realism" as opposed to the more common social realism (122). Doyle contends that the book demonstrates "how socialist realism, using a Canadian subject with international and revolutionary implications, could reach beyond the limited readership of [Communist] Party members and sympathizers toward a mass audience" (225). Doyle also suggests that the critical neglect of the novel "is regrettable, for Allan effectively integrates the technique of socialist realism with such elements of the novelistic appeal as battlefield adventure and romantic love" (123). In addition to the book's demonstrated socialist realism, the book also has much to add to critical discussions of the reportage novel—a literary genre that takes a subjective or partisan stance and imitates or approximates a piece of journalistic or factual writing. Not only is *This Time a Better Earth* exemplary for its reportage stylistics, it puts the subject of journalism at the forefront of the narrative. The protagonist, Bob Curtis, is a Toronto newspaper journalist prior to his arrival in Spain who is seconded to radio broadcasting for the Republicans upon his arrival in Spain. What is more, Bob falls in love with Lisa, a photojournalist. Indeed, many within the cast of characters Bob meets in Spain are journalists of one stripe or another. But the novel's relationship to journalism represents only one of many possible avenues for enquiry. The novel's representation of Jewish characters and erasure of their Jewish heritage in the fictionalization of the narrative (principally the story of Allan and Taro) deserves closer scrutiny. The representation of antifascist partisanship, the oscillations between national allegiance and transnational solidarity, and the place of the novel within a tradition (Canadian or otherwise) of war novels outside the Spanish context are just a number of critical concerns that *This Time a Better Earth* provokes. There are scores of critical questions to be asked of Allan's novel. The hope is that with this new scholarly edition one of the major global events of the twentieth century—the Spanish Civil War—can be revisited through the perspective of a Canadian author who witnessed the war and who took seriously the making of a better earth.

NOTES

1. An electronic draft of the biography can be found online at http://www.normanallan.com.
2. For information on Bethune, see books by Allan and Gordon, Shephard and Lévesque, Clarkson, Hannant, Lethbridge, Petrou and Stewart.
3. Richard Whelan addresses at length this problem of attribution—which photos were Capa's, which were Taro's.
4. *Gerda Taro* is curated by Irme Schaber, Taro's biographer; by Richard Whelan, noted Capa biographer, photo historian and, until his recent death, Curator of the Capa Archive at ICP; and by ICP Associate Curator Kristen Lubben.
5. For more information on the "Mexican Suitcase" and a larger collection of Taro's photographs visit the ICP website http://www.icp.org.
6. TAF is the abbreviation used in parenthetical notes and the list of works cited to indicate the Ted Allan Fonds (MG 30-D388), Library and Archives Canada, Ottawa.

BIBLIOGRAPHY

Allan, Ted. "A Gun is Watered." Monthly Literary Supplement of *New Masses* 26.3 (11 Jan. 1938): 25–28.
———. "An Interview with Ernest Hemingway." *New Frontier* 2.3 (July/Aug. 1937): 16–17.
———. *Bethune: The Making of a Hero*. Dir. Phillip Borsos. Perf. Donald Sutherland, Helen Mirren, Helen Shaver, Colm Feore. Filmline International, 1993.
———. "Blood for Spanish Democracy." *New Frontier* 1.10 (Feb. 1937): 12–13.
———. "Bombardment at Albacete." *New Frontier* 2.1 (May 1937): 16–17.

———. "Canada's Fascists: Duplessis Lets Them in the Back Door." *New Masses*. 27.13 (21 June 1938): 18–20.

———. *Chu Chem: A Zen-Bhuddist-Hebrew-Musical*. Mosaic to Music by Mitch Leigh. Lyrics by Jim Haines and Jack Wohl. London: Ted Allan Productions, 1966.

———. *Chu Chem: A Zen Buddhist-Hebrew Novel*. Montreal: Éditions Québec, 1973.

———. *Don't You Know Anybody Else?* Toronto: McClelland & Stewart, 1985.

———. *Dr Ah Chu and Jonah's Egg*. Ill. by Philippe Germain. Montreal: R. Davies, 1996.

———. "Dr. Norman Bethune Dies in China." TS. Box 2, file 25, TAF.

———. Introduction. *Hello Canada! Canada's Mackenzie Papineau Battalion, 1837–1937, 15th Brigade I. B.* By A. E. Smith. Toronto: Friends of the Mackenzie Papineau Battalion, 1937.

———. "Lies My Father Told Me." *Canadian Short Stories*. Ed. Robert Weaver and Helen James. Toronto: Oxford University Press, 1952.

———. *Lies My Father Told Me*. Dir. Ján Kadár. Pref. Marilyn Lightstone, Yossi Yadin, Len Birman. Pentimento & Pentacle VIII Productions, 1975.

———. *Lies My Father Told Me: A Play with Music*. Toronto: Playwrights Canada, 1984.

———. "Lisa: A Story." *Harper's* 177.2 (July 1938): 187–193.

———. *Love is a Long Shot*. Toronto: McClelland & Stewart, 1984; Scarborough, ON: Avon Books, 1985.

———. *My Sister's Keeper*. Toronto: University of Toronto Press, 1976.

——— [Edward Maxwell, pseud.]. *Quest for Pajaro*. London: Heinemann, 1957.

———. "That Day in Spain." TS. Box 32, file 30. TAF.

———. *This Time a Better Earth*. New York: Morrow, 1939; London: Heinemann, 1939.

———. *Willie The Squowse*. Ill. by Quentin Blake. Toronto: McClelland & Stewart, 1977; London: Cape, 1977; New York: Hastings House, 1978.

———, and Roger MacDougall. *Double Image: A Play in Three Acts*. London: Samuel French, 1957.

———, and Sydney Gordon. *The Scalpel, The Sword: The Story of Dr. Norman Bethune*. Toronto: McClelland & Stewart, 1952; Boston: Little, Brown, 1952; London: Hale, 1954. Revised Edition: Toronto: McClelland & Stewart, 1971; Boston: Little, Brown, 1971; New York: Monthly Review Press, 1973.

Allen, Jay. Preface. *Death in the Making*. By Robert Capa. New York: Covici-Friede, 1938. N. pag.

Appleby, John T. "Spanish War Novel." Rev. of *This Time a Better Earth* by Ted Allan. *Washington Post* 9 Apr. 1939. Box 4, file 22, TAF.

Beeching, William C. *Canadian Volunteers: Spain 1936–1939*. Regina, SK: Canadian Plains Research Center, 1989.

Beresford, J. D. Rev. of *This Time a Better Earth* by Ted Allan. *Manchester Guardian*, 18 Aug. 1939: 5.

Bock, Dennis *The Communist's Daughter*. Toronto: HarperCollins, 2006.

"The Camera Overseas: The Spanish Civil War Kills Its First Woman Photographer." *Life* 16 Aug. 1937: 62–63.

Capa, Robert. *Death in the Making*. New York: Covici-Friede, 1938.

Clarkson, Adrienne. *Norman Bethune*. Intro. John Ralston Saul. Toronto: Penguin Canada, 2009.

Dix, Edward. "Fighters For Spain." Rev. of *This Time a Better Earth* by Ted Allan. *Saturday Night* 11 Mar. 1939: 20.

Doyle, James. *Progressive Heritage: The Evolution of a Politically Radical Tradition in Canada*. Waterloo: Wilfrid Laurier University Press, 2002.

Flexner, Eleanor. "Novel about Spain." Rev. of *This Time a Better Earth* by Ted Allan. *New Masses* 7 Mar. 1939: 26–27.

Frutkin, Mark. *Slow Lightning*. Vancouver: Raincoast Books, 2001.

Garner, Hugh. *Cabbagetown*. White Circle Pocket ed. Toronto: Collins, 1950. Toronto: Ryerson, 1968.

Goldie, Terry. "Ted Allan." *Canadian Writers, 1920–1959*. Ed. W. H. New. *Dictionary of Literary Biography*. 68. Detroit, MI: Gale Research Co., 1988. 3–6.

H., L. R. "Death on Spanish Afternoons Has Terrible Reality." Rev. of *This Time a Better Earth* by Ted Allan. *Winnipeg Free Press* 20 May 1939. Box 4, file 22, TAF.

Hannant, Larry, ed. *The Politics of Passion: Norman Bethune's Writing and Art*. Toronto: University of Toronto Press, 1998.

Harrison, Charles Yale. *Meet Me on the Barricades*. New York: Charles Scribner's Sons, 1938.

Hemingway, Ernest. *For Whom the Bell Tolls*. New York: Charles Scribner's Sons, 1940.

Hoar, Victor, with Mac Reynolds. *The Mackenzie-Papineau Battalion*. Toronto: Copp Clark, 1969.

Hutton, June. *Underground*. Toronto: Cormorant Books, 2009.

Ivens, Joris, dir. *The Spanish Earth*. Contemporary Historians, Inc., 1937.

Laker, J. H. C. Rev. of *This Time a Better Earth* by Ted Allan. *Perthshire Constitutional* 22 Sept. 1939. Box 4, file 22, TAF.

Lethbridge, David, ed. *Bethune: The Secret Police File*. Salmon Arm, B.C.: Undercurrent Press, 2003.

Lowry, Malcolm. *Under the Volcano*. New York: Reynal & Hitchcock, 1947.

MacGillivray, J. R. "Letters in Canada: 1939: Fiction." *University of Toronto Quarterly* 9 (1940): 289–301.

MacLennan, Hugh. *The Watch That Ends the Night*. Toronto: Macmillan, 1959.

Maspero, François. *Out of the Shadows: A Life of Gerda Taro*. Trans. by Geoffrey Strachan. London: Souvenir Press, 2008.

Muir, Kenneth. "This Time a Better Earth? War, Melodrama and Oranges." Rev. of *This Time a Better Earth* by Ted Allan, *The Mask of Dimitrios* by Eric Ambler, *Learn to*

Love First by Amabel Williams-Ellis, and Golden Apples by Marjorie K. Rawlings. Yorkshire Post 9 Aug. 1939. Box 4, file 22, TAF.

Parker, George L. "A History of a Canadian Publishing House: A Study of the relation between Publishing and the Profession of Writing, 1890–1940." MA thesis, University of Toronto, 1969.

Petrou, Michael. Renegades: Canadians in the Spanish Civil War. Vancouver: UBC Press, 2008.

Rev. of This Time a Better Earth by Ted Allan. Booklist 1 Apr. 1939: 252.

Rev. of This Time a Better Earth by Ted Allan. Books 26 Feb. 1939: 5.

Rev. of This Time a Better Earth by Ted Allan. New York Times 26 Feb. 1939: 7.

Rev. of This Time a Better Earth by Ted Allan. Nottingham Guardian 24 Aug. 1939. Box 4, file 22, TAF.

Rev. of This Time a Better Earth by Ted Allan. Pratt, Autumn 1939: 27.

Rev. of This Time a Better Earth by Ted Allan. San Francisco Chronicle 26 Mar. 1939. Box 32, file 37, TAF.

Rev. of This Time a Better Earth by Ted Allan. Saturday Review of Literature 25 Feb. 1939: 20.

Rev. of This Time a Better Earth by Ted Allan. Times Literary Supplement [London] 19 Aug. 1939: 489.

Richler, Mordecai. Joshua Then and Now. Toronto: McClelland & Stewart, 1980.

Romer, Samuel. Rev. of This Time a Better Earth by Ted Allan. Nation 18 Nov. 1939: 557.

Rushmore, Howard. Rev. of This Time a Better Earth by Ted Allan. People's World [San Francisco] 25 Feb. 1939. Box 4, file 22, TAF.

Schaber, Irme. "The Eye of Solidarity: The Photographer Gerda Taro and Her Work During the Spanish Civil War, 1936–39." Gerda Taro. Eds. Irme Schaber, Richard Whelan and Kristen Lubben, 9–37. New York: International Center of Photography; Göttingen, Germany: Steidl, 2007.

———. Gerta Taro: Fotoreporterin im spanischen Bürgerkrieg. Marburg: Jonas Verlag, 1994. French ed.: Gerda Taro: Une photographe révolutionnaire dans la guerre d'Espagne. Paris: Anatolia-Éditions du Rocher, 2006.

———, Richard Whelan, Kristen Lubben, eds. Gerda Taro. New York: International Center of Photography; Göttingen, Germany: Steidl, 2007.

Shand, Jimmy. "For a Better Life." Rev. of This Time a Better Earth by Ted Allan. Daily Worker [London] 15 Aug. 1939. Box 4, file 22, TAF.

Shephard, David A. E., and Andrée Lévesque, eds. Norman Bethune: His Times and his Legacy/son époque et son message. Ottawa: The Canadian Public Health Association/L'association canadienne d'Hygiène publique, 1982.

Shute, Nevil. Ordeal: A Novel. New York: William Morrow, 1939.

Spadoni, Carl, and Judy Donnelly. A Bibliography of McClelland and Stewart Imprints, 1909–1985: A Publisher's Legacy. Toronto: ECW Press, 1994.

"Spanish War Notebooks: Prison Life, Brigade Story." Rev. of *Spanish Prisoner* by Peter Elstob and *This Time a Better Earth* by Ted Allan. *Inquirer* [Philadelphia, PA.] 29 Mar. 1939. Box 4, file 22, TAF.

Stewart, Roderick. *The Mind of Norman Bethune*. Rev. ed. Markham, ON: Fitzhenry & Whiteside, 2002.

Stowe, Leland. "With the Lincoln Brigade: A Stirring Novel of Americans Fighting in Spain." Rev. of *This Time a Better Earth* by Ted Allan. *New York Herald Tribune* 26 Feb. 1939. Box 4, file 22, TAF.

"The Spanish War Kills its First Woman Photographer." *Life* 16 Aug. 1937: 62–63.

Thomas, Hugh. *The Spanish Civil War*. Revised and Enlarged Edition. New York: Harper & Row, 1977.

Wallace, Doreen. "Spain to the Balkans." Rev. of *This Time a Better Earth* by Ted Allan, *Balkan Express* by Leonard Ross, and *Beauty Absolute* by Guy Fletcher. *Sunday Times* 20 Aug. 1939. Box 4, file 22, TAF.

West, Anthony. Rev. of *This Time a Better Earth* by Ted Allan. *New Statesman & Nation* 12 Aug. 1939: 254.

Whelan, Richard. "Identifying Taro's Work: A Detective Story." *Gerda Taro*. Eds. Irme Schaber, Richard Whelan, and Kristen Lubben, 41–51. New York: International Center of Photography; Göttingen, Germany: Steidl, 2007.

———. *Robert Capa: A Biography*. (1985). Rpt., Lincoln: University of Nebraska Press, 1994.

———. *This is War! Robert Capa at Work*. Göttingen: Steidl, 2007.

Wilson, John. *Norman Bethune: A Life of Passionate Conviction*. Montreal: XYZ Publishing, 1999.

"Woman Photographer Crushed by Loyalist Tank." Trading Card. *True Stories of Modern Warfare*. No. 89. Philadelphia: GUM, INC., 1938.

Zuehlke, Mark. *The Gallant Cause: Canadians in the Spanish Civil War 1936–1939*. Vancouver: Whitecap Books, 1996.

This Time a Better Earth

A *novel by*
TED ALLAN

One generation passeth away, and another generation cometh: but the earth abideth forever. *Ecclesiastes*

The song *Abe Lincoln* by Earl Robinson and
Alfred Hayes, quoted on page 34 and 35, is by
permission of the copyright owner, Bob Miller,
Inc. The sonnet on page 163 and 164 is by Joseph Seligman,
killed in action in Spain at the age of 23.

FIRST PUBLISHED 1939

All names of characters are fictitious, except names of Spanish leaders, generals, or civil personages: Largo Caballero, Juan Negrin, José Miaja, Francisco Franco, Queipo de Llano, Colonel Gonzales (El Campesino), Colonel Enrique Lister, Dolores Ibarruri (La Pasionaria).

This Time a Better Earth

PART I

1

Slowly the sun was dropping beyond the mountains and slowly we climbed the narrow winding path leading to the top of the hill. It was high in the Pyrenees. The air was fresh with the moisture of the clouds. The sky was a rainbow of colours fading quietly into night.

The beauty of the surroundings was lost to us. We were tired and hungry. Our minds were filled with a million thoughts of the past, the present and what was to come. Home and yesterday were like a dream, and to-day was a dream and to-morrow was real. That's how it had been for a week now since we had left our homes in Canada and the United States.

Climbing the mountain, I thought to myself that all of us had been too young to know what life was and too young to believe we could die. And now we were on our way to life and death. To life, because we were going to fight for what we believed in. To death, because one dies fighting for what one believes in.

These are strange thoughts to think while one is climbing a mountain. They are strange thoughts to think, anyway, for us, young men in our early twenties.

What had Spain been to us? Nothing but a coloured space on the map and unclear pictures of señoritas and Don Juans playing guitars, and castles and bullfights and red wine and olives. We were conscious of Spain for the length of time it took us to read the newspapers or the pages of a book. Then Spain ceased to exist. It played no part in our existence or development. Perhaps we dreamed of castles and romance, but we had grown up and lived and thought and laughed and suffered without Spain—and now Spain was where we were going to live or die.

It is good to laugh at yourself. I tried to laugh climbing the Pyrenees, but somehow I could not laugh. I tried to see myself as one of sixty American and Canadian boys grunting and panting on their way to Spain, and I wanted to see how funny it was, me being here. But it wasn't funny and it frightened me. It frightened me because I could not laugh and say: "What the hell."

When I was a little boy going to school and things went wrong, I tried hard to smile and say, what the hell, there's lots of time, I'm little. And when I got older and had to look for a job and couldn't find a job because there were too many of us, even then I could laugh at myself and say, what the hell, there's lots of time, I'm young yet. I could say, like all of us had to say, wait, some day you'll find a place for yourself in this world and you'll look back at now and laugh. Always I had been able to say that to myself—there's lots of time.

But it hit me suddenly like a blow on the face that I could say that no longer. There was no more time...for me or for them.

We who were climbing into Spain had told ourselves that there was no place in the world for us as long as the world was what it was. But now we had a place and it frightened me because I knew that I could not laugh any more and say, what the hell.

We were young enough to feel that here in Spain we would learn to know ourselves; we would find ourselves. There was more. There was the feeling that we were helping change the destiny of the world.

I thought of this. I thought of life back home. It had been good sometimes. There were things that tickled you and gave you joy. Little things, like a walk in the park on Sunday, or the way a bird sang, or the way a butterfly looked in the sun, or flowers and the feel of grass on your bare feet, or words uttered by friends, or even a street or a house.

I became conscious of it as I climbed. Those things I had accepted the same way as I accepted breathing. There was music and books and ideas and things to learn. There were always things to learn, about men and animals and plants, about science and history.

My thoughts were confused. I have so many things to learn yet and so many things to see.

The individual and society, I kept muttering to myself. Is that what the writers meant? The conflict between the individual and society...was this it? Was my fear an expression of that?

What was it that had suddenly made me afraid? I asked myself. The closeness of it?

Again I thought of life back home. There had always been a sun by day and a moon and stars by night and spring came when winter was over and summer followed spring and then the leaves fell to the ground. And every year it was the same and would be the same year after year.

But it was *not* always the same. I knew *that*. Men could change the world. *We* could change it.

I thought of my boyhood and then suddenly becoming a man. There had been no happiness in adolescence; only pain and more confusion.

I thought of all this as I climbed. I saw familiar faces of my childhood and my youth and saw my father and my mother and pitied them because they did not understand.

But was it the prospect of death frightening me now? I didn't know. I knew that now I could no longer say there was time: weeks, months and years. There was no turning back now. Always I had been able to turn back, but now there was no turning back. To turn back now would mean that my words were like the air hissing out of a toy balloon.

The sunset was fading swiftly into evening and I saw the first stars glittering in the sky.

I am not a fake, I kept telling myself in my new bewilderment on the mountain. I am not.

And my friends. What were they? They were different from me and yet the same. We were of the same generation, the new generation.

And as we climbed and our breathing came in short painful spurts, I thought of each of them. Of Alan Linton, Lucien Poirer, Milton Schwartz, Harry Sills and Doug Rollins. We had become friends on the ship. We told ourselves that we were the vanguard of our generation. We used these words, not to dramatise ourselves, but merely to tell each other that we understood why we were going to Spain to fight.

Were we brave? I asked myself. Were we braver than the others who did not come?

No. We were not braver. We understood. That was all.

And I who had always laughed to hide my fears could no longer laugh, so I said to them as we climbed: "Let's sing a song."

"Okay, Bob, what?"

Alan Linton was six foot three when he stood up straight. He had been an actor in Boston and the kind of a guy Harry Sills said he wouldn't have liked back home, because back home Harry would have thought Alan a "bohemian." And "bohemians," according to Harry, "do nothing but waste good time," so Alan couldn't possibly be a "bohemian" because he was on his way to join the Abraham Lincoln Battalion.

Alan had a mellow tenor voice and a sort of charm that made Harry say he was the kind of a guy that you knew would never get married. But Alan happened to be married, had been for a year, and so you were wrong again about Linton. He was twenty-three years old.

Harry Sills had been a coal-miner in Alberta and secretary of his union local. He was husky and squat and when he didn't speak through the side of his mouth you could hear him say things about philosophy and political economy and music and literature and trade unions. He was older than any of us, being twenty-eight, and had been married six years. He had two children, a boy and a girl, and he always told the story to anyone who would listen of how Jimmy had asked him to: "Bwing back free fathists, Daddy."

"Why three?" Sills had asked.

"Well, one for mommy, one for Edith and one for me," had been his son's answer. Harry showed us their pictures every time we were willing to look. That seemed to be his only weakness.

As we approached the summit of the hill, Doug Rollins, the negro stock-yard worker from Chicago, started to sing one of his songs. Doug had a clear baritone voice, "from imitating the hogs," he told us. "Contrary to what one would expect," he said, "I like the stock-yards." The reason he gave was that the wind coming from the south-west stank up the eastern section of the city where the rich lived, "making Chicago the only city in the world where the rich got a good whiff of the slums." He chuckled when he said it. He was always chuckling or laughing about something. He had the kind of laugh that started deep in his stomach and made his eyes close when it finally came out of his mouth. It was good to hear him sing.

Religion is somethin' for de soul,
But preacher's belly done get it all,
Preacher's bell-ee done get it all dey say—yip!

He had taught the song to us on the ship. We all joined in. You had to hiccough at the end of each stanza and each of us tried to hiccough louder than the other, but Milty was usually louder than any of us.

Milton Schwartz hailed from Brooklyn. He had been a member of the National Guard and was the only one of the six who knew anything about anything concerning a war. According to himself, he was the finest machine-gunner in the National Guard and could take a gun apart and put it together in the space of a split second. Milty said he wanted two things in Spain, a Soviet machine-gun and a speedy conclusion to the war because he had to get back and marry his girl, Susie.

"What makes you so sure you're going back?" Alan had asked.

Milty was surprised at the question. "There isn't a bullet made that has my name on it. They can't kill *me*." His confidence left us a little bewildered. "And another thing," he said, "Susie wouldn't like it if I didn't get back soon." That settled that.

Back home Milty had always wanted to be a radio announcer. So, on the boat and climbing the mountain he was continually practising. He practised by cupping his hands and prefacing almost everything he said with: "Good evenin', folks, this is Milton K. Schwartz comin' to youse tru the kertesy of the Haiseh Baigles Incorporated." Sometimes he changed the name of the sponsor. He had a stock number of radio jokes, like the one about using a razor-blade on your neck and so doing away with shaving for ever, and you laughed every time, not at the joke but because you were taken so by surprise.

We got to the summit of the hill panting and cursing. There was a three-quarter moon. It had become night so swiftly that you felt you had walked into it through a door. The Spanish guide raised his hand.

"Count off!" he shouted.

"One—"

"Two—"

"Three—"

"Four—" all down the line up to "Sixty."

"Bueno," said the guide.

Below us in the light of the moon we could see a church spire and the thatched roofs of homes. The town was nestled in a valley.

"Looks like a Hollywood setting," said Alan.

Beyond the town, on a rising hill, we saw something that looked like a castle. It turned out to be a fort. It was in this fort that we spent our first night in Spain.

A short distance down on the main highway were waiting trucks. We had successfully evaded the non-intervention patrols. We cut through a forest, off the path, and made our way to the road.

Lucien Poirer, the French-Canadian longshoreman from Montreal, suggested that we sing *Alouette*. Everyone wanted to sing. Singing somehow took away the strangeness.

Lucien had a nervous twitch of the eye and he didn't say much. But when he did, each word was given added meaning by an emphatic shut of the eye. Alan told him that the reason for this twitch was that he hadn't led a regular sex life. Lucien answered that the reason his eyes twitched was that he was trying to shut out the bad things in the world.

"An escapist," muttered Alan.

But the explanation was too simple. Milty said that if the explanation were the right one, Lucien would keep his eyes closed permanently after their first bombardment.

As we walked towards the highway, I thought of each of them and then suddenly wondered what the word "bombardment" really meant.

We sang *Alouette* and I looked up at the moon and wondered if it were the same moon I had always seen.

Then we came to the trucks and the Spanish chauffeurs hailed us and shouted: "Viva Norteamericanos." We piled in with a few tired whoops and cheers.

We had crossed the frontier.

2

The smell of the dormitory was so sharp it hurt your nostrils when you took a breath. We sat on our cots and groaned. It was hard breathing.

"Whew! It stinks!" Milty held his nose and took deep breaths through his mouth.

"Reminds me of Chicago." Doug had his nose in the air as he compared the odours.

The comandante of the fort introduced himself as Kuller. He was a little man, who spoke English with a German accent and who looked more like a poet than a soldier. He smiled sympathetically.

"The smell is bad, I admit," he said, "but it could not be helped. I believe this fort was built originally by the Romans and the toilets have never been changed since their day."

"How about giving us some gas-masks?" suggested Milty.

"That would not be such a bad idea, but we haven't many gas-masks, and those that we have are at the front." He smiled.

"Whew!" said Milty again.

"Now, not too much noise. Try to sleep. The other volunteers have travelled far and they are tired. You will not be here long." He said good night and went off.

There were about five hundred bunks, four hundred of which were already occupied by the volunteers from the European countries. The walls of the dormitory were about thirty feet high and there were ten little barred windows near the ceiling which were supposed to let in air.

Two small lamp bulbs hung from the centre of the ceiling, casting a sickly yellow glare on the forms of the sleeping men. There was a long narrow sink attached to the wall opposite the toilets. The toilets were not only unwalled, they had no seats. A water-pipe, creeping like grape-vine on the wall, supplied water for twenty-five taps hissing and trickling into the sink. It harmonised uncannily with the snores and sounds of the sleeping men.

"The stink symphony," grunted Milty.

On the walls were inscriptions in every language under the sun. The words *No Pasarán* were written everywhere and under them the equivalent in the native languages of the inscribers.

In the wing assigned to us were inscriptions in English. We could read them from where we sat on our bunks.

One read: "James O'Rourke. Born New York, 1914. Seaman. Passed through this perfume factory February 2, 1937. May Marx, Lincoln and Browder bless those who follow me. Salud and No Pasarán."

To the right of this we read: "Walter Kent. Born Winnipeg, 1916. Passed through this historic fort February 2, 1937. Long Live the People's Front of Canada and of Spain."

Under this, in a scrawly, shaky handwriting: "Isadore Gottlieb, Brooklyn, New York. Long Live the International Brigade. Long Live Democracy. But why they have toilets with no seats I'll never know. Salud."

Across the entire wall ran an inscription printed in block letters. We read this one out loud in unison:

"THIS PLACE STINKS. BUT SO DO A LOT OF THINGS IN THIS WORLD. REMEMBER WHY YOU CAME. KEEP UP YOUR SPIRITS. HOLD YOUR NOSES AND NO PASARÁN."

There was no signature.
We got under the covers.
"Good night..."
"Good night..."
After a while we fell asleep.

3

When I awoke next morning the sun was fighting hard to get through those ten little barred windows, but it was a losing fight. Ten miserable rays of sunshine flickered through like flashlights whose batteries were going dead.

My mouth felt like the morning after my first drunk. I spit up the dust and phlegm which had settled in my lungs during the night. There was noise of some five hundred men talking in almost every language on earth and the familiar sucking sound of soap under armpits as they washed at the sink.

I shook my head. My eyes were heavy. I listened to the sound from the washrooms. There was laughter. Men smacked each other across the buttocks. They were like children playing.

They were happy, happy to be here. It made me feel good looking at them.

The gang was up.

"Good morning. How'd you sleep?"

"Like a log. Whew! Let's get into some fresh air."

Milty decided to do setting-up exercises. He pranced around the cement floor and pounded his chest and let out loud ah-ah-ahs.

"Sounds like a whore putting on an act," said Alan.

Milty paid no attention and began shadow-boxing. "Got to keep in trim. My captain always said, he said: 'Boys, keep in trim.'" Milty flicked his nostrils with his thumbs in the manner of prize-fighters. Harry gazed on puzzled, shaking his head.

"So that's America," he finally said.

Alan grinned. "No. That's Brooklyn. Stop it, screwball. They think we're all like you."

Milty paid no attention. The Europeans gathered around him, open-eyed.

Milty's fists shot into the air. He let go a few powerful left jabs and a couple of lightning uppercuts and almost swung himself to the floor. Everybody laughed, but Milty was very tired.

Doug had his chin on his hand. "Tired?" he asked gently.

"Nope." Milty started touching his toes.

Doug and Alan made a dash for him and dragged him towards the taps. He howled. They stuck his head under a tap. "Achronists!" he yelled.

"Anarchists," Alan corrected, still holding his head. "Now, have you cooled off?"

"Aw, what the hell's the matter with you guys?"

"The honour of America is at stake," proclaimed Doug solemnly.

"Is there no freedom here? No free speech?" Milty asked.

"You're in the army now, boys," said Alan.

"Okay, okay…" His hair was dripping. "If I catch pneumonia…well, my death is on your hands."

"*You* can't die," said Alan.

The Europeans had been watching the little by-play with pleasant smiles.

All of us washed, but the proximity of the toilets made us lose our appetites for breakfast.

Lucien, who had taken part in the morning's proceedings with much batting of eyelashes and with no words, unburdened himself as we walked up the corridor into the square. "You know something?"

"What?" I answered.

"It stink," he said.

4

Breakfast turned out to be another test for us. It consisted of fried eggs and coffee and a hard cement-like bread. The men serving us told us it was coffee and we didn't argue, but the eggs swam in olive oil, rancid at that, and to drink the coffee you had to close your eyes and gulp fast. There was no sugar.

Lucien was doing the only talking for a change. "C'est la guerre," he kept repeating. "C'est la guerre."

We made our way from the mess-hall into the square of the fort and took long, deep breaths. A cool breeze came down from the Pyrenees and a rising morning sun was trying its best to make things pleasant for us.

The fort was surrounded by huge walls about thirty feet wide and fifteen feet high. There was a flight of stairs leading to the top of the walls in each corner of the square. We climbed to the top and sat down. From here we could see a green, peaceful-looking valley. Below us was the town with its pointed church spire flashing in the sun. A moat encircled the fort and a drawbridge connected a narrow road leading to the fort's wide red gates.

"It's just like in the movies," commented Milty.

Sitting there, I expected suddenly to see men in armour marching up the road led by knights on horses, and I could almost hear the sound of trumpets. But all we heard was the sound of birds and the rumble of men's voices from the square, and all we saw were ploughed fields stretching as far as the horizon.

In the distance were the Pyrenees rising high into the clouds.

"We're in Catalonia now, ain't we?" Milty asked.

"Yes."

"Hard to believe that we crossed that yesterday," said Harry, nodding towards the Pyrenees.

"It was a lousy climb," said Milty.

"Helps you keep in trim," said Alan.

"How far are we from Barcelona?" Milty asked. He waited for an answer.

"I don't know," said Harry. "Have any of you heard when we're going to get an address our folks can write to?"

"No. Probably find out this afternoon."

"Wonder if the food gets better at the front, or worse," said Doug.

"How far are we from Madrid?" Milty wanted to know.

"I don't know," Harry said. "What the hell is the difference?"

"I always like to know where I am, that's all. We shoulda bought a map."

"We'll have to buy some dictionaries first chance we get," mused Alan. "I'm going to try to learn as much Spanish as I can."

"My Spanish is good enough to get me along," said Harry.

"How do you say 'water'?" Milty wanted to know.

"*Agua.*"

"'I want'?"

"*Quiero.*"

Milty was satisfied. "Qu-i-ero awah. I'll have to try that out on some Spaniard."

"Try out '*cojones para tu,*'" suggested Alan.

Harry smiled.

"What's it mean?" asked Milty

"Try it out," insisted Alan.

"In Spain it's not such a bad word to use," said Harry. "One of the Spaniards who used to work in the mines with me used it the same way we use the word 'guts.' A man with cojones is a man. A man without it is a coward."

"I still don't know what it means," said Milty.

Harry told him what it meant.

"That's a good word to know," said Milty.

"Yes…"

"How long do you think it will last?" Alan asked suddenly.

"Who knows?" Harry shrugged. "Maybe a year. Maybe more. Your guess is as good as mine. It depends on so many factors…what England will do…what France will do…what America will do. If they decide to make a deal with the Fascists and then gang up on Spain and then on the Soviet Union, there will be years and years of undeclared wars. If they keep on sending more Italian troops, more German planes and munitions…you know the answer as well as I do."

"I betcha it doesn't last more'n a year. We'll run the bastards out on their asses before the year is up," said Milty.

"I hope you're right," said Harry.

Lucien fingered his chin. "I figure two year and den, going to be another world war."

I saw Alan staring ahead of him. "If I get it I want it clean. No steel. A nice clean bullet. Fast. Like that." He snapped his fingers.

"Anything special you want us to do after you get it?" asked Milty.

"Yeah, bury me. Don't let me lie on the field too long and decompose. I'd hate to think that I'm going to smell after I die. Let me die heroically, nicely, no mess." He stretched and yawned. "I'll have a few good last words on my lips. See that you guys hear them. My bones will fertilise the soil of Spain. Now there's a thought."

"If you're going into the trenches with such a fear of death," said Harry, "you'd better try to get transferred to a different kind of job."

"Aren't you afraid of death?" Alan asked him.

"Yes…we all are. But I'd stop talking about it if I were you."

"That's a damned good idea," I agreed.

"You'll excuse me, I have to leave the room," Lucien got up.

"And don't do anything around here. Go down to the wash-rooms," said Harry.

Lucien chuckled. "Don't worry." He made his way down the stairs.

We heard a burst of laughter. It came from Doug.

"What the hell are you laughing for now?"

"I was just thinking." Doug's shoulders shook. "Jesus! I was just thinking if suddenly I should be walking near the trenches and the Spaniards mistake me for a Moor."

"Very funny," said Alan. "They'd blast you full of lead."

"Well, it would be funny. It sure would be funny," said Doug. "I'll have to watch out.

We puffed at our last few remaining cigarettes we still had from home. Harry pulled at the grass. "You're like a bunch of kids on a picnic," he said.

Alan flicked his pipe against his teeth. He was the only one of us who smoked a pipe. We all smoked cigarettes except Lucien. He didn't smoke at all.

"Be sad if I die." Alan tapped his teeth with the stem of his pipe and smiled.

"Be sad if any of us die, but I'm not going to die so soon. I've got a lot of time on my hands yet," said Milty.

Alan grinned. "Well, you see, I'm the last of the Lintons. Ever hear of the Boston Lintons?"

"Naw. Ever hear of the Brooklyn Schwartzes?"

Alan drawled on. "The Boston Lintons who came to America on the *Arabella*. That, my friends, was the ship that followed the *Mayflower* by a few months or so."

"I've got a couple of brothers, so I guess it'll be all right," said Doug. "They can carry on the fair name of Rollins. Only one of them is a damned fool. The other is coming along fine. He'll carry on the name okay, I guess."

"And I've got a son," said Harry.

"My family name Curtis doesn't go out of extinction either if I die," I said. "I don't know about Lucien. But we'll have to preserve Alan for the sake of the Boston Lintons."

That seemed to be the cue for Milty to jump to his feet. "Ladees and gentlemen." He sounded like a circus-barker. "This is Milton K. for Kaker Schwartz, comin' to youse tru the kertesy of the Spanish Onion Incorporated Limited. Milton Schwartz of the Brooklyn Schwartzes what came over on the *Berengaria*, which you will kindly remember followed the *Arabella* around by a few weeks or thereabouts."

"Sit down, screwball," said Doug.

The dinner-bell rang for lunch.

"One more smell of olive oil and I join Franco," said Alan.

There was thick barley soup, lamb stew and hardly any olive oil at all, so we ate well.

Lucien announced proudly that he was learning how to use the toilets. Harry told him we were all very happy to hear about it.

When we got back to the square we saw the European volunteers drilling. They were divided into their national groups.

"Let's show 'em," said Milty.

He elected himself sergeant. About thirty American and Canadian boys formed into fours under his command.

"Count off!" barked Milton Schwartz.

"One—"

"Two—"

That part of it was easy.

He began barking out commands and things didn't go so well from then on. Some of us left-turned and some of us right-turned and bumped into each other. Sergeant Schwartz held his cheeks in his hands and moved his head back and forth in silent agony.

The Germans marched by us, chins in, chests out, arms swinging, all in perfect time. The beat of their feet echoed across the square. Milty decided it would be better if he had us standing in one place.

"When you march," he roared, "you look more like a picket line than a bunch of soldiers."

"Calm yourself, boy," advised Harry, "these days they move you around in trucks."

"With that army the war will last for ever," snorted Milty.

It was too hot for drilling.

"Halt and break ranks and go break your legs," was Milty's last command. He was sweating.

We went into the canteen, which was in another building facing the dormitory. A Frenchman was behind the counter. Orange pop sold for four centimos. There wasn't much sugar in the pop. Harry bought Milty a bottle of pop and patted him on the shoulders and said: "You did a fine job, considering." Milty looked disgusted.

We took our pop and sat at a table.

We noticed a large sign hanging on the wall.

"Your mailing address is c/o International Brigade, Albacete, until further notice."

"Must have put it up this morning. I'm going to write the wife and kids immediately." Harry got up from the table and came back with some post-cards and writing-paper.

All of us got down to the business of writing. I described to my mother how lovely the weather was, how beautiful the Pyrenees had been, and that I had already gained two pounds and was getting tanned fast.

"Are we allowed to mention the place we're at now?" Doug asked.

"Better not mention any places. Just write 'Somewhere in Spain'," Harry told us.

Milty managed to send off ten post-cards. He sent two to Susie because they had nice pictures and the remainder went to a host of friends.

By this time we were all out of our American and Canadian cigarettes. All we could buy now were a type of Spanish cigarette that we immediately nicknamed "pillow-slips" because they were loosely packed and the paper wasn't glued. Each end was twisted and the idea apparently was to buy real cigarette paper and roll your own. But the canteen was out of cigarette paper. Saliva had to serve as glue, and that dried up by the time you were half-way through a cigarette. The tobacco was strong and dry. Alan watched us smoking with a detached air while he quietly poured the loose tobacco from the "pillow-slips" into his pipe.

"We'll have to take up pipe-smoking," I said.

"Better stop smoking altogether," said Lucien. "It is not healthy, anyway."

"How about sleeping on the wall to-night?" Alan suggested to me.

"That's a good idea."

The others said they would rather stand the smell than the cold.

"If I spend one more night in that dormitory," I said, "my smelling apparatus will get so impaired that I won't know poison-gas from eau-de-Cologne."

While we were talking, Comandante Kuller walked into the canteen. He waved his hand in greeting and said Salud. He began distributing questionnaire cards. We were to fill them out and bring them to his office.

"How long do we stay here?" I asked him.

"You leave to-morrow morning," he answered.

"To-morrow morning!" Milty looked pleased. "Geez that's swell. We'll soon be in the trenches."

Alan and I eyed each other.

"Yes," said Kuller, "and to-night we are going to have a concert in the hall next to the dormitory. It does not smell so bad there. Each group will sing their national songs."

"That'll be great," boomed Doug.

"In your letters," Kuller said before leaving, "be sure and do not mention the names of any towns."

"Okay...."

"To-morrow," I said. "I wonder if we're going to get any training."

"That'll probably depend on the military situation, if we're needed right away, I don't think we'll get much training," said Harry.

"I'll teach youse how to handle a gun," Milty assured us.

"The faster we get into trenches, the faster the war will be over," said Lucien. We looked at him and smiled.

"That's the spirit," said Harry, "and don't worry, kids, we can't lose. Whether we live or die, we can't lose."

5

I got away from the others and walked by myself around the square and watched the sun dropping in the sky. The guys were playing cards in the canteen. It got cooler. I stared at the massive walls and at the groups of men conversing, and kicked at the sand. I felt lonely.

The walls had a depressing effect. I climbed to the top of one and looked down. It felt better being on top than in the square and not being able to see what was outside.

I'll be okay, I kept saying to myself. It's normal feeling this way.

To-morrow....I tried to picture in my mind what the trenches would look like. Sandbags. Barbed wire. I remembered some of the moving pictures I had seen.

Now, ole Abe Lincoln, a great big giant of a man was he...
Oh, you push the first valve down and the music goes round and round wo-ho-ho hoho and it comes out here.

I kept humming to myself.

Is it true what they say about Dixie?
Does the sun really shine all the time?

I sang song after song to myself. First the jazz songs and then some of the school songs.

In days of yore the hero Wolfe
Britain's glory did maintain
And planted firm Britannia's flag
On Canada's fair domain...

I looked around to see if anyone were listening.

O Canada, our home, our native land,
True patriot love in all thy sons command.
With glowing hearts we see thee rise,
The true north strong and free,
And stand on guard, O Canada, we stand on guard for thee.
O Canada, glorious and free,
We stand on guard, we stand on guard for thee.

If I keep this up I'll start weeping, I said to myself.
I wish Alan were here. He knows some music to the Rubáiyát.
I lay on my back and watched the sunset.

Come fill the cup and in the fire of spring...

I used to recite it to my girl friends. It impressed them.

Your winter garments of repentance fling,
The bird of time has but a little way to flutter
And the bird is on the wing.

What were the other poems I knew?
The quality of mercy is not strained...I had forgotten most of my Shakespeare... it droppeth as the gentle rain from heaven Upon the place beneath: it is twice blest...
My heart aches and a drowsy numbness pains my sense as though of hemlock I had drunk and Lethe-wards had sunk...
I had played the part of Bottom in second-year high school. The only thing I could remember was, the raging locks and shivering shocks shall break the locks of prison gates, the raging locks and shivering shocks...
I got up slowly and shook my head.
If I keep this up I'll be put in a strait-jacket before I see the trenches.
I made my way to the comandante's office. He was not in. I was about to leave the questionnaire card on his desk when I noticed someone sitting on a chair in the far end of the office.
It was a girl. She looked about twenty-one or twenty-two.
I stared.
She had blonde hair and was small and slim. She saw me staring at her and said something in German. I didn't answer. The session with myself on top of the wall still had me dazed. I wasn't sure I was seeing right.

"Eh, don't understand," I said finally. "Do you speak English?"

"Yes," came back the answer.

I approached her and fumbled with the card in my hand. She was wearing a white shirt open at the neck.

"Nurse?" I asked.

"No." Her lips were small and full. "Photographer," she answered, smiling. She had a row of white, even teeth. Her lips were moist, with the faintest suggestion of lip-stick.

"Too bad. I would have got myself wounded right away."

She smiled.

"My name's Bob, Bob Curtis. I'm from Toronto."

"Yes? I am from Berlin at the beginning...how you say?...at first, yes?"

"At first?"

"Mm," she pursed her lips and placed her forefinger on them. It was a small slender finger. "How you say?...oh yes, originally. I am from Berlin originally." She looked pleased that she had found the word. "But now I am from Par-ee. My name is Lisa Kammerer."

"Kammerer," I repeated, "that's a funny name."

"What is funny?"

"Kammerer...I don't know. It sounds funny. Lisa...I like Lisa. I didn't expect to find a woman here. It took me by surprise. You must forgive the way I stared at you at first."

"I thought you knew me, the way you looked at me," she said.

"Are you going to be here long?"

"In Spain? I think so. The comandante is getting for me a car to go to Valencia. Is that not fine?"

"That's very fine."

Kuller walked in. She got up and he said something to her in German and she looked happy. I gave him the card.

"Filled out?"

"Yep."

He read it out loud. "Robert Curtis. Twenty-one. Canadian. Birthplace, Toronto. Journalist. No military experience." He looked up. "Most of the Americans and Canadians have no military experience." He started to read the card again. "Member of the Communist Party...quite a few Communists from the United States and Canada. Also quite a few volunteers who do not belong to any political party."

"Yes..." I was half listening to him. I stared at her. "Yes, quite a few non-party people, yes."

He smiled. He spoke in German again to the girl and walked into another office.

"He has the car for me," she said.

"When do you leave?"

"Right away...."

"Well, I hope I see you again." I began to edge backward.

"I hope so too." She bent down to get her film camera lying underneath the chair.

"Perhaps I could write you," I said in as off-hand a manner as I could.

"Yes, of course." She took out a little book from her purse, tore out a page and wrote something down. "You can always write me care of the Prensa department, either Valencia or Madrid."

She looked uncomfortable under my direct stare.

"You're not married by any chance, are you?" in that same—what I hoped—off-hand manner.

She let out a peal of laughter. "No. Not yet. Are you?"

"No."

I kept edging backward. We shook hands and I said Salud and she said Salud and I realised I was holding her hand a little too long, so I dropped it and said good-bye a few more times and somehow found myself back in the square.

I took a deep breath.

I walked to the canteen. Alan was leaning against the wall outside.

"What's the matter, have you got cramps or something?" he asked.

"No...I was on the wall reciting poetry to myself and then I walked into the comandante's office and then I saw her."

"Saw who?"

"A dame. A blonde, a lovely blonde girl."

"In the comandante's office? He's doing well for himself."

"No, she's a photographer. She's on her way to Valencia." I shook my head. "That sure took me by surprise."

"I was wondering where the hell you had disappeared to. You say in the comandante's office? I think it's time I handed in my card. Did you get her name?"

"Lisa, Lisa Kammerer."

"You didn't waste any time." He started towards the office. I waited for him outside the canteen.

He came right back. "You've got something there."

"You saw her?"

"Yep. She's lovely."

"Did you speak to her?"

"Nope. I just saw her go into a car."

"Then she's gone?"

"Yep. Tough. Anyway, she was nice while she lasted."

Then the dinner-bell rang and we joined the gang in the mess-hall.

6

That night, before entering the dormitory, we made Alan light his pipe and puff fast. When he smoked the Spanish tobacco fast enough the smoke barrage could neutralise the smell of the toilets. We made our way between a row of bunks, passed through a door and entered a long low-ceilinged room.

Five planks across some chairs served as an improvised platform. The men were gathered five hundred deep and the place was fogged with cigarette-smoke. There was a low rumble of voices and an undercurrent of excitement.

Kuller climbed to the platform and beckoned for silence. He wiped his sweaty face with a big red handkerchief and announced in French, German and English that he would say a few words in each language. He spoke quietly and simply. When he finished his speeches in French and German, he blew his nose and cleared his throat, while we applauded.

"Volunteers from England, Canada and the United States," he began slowly, "it is my privilege to be the first to welcome you in the name of the People's Front of Spain and the glorious International Brigade. I do not have to say very much to you. I need not explain the situation. If you did not know the situation you would not be here now. The volunteers from North America are the second group to arrive. You are joining the ranks of a brigade which has become world famous in a few short, epic months. The volunteers from England, Germany, France, Italy and the other European countries came to Spain in those eventful November days when all seemed lost, when the fascists had entered the suburbs of Madrid. The people of Madrid then issued the slogan that has been heard around the world, No Pasarán. They shall not pass. They have not passed. They shall not. We have come here because we know that, on the battlefields of Spain, not only is Spain's future being decided, but the world's. Spain must become the tomb of fascism."

He stumbled for words. "I have just this to say to you and then we will go on with our concert. In the International Brigade there are no politics and no parties. There are no Communists, Socialists, Anarchists, Republicans...there are only anti-fascists. That same ideal which has brought all of us here is the basis of our discipline. You are enrolling in the People's Army of Republican Spain. Our job has just now begun. How long we will be needed I do not know. But as long as we are needed, that long we will stay. The military situation is still serious. We are outmatched in planes, in munitions, in all mechanical materials of war. But we are not outmatched in bravery and determination. Up till now the democratic nations, or better, the heads of these democratic nations, have seen fit to forsake Spain. We are answering for them. Internationals," a long pause, "this speech is longer than I wanted it to be. You know what I am trying to say. May our fight end in speedy victory."

We cheered.

Kuller beckoned for silence.

The concert was on.

A young German boy with flushed rosy cheeks was pushed forward by his comrades. His voice was low and hoarse and he was shy. He sang with his eyes gazing ceilingward. He was singing *Die Moorsoldaten*, the *Peat Bog Soldiers*, the song of the German concentration camp prisoners.

It was the first time many of us had heard the song. I felt a little choked inside, listening to this German boy singing it. The music had a low, haunting quality, and as I turned from the face of the boy and watched the guys, I saw they were tense, listening. And then his voice dying off, *Ins Moor, ins Moor*. He jumped off the platform and there was a silence and then the place shook and trembled with the cheers. The French group, the largest, made the most noise, shouting for an encore, but the German boy wouldn't sing again. He was too embarrassed. Kuller beckoned for silence again.

A man was pushed forward and hoisted to the platform. He was grinning self-consciously. Then he began to sing. He was an Arab and he sang a song that sounded like a Hebrew lament, only it was a happy song. The boys began to swing their bodies from side to side and laugh and clap their hands.

The Arab clapped his hands to keep time and the room was filled with laughing, clapping men. When he finished they wouldn't let him off the platform. He had to sing again, but this time he wasn't shy. His song was faster and he waved his hips and the men swung to and fro and some held each other and danced and everyone laughed.

I looked from face to face and each face smiled at me. I stared at a German, a Pole, a Frenchman, an Italian, and they laughed and nodded to me when they caught my eye. Milty, Harry, Doug, Alan and Lucien were grinning and keeping time with their hands. Milty started to dance with Harry and we all roared at the top of our lungs. We all looked at each other and laughed and swayed and hummed. There were no words spoken.

We began to push Doug to the front after the Arab had finished. Doug protested and said that he had a cold and that his voice was hoarse. We kept pushing him forward.

"Chantez!" roared the Frenchmen.

"Zing!" shouted the Germans.

"I never sung before so many people. Aw, listen, guys..." he pleaded.

We hoisted him to the platform. He fixed his pants and shuffled his feet and scratched his head.

"Honest-to-God I got a cold..."

"Sing!" we yelled at him. "Come on, sing the Abe Lincoln song."

That was Doug's song. It was Alan's too. They had taught it to us on the boat.

"Go ahead," said Alan, "I'll help you."

"Okay...okay..."

We surged closer. Doug licked his lips and kept on scratching his head. "Don't forget to come in at the right time..."

"Begin!" we shouted.

He cleared his throat, flashed us a sheepish smile, and began:

Now, ole Abe Lincoln, a great big giant of a man was he,

Those of us who knew the song declaimed: *Yessir!*

He was born in an old log cabin and he worked for a living,
Splittin' rails.
Now, Abe he knew right from wrong, for he was as honest as the day is long,
And these are the words he said:

We all came in on the chorus:

This country with its institutions
Belongs to the people who inhabit it,
This country with its constitution
Belongs to those who live in it,
Whenever they shall grow weary
Of the existing government,
They can exercise their constitutional right of amending it,
Or their rev-o-lution-ary right to dis-mem-ber or overthrow it.

By the time we had finished the chorus every man in the room was going wild and the excitement mounted like a wave pounding over a ship. Doug grinned from ear to ear and when we finished the chorus, he started another verse:

> *Now Abe was close to the ground tho' he towered up six-foot four,*
> *Bare feet.*
> *And his heart was as big as the whole country with room for more,*
> *Black folk too.*
> *He never forgot from whence he came tho' he landed in the White House and got*
> *great fame,*
> *For Abe was a working man.*

When the last notes of the chorus had died down the smell of the fort was forgotten and so were the flippancy and the jokes and the words and the fears.

I felt a strength in me. I wanted to hug everyone and kiss everyone. We all grinned at each other and patted one another on the back and said things in strange languages and said Comrade or Camarada or Salud or No Pasarán, or said nothing, but smiled and shook hands.

Something warm bathed my insides.

Kuller stood on the platform and beamed. He kept wiping his face with the back of his hand. He looked like a mother watching her brood.

"Ach, ist gut," I heard him say, "ist gut."

Milty looked at me and said quietly, "Geez…"

Alan was trying to be calm, but he kept brushing his chin, and Harry beamed at us and suddenly someone began to sing the *International*. We all sang it, because we all knew it. It was never sung like that before. Anywhere. We stood erect and straight as we sang, and proud. We shouted it out, and our fists were clenched tight as we sang the chorus. Five hundred men going into the trenches singing one song in eleven different languages.

> *Arise ye prisoners of starvation*
> *Debout les forçats de la faim*
> *Das Recht wie Glut im Kraterherde*
> *Il tracollo non è lontan*
> *Sterft gij oude wormen en gedachten*
> *Snart verden Grundvold sig forrykker*
> *Boz to jest nasz ostatni*
> *We have been naught, we shall be all!*
> *'Tis the final conflict.*
> *Let each stand in his place,*
> *The International*
> *Unites the Human Race.*

Comandante Kuller looked at us. He was not smiling now.

"There is nothing for me to say. We shall win."

We filed out of the room into the dormitory, most of us silent. We undressed slowly. The water still hissed in the pipe and trickled out of the taps, and the toilets were still unwalled, but Alan and I decided not to sleep on the wall that night, because somehow the dormitory didn't seem to smell so bad now.

7

Again, morning with the sloping shafts of anæmic light and a bugle-call off-key and the water splashing out of the taps. Then breakfast, with hurried gulpings of coffee.

Then the march down the dirt road leading from the fort to the town. Grass grew along the road and the fields were newly ploughed. There was no sun that morning and a grey mist hung over the earth. We were sleepy-eyed and we marched slowly, kicking at the stones. Doug started to sing *Hold the Fort*. We joined in and marched to its beat.

> *Hold the fort for we are coming,*
> *Union men be strong,*
> *Side by side we'll battle onward,*
> *Victory will come.*

Milty imitated a drum. Pum-pum purarum pum-pum.

A half-mile or so down and the paved streets of the town began. Wooden cottages and small gardens. People waved to us from windows. Suddenly, there was a noise. Music. Cheers. Shouting. Men and women and children shrieked out cheers. Roars of "Viva Brigada Internacionale! Viva Democracia!"

Little boys ran beside us and shrieked, "Norteamericanos!" Some didn't seem sure about it and asked, "Sí, sí, Norteamericanos?"

I wanted to make the distinction that although we came from North America there were some of us who came from a country called Canada, but they didn't seem interested in such distinctions.

We marched around the main square of the town four times, so that the people could take a good look at us. A few of us were still wearing our fedoras and we offered to exchange them for berets. The march was temporarily disorganised while the barter took place, and I marched the rest of the way with a beret set rakishly on the side of my head. The boy who got my fedora had a small head and as he thanked me it fell over his ears.

Young girls looked down from balconies and we waved to them and they waved back to us. The balconies were small and looked as if they had been taken from the scene of *Romeo and Juliet*.

We swaggered a little. The little boys running alongside of us giggled when we tousled their hair. Suddenly one little black-eyed kid began pointing and started to shriek, "Moro! Moro!"

"For Chrissake," said Doug.

A group of kids gathered and stared at him and ran back to the sidewalk and pointed.

Doug laughed.

"They think you're a Moor."

There were seven other negro volunteers in the entire group and their black faces stood out. They became the centre of attention.

The older people laughed at the children and we saw some of them bend down and apparently explain that they were negro anti-fascists, not Moors. But the little black-eyed youngster who started the excitement kept staring at Doug and followed from a safe distance. Doug and Harry walked out of the line and spoke to him.

"El no Moro, pero camarada negro, camarada Norteamericano," explained Harry. The little boy stared at Doug's face. Doug was grinning from ear to ear.

"Me anti-fascista," he beamed.

The kid's eyes opened wide. Doug laughed. He turned to us. "What did I tell you? I'll have the whole Spanish army running after me. Me anti-fascista," he said again to the kid.

"Here," he took out a piece of chocolate he had bought in the canteen and offered it. The boy looked at it shyly. "Here, take," said Doug.

"Gracias," said the boy.

Doug hoisted him to his shoulders and the boy clapped his hands. "Mira! Mira! Look! Look!" he shouted. The people on the sidewalks waved to him. Doug looked up at him solemnly and said in English, "I am not a Moor. I am an American negro and I am an anti-fascist. And we don't spout the theories of white and black fighting side by side, we live them."

"Sí, sí!" shrieked the boy. He let loose a torrent of Spanish. He lisped and we heard words like "fathista" and "no patharan."

"No patharan?" mimicked Doug.

"Sí, Camarada."

The kid's eyes were as black as coal and his skin was almost brown. Doug squeezed him and he giggled. He caressed Doug's cheeks and Doug hugged him. Doug asked him his name, but Harry's Spanish was a little better and the boy answered, "Miguel."

"Miguel," said Doug, "Bueno. That's a good name."
"Sí, sí," giggled Miguel. "Y tu?" he asked.
"Douglas."
"*Dooglas?*" His eyes opened wide.
"No. Douglas. Not *Dooglas*."
"*Dooglas*," he repeated, his lips now brown from the chocolate.

At the railway station Doug placed Miguel on the ground and both of them shook hands solemnly. "Salud, comrade," said Doug. "Thalud y No Patharan," answered Miguel in a piping voice.

The brass band marched to the head of the platform and struck up a few more march tunes.

"Their best players must be at the front," Alan said, making a grimace.

The band stopped playing while the mayor (*alcalde*) of the town, a short and red-faced man, made a short and fiery speech. We didn't understand much of it, but the sincerity of his welcome was obvious. We cheered. Then the band played again. We filed into the train and found seats. As the engine started, the people let out a roar and kept waving to us until we were out of sight.

The train crawled. By noon we had passed ten villages and made three stops. At each stop people gathered at the station and offered us bread and oranges. They rushed to the cars with baskets filled with oranges and poured them into our laps. "Viva Brigada Internacionale!" they shouted. Farmers in their fields saluted us. One peasant ran to the top of a boulder as our train chugged by, and shook his sickle in the air. It flashed in the sun. We roared "Salud!" and it must have been heard all over the Catalonian countryside. The peasant laughed and kept waving his sickle. A tired mule grazing in a field raised his head to see what all the rumpus was about.

We smelled the fragrance of orange-blossoms as we passed the groves and then suddenly, without announcement, we saw the Mediterranean and the soft, golden sands of the shore.

"There it is!"

It was blue, as we had read it would be. The waves lapped quietly on to the shore, making a sound like the rustling of leaves. We stared and listened, and said nothing.

The sun was just beginning to break through the clouds and there was a streak of red through the blue.

"Be swell going in for a swim," said Milty.

The train took a turn and the scene got greener and we saw trees and then vineyards and soon we could no longer see the Mediterranean. We sat back in our seats and stopped looking out of the windows.

It became night again and our bones ached on the hard wooden benches and we spoke of home and puffed at the dry Spanish cigarettes and moistened our lips by sucking at the oranges.

Lucien got into a conversation with a Frenchman who was coming into Spain for the second time. He had been recuperating in Paris from a wound received during the November fighting on the outskirts of Madrid. He showed us his wound, an ugly crooked gash on the side of his leg. I made a face and he laughed. "Ce n'est rien—it is nothing," he said, "you should see some of the ones I've seen."

"Ugh." I was fascinated by the depth of the wound.

"Can you walk all right?"

"But of course. Look." He stood up and stamped his foot a few times to demonstrate.

"Aren't you afraid to go back after getting wounded?"

"Afraid? I am always afraid. But not that afraid."

"Have we enough guns?" Harry asked him.

"Have we enough guns?" he snorted. "If we had enough guns we would win the war in short time. But I hear that soon some new Mexican guns are coming in."

"Mexican?"

"That's the Russian for anything here—Mexican," he said with a laugh.

"Is there much Soviet material coming through?"

"Now they are starting to come, but it is a difficult job getting them into Spain...the sea blockade, and now they have closed the frontier."

"Are there many French volunteers?"

"Certainement. What would you expect? There are more Frenchmen in the International Brigades than any other nationality." He said it proudly.

Then he began asking questions about the United States and Canada. He wanted to know about the C.I.O. and the Labour Party and how soon we were going to have a Popular Front in America. He offered us his French cigarettes, which were a little milder than the Spanish. Then he took a bottle of cognac from a bag and took a sip. "My wife gave me this bottle before I left. She has organised a group of working women to make stockings for the volunteers," he added with quiet pride. He offered us his bottle of cognac and we accepted with many "merci beau-coups."

I had been listening to the conversation with my eyes half-closed.

For some reason the melody of the *Light Cavalry* kept running in my head. Then I realised that I was unconsciously keeping time with the rhythm of the train-wheels.

A dullness was taking possession of me...I heard their voices like a man in a stupor...Mais oui...votre nom? Lucien Poirer?...I'm getting cramps from those oranges...Bob's asleep already...He needs a shave bad...We all need shaves... shave bad shave bad shave bad shave bad shave bad...*O night of nights, O nights of splend-or*, Milty was singing...But the theatre has seen a revival, Alan was saying...last season bury the dead waiting for lefty it's been a wonderful season...we need a good people's theatre in Canada, Harry said...you guys got cramps? I got cramps...Mais non, il est nécessaire d'avoir un gouvernement très fort...we're getting closer to the trenches, eh?

We're getting closer to the trenches, the wheels kept saying...*closer to the trenches closertothetrenches closer-to-the-trenches...closer...to...the...trenches...closer closer closer closer closer...*

I was awakened by someone shaking me. Alan was standing in front of me. "Wake up. Barcelona. We get off here."

"What time is it?"

"About six o'clock."

We marched along cold, empty streets and into a large barrack, where they served us hot coffee. Then we marched back to the station and that was all we saw of Barcelona.

"Nice place, eh?" grunted Milty. "I didn't even have time to have my coffee."

"You shouldn't have eaten so many oranges."

Night had fallen when the train pulled into the Valencia station. My bones ached and my mouth felt raw. We stumbled out of the train and stretched ourselves.

We noticed that the station was crowded with people. A train on the next track was full of what looked like household belongings. Women holding children sat on the train steps. The wail of infants echoed faintly across the station. Otherwise, a death-like stillness.

"What the hell's the matter? Who are they?"

There were groups of children huddled together staring out in front of them. They didn't speak.

We walked along the platform staring.

"Qué pasa?" Harry asked a woman sitting on a step.

She looked at him quietly. There was no expression on her face. Just a weariness. Her eyes looked slowly at each of us and then she turned her face and said in a monotone, "Todos muerte, todos. All dead, all."

Harry turned a bewildered face.

Alan walked to one of the groups of children. He crouched and tried to make them smile. He blew with his mouth, crossed his eyes, imitated a gorilla. They huddled closer. He stood up and passed his hand slowly through his hair.

"They look like corpses." Doug began turning his head excitedly, "Can't we do something?"

"Shh...."

"What the hell is the matter? What's happened?"

An Englishman with an uppish accent, who told us he was attached to the Scottish Ambulance Corps, related what had happened.

"Refugees from Málaga. Málaga was captured by the Italians a week ago. Fell without a fight. These are some who got away. They were machine-gunned by planes on the highway. Our ambulances have been working day and night helping the old people and wounded. They have no place to go. The city is flooded with refugees. They are making preparations to move them on to Barcelona. The problem now is to feed them. Ghastly business."

Young Spanish women wearing Socorro Rojo armbands distributed milk to the children.

"Sonsobitches," said Milty.

"I beg your pardon?" said the Englishman.

"Fascist sonsobitches," repeated Milty.

"War is war," said the Englishman.

"And is war machine-gunning women and children?" muttered Alan, half to himself.

The Englishman had a tiny moustache, which he kept brushing with his little finger. "Americans, I presume?"

"And Canadians," I said.

"You arrived at a very bad time," he said.

"Yes?"

"Things look very black indeed. Political dissension in the rear. Chaos at the fronts. The Communists are accusing the generals of having sold out Málaga. The Communists are fighting the Anarchists and the Poumists. They're cutting each other's throats and Franco keeps winning battles."

"We understand there is a Popular Front here," Harry said quietly.

"Of course, but the Poumists say they want a proletarian dictatorship, or whatever they want, and the Communists and Socialists say win the war first and then settle these things. There will probably be a civil war within a civil war." He looked pleased with himself.

"First of all, this war isn't a civil war," said Harry, still very quietly. "It's an invasion. And second, don't you think you've exaggerated the picture a little bit?"

"No, I don't think so. It's really simply unbelievable. No general staff at all. One general doesn't know what the other is doing. It makes you laugh sometimes. The workers were good fighters when it was a matter of fighting on the barricades, but trench warfare, that's a different matter altogether. There's positively no discipline in the army. Except around Madrid, of course. But Madrid isn't Spain."

"Then it should be all over in a couple of weeks," said Alan.

"Well, perhaps not so soon, but it can't go on very much longer," said the Englishman.

"This guy gives me the willies," said Milty.

"He reminds me of his Prime Minister," said Doug.

"Sorry, old chaps, but I thought you wanted to know how things are."

"We know," said Harry. "And thanks."

"Not at all. Give my regards to the British Battalion, what's left of it. Was speaking to two deserters from the British Battalion, and they told me it was practically wiped out on the Jarama front."

"You're a goddamned liar," shouted Milty. "There aren't any deserters in the Brigade."

"My good man," he had a smirk on his face and his moustache twitched as he said, "Don't be so naïve. There are deserters in the best of armies."

"Come on, this guy smells," said Milty. We began to walk away.

The Englishman took out a packet of English cigarettes.

"Say, he's got cigarettes," I announced, smiling.

They walked back.

"Well, that's damned nice of you, old chappy," said Alan.

The Englishman held out the packet without a word. We took a cigarette apiece.

"Got a match?" asked Milty.

"No," answered the Englishman

"I've got a match," said Doug.

We lit up and exhaled loudly. "Ah...."

"You certainly are a life-saver."

The Englishman walked away.

"Bastard...he should be kicked out of Spain," said Milty.

"He's just a damned fool. Wonder what the hell a guy like that is doing in Spain?" said Alan.

Harry examined his cigarette. "A guy like that gets around a lot. He could be an agent for the British Government. No use reporting him, because the Government probably knows exactly what's what about stinks like that one."

"He certainly painted a pretty picture," I said.

"To hell with him," said Doug, "let's chip in some dough and give it to the Socorro Rojo."

We began to empty our pockets.

"Keep a few pesetas," cautioned Harry.

We gave Harry the money and he stopped a girl with a Socorro Rojo armband. She shook her head.

"What's the matter?" I asked.

"She won't take any money from the Internationals, she says we're giving enough."

"Tell her we have plenty of money," shouted Milty.

The girl looked at us and smiled. Harry offered the money again. She shook her head and took a few steps backward.

"Tell her we'll feel bad if she doesn't take it," I said.

Harry spoke to her. She stopped smiling. He held the money in his two hands and she lifted her apron and he dropped it.

"Gracias, muchas gracias," she said. She held her apron with one hand and with the other saluted us with a clenched fist. We saluted back. She walked away.

"She was pretty," observed Milty.

We stared at the refugees.

"How long do we stay here?" I asked.

"Until we get our orders."

"If we spend a couple of hours here, maybe we'll be able to look up Lisa," I said to Alan.

"If we spend any time here, all we'll be able to look up will be a barrack wall," he answered.

Watching the refugees made us jittery.

"If we could only do something for them." Doug put it into words for us.

"I hope we get into action fast," said Milty.

It turned out that we saw nothing of Valencia, and the train pulled out an hour later with us staring out of the windows and being very quiet.

Our next stop was Albacete, base of the International Brigade.

8

The days in Albacete were boring and pleasant. The barracks in which we were quartered were white-washed inside and out, and our dormitory was spotlessly clean. The sheets on our cots were clean. The toilets flushed and had seats. There were soap and towels. The nights were languid and lazy and the days were hot. The food was good and life became a routine of going to bed when it got late, getting up, eating, browsing around the city, reading war posters, learning Spanish, buying strange foods in the market-square, sipping wine at the Brigade Club near one of the city's parks, and writing long letters home.

On the second day we had been given our uniforms. They were good fits for all of us except Alan, who had a bad time of it. His trousers were too short and the sleeves of his jacket came within two inches of his wrists. When he passed a window and saw a reflection of himself he doubled up with laughter. He had had a hair-cut given gratis by one of the Brigade barbers. His long mane of hair that had made him look like Abraham Lincoln was now closely cropped.

"I look like a caricature of a man in uniform," he chuckled, examining himself in front of the window-pane of the comandante's office.

His six-foot-three frame had been a surprise to the supply department. He walked around in his bad-fitting uniform for a few days and then protested to the comandante.

"If I can't get a pair of pants that fit me, at least let me wear puttees."

Comandante Motril, an American from San Francisco, agreed. "If you can find puttees, go ahead."

Alan found puttees. There was one pair in the supply department. Our uniforms didn't need puttees, because the pants were like ski trousers, coming down to our shoes. There was nothing else to be done about Alan's uniform.

"In that uniform and with that hair-cut," I told him, "you look as if you'd just gone through a ten-years' war. You were a handsome guy before you got that hair-cut."

"I'm the comic relief," Alan said dryly.

"How about taking a picture of yourself and sending it to your wife?" Doug suggested. "After she sees you like that, it won't matter a damn to her what happens to you."

"That's not such a bad idea," said Alan.

We had no idea how long we were going to remain in Albacete. All Motril told us was, "You stay here until the order comes for you to leave."

We were first given our rifles when we had to do guard duty. The rifles were unloaded, but walking back and forth in front of the barrack gates gave you a feeling that you were in the army.

One day Milty announced that he had found out where there was a "swell brothel, government-inspected."

Harry told us to lay off.

"But it's government-inspected," insisted Milty.

"Better ask Motril about it first," said Harry.

"Okay." Milty went to ask Motril.

"Motril says to go to the Brigade hospital first and get all the necessary precautions," Milty announced, very pleased.

"If you guys don't mind, I'm not in on this. I don't go to brothels," said Harry.

"Well, I've only been to about two in my whole life," I said, "but we're going to be in the trenches soon."

"It's okay with me. Go ahead if you want to. I don't go to brothels, that's all."

"Me neither," said Lucien.

"Nor I," said Alan.

So the three of us went, Milty leading the way.

The cat-house, as Doug called it, turned out to be a clean-looking five-room apartment-house in the downtown section of the city. We walked up four flights of stairs, rang the bell and waited.

"If they're old and ugly, I'll wait till you guys are finished," Milty said.

They weren't old and ugly. The door was opened by a charming young girl who could have been anybody's sweet sister. She said Salud and we walked in. Half-clad women were walking back and forth. Twelve soldiers in the front room were engrossed in an argument on the political situation and completely oblivious of the women who passed by them.

"This ain't a brothel," said Doug. "It's a debating club."

A girl approached us and introduced herself as María. She was pretty.

"Are you sure we're in the right place?" I asked Milty.

"You're in the right place," one of the seated soldiers said. "The price is twenty-five pesetas."

"You guys make yourselves at home all right," said Milty.

"Why not? It's a better place than the Brigade Club. The chairs are softer."

"That is an advantage," I said.

We each chose a girl, Milty going off with María.

On our way out the twelve guys were still arguing. "But if the Jarama sector holds, then Madrid is safe."

"How about the north?"

"How about it?"

"It will resolve itself into a war of positions."

"Yeah..."

Back at the barracks, Harry wanted to know if everything was okay.

"Fine, fine!" we answered.

That evening Motril had us gather in our dormitory and delivered a short talk.

"I understand that in the city men have come in contact with elements who talk about the Brigade being wiped out. The Brigade has been 'wiped out' about fifty times since it has come to Spain, but still it manages to play an important role in the army. I don't know what effect these silly rumours have on you, but someone asked me to-day if it were true about the Brigade being wiped out. There is a good reason for such rumours making headway. It is an attempt to demoralise us. Spies start them and fools spread them. As for the truth of the report, I suppose it all started in a dream of our friend Franco. That is all. If there are any questions..."

"Yeah," a voice shouted. "When the hell are we going to the front?"

"That I do not know. But you'll get your orders to stand by about fifteen minutes before you're ready to leave. Any more questions?"

"Are there any American cigarettes arriving?"

"Not that I know of. Some organisations in New York have started a campaign to send us cigarettes. They should be arriving soon." He waited for more questions.

There were none. He said good night.

On Saturday night we decided to see a movie. Lucien was on guard duty, so we five went without him. It was a Spanish movie that didn't have much of a plot. The women tried to imitate American sirens and they spoke fast as hell. But there were a few good songs and it wasn't too bad. Mickey Mouse in Spanish was something to write home about and there were news-reel pictures of the war.

We slouched into chairs in the Brigade Club after the show, and ordered drinks.

"Life is becoming boring as hell," said Alan.

"Hold your horses, you'll get more excitement than you've wanted very soon," said Harry. "I spoke to Motril this afternoon, and he said it was more than likely that we would be sent to Jarama."

"Where's that?" Milty asked.

"Somewhere near Madrid. It's a sector protecting the Madrid-Valencia highway. That's where the Lincoln Battalion is fighting."

"How many of our guys are going into transport?" Doug asked.

"About thirty. That leaves half of us for the trenches. There must be a hell of a need for truck-drivers."

"That's what Motril said. They're reorganising the entire transport service. They need truck-drivers as badly as they need reserves for the Brigade."

"Well, the guys'll make good drivers."

"They'll make good soldiers too," said Harry.

"I'd like to see María again to-night," Milty said.

"Not to-night. We've got to be back at the barracks by ten o'clock."

"It happened again yesterday," said Doug. "Four kids this time, following me and shouting 'Moro!' I wish I'd learn Spanish faster, so's I could give 'em a good talk. One of these days I'm gonna put a turban on and give 'em the scare of their lives."

"This is the lousiest whisky I've ever tasted," said Alan.
"Never drink the stuff. Not until I got here," said Milty; "I like beer."
There was no beer to be bought at the club.
Alan got up. "Come on, let's get back. Our minds seem to be getting dulled. There doesn't seem to be anything to talk about. What a war! Nothing happens. You sit around and grow fat. Makes me feel like a pig being prepared for slaughter. What the hell is the sense of our lying around this town? It's been a week now, or has it? I've forgotten."
"Six days," said Harry.
There was a full moon. It lit up the streets. People passing saw our Brigade uniforms and shouted Salud. We checked our names at the office when we came back. Lucien was waiting for us. "Good show?"
"Lousy."
We pulled our mattresses into the square. Most of the guys were lying on their mattresses, taking things easy.
"Looks more like a rest-home than a barracks," I said.
I flopped and stared up at the sky. There was a warm wind. Things seemed to be standing still.
But the night was too lovely. You couldn't possibly feel bad on a night like this. If you looked up at the moon and let the warm wind play with your hair, you could think of the most wonderful things. I got visions of castanets clacking and music playing and Spanish girls dancing. There was no use trying to sleep.

The moon shines bright: on such a night as this
When the sweet wind did gently kiss the trees
And they did make no noise—

Alan was reciting.
"What's that from?" I asked.
"*Merchant of Venice.*"

—in such a night,
Troilus, methinks, mounted the Trojan walls
And sighed his soul towards the Grecian tents
Where Cressid lay that night...

Milty was shouting out the time. He had been doing it all evening. "Eight o'clock, all's well. Nine o'clock, all's very well. Ten o'clock, it's a night for love."

"Oh, swear not by the moon, the inconstant moon—blessed, blessed night! I am afeard being in night, all this is but a dream...."

Then we heard it.

First a drone. Then louder.

"What's that?"

"Just a truck," someone answered.

Then we heard the air-raid sirens screaming in the city.

"Air raid!"

"Take it easy."

"What do we do?"

We stood up, listening. We were breathing hard.

"Lie still. Take it easy." Harry was up on his feet. "Get the mattresses back into the dormitory. I'll get instructions from Motril."

We ran into the dormitory.

The drone got louder. Menacing.

Harry rushed back to the dormitory. "Motril wants us to line up against the wall in the square." Then to us in a quiet voice: "He told me that there wasn't an anti-aircraft gun in the whole city. There are no spot-lights either. Our planes are being used on another front. Looks like some espionage. They'll probably go to town to-night. Nothing to stop them."

"Ah's a muggin, ta-da-di-ada." Milty felt like singing, for some reason. Someone struck a match to light a cigarette.

"Put it out! You damned fool!"

The match was thrown to the floor and stepped on.

The city was awake. The sirens pierced through the night. There was the sound of hurrying feet. People were running to the fields.

Then came the first blasts of the bombs. One! Two! Three! Four! The earth seemed to split in two. Then quiet.

"Ladies and gentlemen, for the next couple of hours you will hear an air bombardment through the courtesy of Franco, Hitler, Mussolini and Company. When you hear the gong it will be half-past nine and time to scram." Milty was rubbing his hands.

"Shut up!" Alan said. I saw him bite his lips.

Again the thunder. Again. Then you could not distinguish the bombs as they dropped. It was like something insane smashing itself against the earth. The roar swept through my head and faded slowly, slowly, until the next series of bombs dropped and it began all over again. They were coming closer to the barracks.

"My God!" someone was saying. "My God! My God!"

We could hear men and women screaming in the streets.

My clothes stuck to my skin.

Someone was shouting. It was Motril. He was standing in the middle of the square.

"We need relief squads to go into the city. I have just received a call from the *alcalde*. Volunteers step forward. Come, comrades, quickly."

With each bomb something inside of me trembled. There was a sharp pain in my chest. Something clutched at my stomach. The insides of my head were trying to burst through my ears. My mouth was dry.

The drone of the motors kept getting louder, then softer, louder and then softer. You could hear the beginning of the bomb sounding like a million popcorns cracking and then like a hammer hitting a huge drum against your ears, and then the noise of heavy things breaking and falling. Then all I could hear was a ringing in my ears. I saw men talking, but I could not hear them. I was deaf.

And then, as in a dream, I heard a soft murmur of voices and heard men shouting and I could hear again. The wall behind us began to crack. The screaming from the streets became worse than the sound of the bombs. People make such funny noises when they die.

The comandante was waiting.

"Sweet night," I said through my teeth. "Recite some of your Shakespeare, Alan." Recite something sweet and gentle and appropriate. God, how my ears hurt!"

"O comfort-killing night," obliged Alan, his face white, "image of hell, dim register and notary of shame..." His jaw-bones quivered.

Harry turned to us: "They need relief squads. Coming?"

A shiver began in my knees and I felt it in my wrists and in the back of my neck.

"Coming?" said Harry again.

"Yes, I'm coming."

Something was cracking inside my head.

They started to walk toward a pile of picks and shovels lying near the comandante. I felt myself moving forward. My feet seemed detached from the rest of my body, and with each step I felt a sharp pain in my chest. My clothes were soaking wet with sweat.

When I placed my hands on the handle of the pick, the band around my chest gave way. I took a good grip and flung it across my shoulder. Lucien said: "Bons garçons," and Milty said: "Bone nuts."

Then we ran single file into the streets.

The planes were coming in relays. We had not seen any of them yet. Harry said there were about ten of them. Lucien said: "No, only five or six." Milty said there were a hundred.

We ran crouched low along the sides of the houses. The clap-trap of our feet sounded strange after that noise. I remembered the silence of the city and the sound of our feet in the streets only a few hours before.

The sound of our heavy breathing mingled with the distant noises of the city.

Milty began yelling out the time again. "Eight o'clock, all's well; nine o'clock, all's very well. Ten o'clock, all's screwy. Eleven o'clock, my God!"

We stopped at a baby-carriage and looked in, but it was empty. The streets were heavy with smoke and dust. We saw the ruins of houses, smouldering. A telephone was dangling in the air and we followed the wire to the gaping side of a house. Beds and furniture were still standing on what was left of the floors. Pictures were still hanging on the wall. There was an unpleasant chemical smell and glass was strewn all over the pavement.

Ambulances and trucks hurtled through the streets. There was the sound of many people running.

Then came the drone again.

We looked up.

We could see ten bombers distinctly. They seemed to be moving very slowly.

There was a noise like canvas being ripped by a knife. We fell flat to the ground. I closed my eyes and felt my nails coming through the palms of my hands. Then the bomb exploded. The earth shook. Things flew over me. I tasted blood. I had bitten right through my lip. It became quiet, but I could hear my heart pounding against the pavement.

"Everybody okay?" No one answered.

Milty shook his fist at the planes. "Bastards, come down and fight."

A cat streaked by us and disappeared.

A Spaniard ran toward us and pointed to the ruins of a house, his eyes wide, his hand trembling.

"Come on," said Harry. We ran to the ruins and began to dig.

"Think any were caught here?" I asked.

"Who knows?"

Again there was the swishing sound of a bomb falling.

"Lie down flat on your stomachs until they've gone," said Harry.

There was thunder and I felt the earth heave under me. Hot fire on my lips. Blackness. A flash of light. Thunder in my head. A sharp pain. Then quiet.

"Everybody okay?"

"That was close."

I heard one of them laugh, a low laugh.

I felt something warm on my hand. It was blood.

"Look, Bob's arm is bleeding."

"It's nothing," I said, "just a scratch."

"Let's see," said Harry.

A piece of shrapnel had cut a gash above my wrist.

"Better go to a hospital and get it attended to," said Harry.

I took out a handkerchief and Harry tied it round my wrist. I did not want to walk those streets alone and I did not want to tell them that. "It's only a lousy scratch," I said.

"It may get infected," said Alan.

"For Christ's sake, it's just a scratch." I was trembling.

"Better sit down for a while," said Alan.

"I'm okay," I said.

We started to dig again.

9

For five hours the planes came and dropped their bombs over the city, and then they were gone and the full moon was gone too and the dawn came up. It was a grey, streaky dawn with no sun. There was the noise of men working on the ruins and the shriek of ambulances running through the streets and their sirens full blast, and the sound of rumbling trucks that came to take the dead, or what was left of the dead.

We shivered with cold.

My muscles ached. My ears still rang. The handkerchief on my arm was soaked with blood.

"Bob, better get your arm taken care of," said Alan.

"I'll wait till we all go back."

Milty had gone to get a truck to pick up the dead we had taken from the ruins. The others were digging quietly. My hands were blistered. A few of my fingers bled under the nails. Every time our picks touched something soft we had to dig with our hands.

We would take time off for a cigarette or walk away a few blocks to get a whiff of fresh air.

My pick touched something soft again. I got down on my knees and began to dig away the dirt.

"That's the fifth kid," said Harry; "this place must have been a nursery."

The rest of them came over, and gently we pulled the kid out. I tried not to look at it.

"Boy?" asked Lucien.

"What the hell's the difference?" I began to spit.

We carried the kid to the sidewalk and placed him beside the others. I noticed a Spaniard, unshaven and tired-looking, staring at us. "Come on and help us," I said. He nodded, not understanding, and said something in Spanish.

"What's the matter?" asked Harry.

"Nothing. I just want this guy to help us. He stares and does nothing."

"Where the hell is Milty with that truck?" asked Doug.

"Maybe he got lost," said Lucien.

"That guy couldn't get lost," said Alan. "He's probably boozing somewhere." Alan sat on the handle of his shovel, his long body bent double, staring at the ground. Harry was wiping his face with a dirty handkerchief. I lit a cigarette and passed my packet round. Alan gave me back an empty packet, crumpling it as he gave it to me.

"Thanks," I said.

"Don't mention it."

"What do you think is better, breathing through your nose or through your mouth?" Doug asked.

"Through mouth," said Lucien.

"Same damn thing," I said; "it smells either way."

"Good to have gas-masks when you do this kind of work," said Lucien.

"The trenches will be a picnic after this."

We began digging again.

"Maybe there were only eight," I said. "See, there's the father and the mother, four kids, and maybe there's another father, and..."

"Two fathers, hmm?" said Alan.

"I mean another father from another apartment. You can see that this was an apartment."

Lucien began to count: "Two men, one woman, three boys, two girls."

"We can count," said Alan.

"I bet that's all there is," I said.

The sun was coming up. It was going to be a warm day. The Spaniard who was watching us walked over to the eight bodies and stared at them.

"You'd think he'd help instead of gazing at us as if we were doing an excavation job, or something," I said. I climbed down to the sidewalk and offered him my pick.

"No," he said.

"You son-of-a-bitch. Why not?"

"How do you expect him to understand English?" said Lucien.

"Why not?" I said again to the Spaniard.

"No, no..."

"Aw, leave him alone," said Doug. "He looks tired as hell."

"*He* looks tired as hell. We've been here all night and he looks tired as hell."

"Leave him alone," said Lucien.

"I didn't ask you," I said. "When I ask you you can say something."

"Stop getting bitchy," said Harry.

"I'm not getting bitchy. It makes me sore, that's all. Why should he stand there doing nothing watching us? Let him go home then."

The Spaniard began talking fast.

"Harry, come down and speak to this guy." I climbed back to the debris. "Why the hell isn't Milty here?"

"Take it easy, kid," said Harry, passing me as he went toward the Spaniard.

"Milty's probably drunk or in some brothel," said Alan.

"He knows we're waiting for him. They're beginning to stink. I want to get away from this..."

A truck pulled up and Milty jumped out of it.

"Where the hell were you?" Alan asked.

"I was helping first aid." Milty looked tired.

"Oh, yes?" said Alan. "Some whore cut herself?"

"They found two kids. They were still alive. I had to help."

"It took you an hour, eh?"

"Then I went for a drink. And then it took time to get the truck. They couldn't spare one until now."

"I thought so," said Alan, "boozing around while we had to do this." He waved to the bodies on the sidewalk.

"I'm sorry, guys. Honest."

"It's okay," said Alan. "I don't know what the hell's got into me."

Lucien climbed down and helped Harry and Milty pile the bodies into the back of the truck. Then Milty vomited. We didn't say anything.

"I don't feel so good," said Milty. "I'm going back to the barracks."

We stared at him until he turned the corner and then we began digging again. Harry was standing on the sidewalk talking to the Spaniard.

"I need a good drink," I said.

"And you'll vomit like he did," said Alan.

"No, I won't." I nodded my head reassuringly.

"What's he saying?" Doug asked Harry.

"He talks too fast," answered Harry.

"Tell him to talk slower."

"I'm not sure," Harry began, "but I think he says he lived in this apartment. I think he's saying something about a sister. Wait a minute and I'll make him say it over again."

They were both gesticulating with their hands.

"Yeah, he says the eight bodies we found were the Hidalgo family on the fifth floor. Mrs. Hidalgo's brother was the other guy. He lived with them. I don't know which was which. It doesn't matter, I suppose."

We aimlessly picked at the dirt and rocks with our shovels while we listened.

"Yeah," went on Harry, "he says that he thinks his sister's still here. She was pregnant. Eighth month, I think he says. Her husband's fighting. She was in her room. He came back for her after saving his family. He thinks everybody but the Hidalgos got away, but he's not sure about his sister. When he came back from the refugio, the place had been hit and he has been waiting to see if we find his sister."

"Better tell him that's all there is. Even if we find her there's no use him being around. Tell him to go back with his family," I said.

Harry turned to him and it was then that I touched something with my shovel. "Alan..."

He came over, "A woman?"

"Yes—hell—"

We began to dig with our hands. A section of the debris gave way.

"Oh, Christ! Let's leave it like this now and cover it with the dirt." I wanted to get away fast.

"Tell that guy to go away," I said to Harry.

"Is it her?"

I was getting a headache. "Take him away."

The Spaniard did not want to go away. He got excited and began wringing his hands.

"Solamente ocho," Harry kept saying. "Only eight. Better go home."

After a while the Spaniard caught on. He sighed and hunched his shoulders. Then he looked at each of us and shook his head slowly and walked away.

"Let's get a drink and come back," I said.

"Okay," said Alan. "It's a fine war...."

"It'll be a warm day," said Doug. "We better get back fast."

10

"Why didn't you come to me with this before?"

"I was doing rescue work."

"You could have left it. Trying to be a bloody hero? That arm looks infected."

The doctor chewed gum as he spoke. He was irritated. "Damn fool," he said. He poured alcohol over the wound. It burned. "Ouch!" I said.

"So you wanted to be a hero, eh?"

"Hero, nuts. I was afraid to walk back through those streets alone. Those damned planes..."

He smiled. "Oh, that's it. Want a piece of gum?"

"Thanks."

"Your first bombardment?"

"Yes. And I hope my last."

He chewed loudly. "It was pretty bad. Worse than anything I've been through yet. I was in one in Madrid, but we had anti-aircraft guns and planes to fight back. That made it feel better."

"Many people killed last night?" I asked.

"Hmm, about a hundred."

"A hundred? We picked out eight, no, almost ten. There was a woman pregnant."

"Dead?"

I shuddered. "Ugh. Yes. Dead. The baby came out. We had to go get a drink."

He began to bandage my arm. "Say, that hurts. Take it easy," I said.

"Those shrapnel wounds are fascinating. Yours is only a scratch, but it looks infected. We need more surgeons here. A few of us worked right through the night. And listen, kid, try to forget last night. Your nerves are in a hell of a state."

"Well, you don't seem to be particularly calm either."

"I worked all night."

"So did I."

"This is an idea of what the next world war will be like. There will be more people insane from air bombardments than soldiers killed. We should get a few of our psychiatrists here and let them study a new kind of neurosis."

"They can start on me," I said. "That arm burns. It didn't burn before, only after you started to cure it."

He chuckled. "I was chief surgeon in my hospital in New York, but I don't suppose that means anything to you guys."

"My arm still burns."

"It's going to burn more than that. That's what you get for trying to be a bloody hero."

"I..."

"I know. I know. Anyway, you'll stay over a few days and get it treated."

"But we may have to move up any day now."

"I understand the boys are leaving to-morrow morning. You'll stick around here and get that arm treated. We don't want tetanus to set in. I'm going to take you down to the hospital this afternoon and give you an injection. I haven't the stuff here. Probably too late to help, anyway. If you're going to get tetanus."

"Cheerful kind of a guy, aren't you?" I said.

He grinned. "I've been here two months. The things I've seen—never mind. Sure, I'm a cheerful kind of a guy. You're going to get as cheerful as I am in a few short months—if you live that long."

I didn't answer.

"How old are you?" he asked.

"What's the difference?"

"Seriously. How old are you?"

"I'm twenty-one."

"Twenty-one! Children. All children. The children are fighting our wars. I'm forty. I don't look it, but I'm forty. Almost double your age. Twenty-one!" He sucked at his teeth. "If they agreed to allow only men over forty to fight, it wouldn't be so bad. Twenty-one! I was going to college at that age. What did I know then? Nothing. And here you're twenty-one and you've lived your life and you're ready for death."

"I'm not ready for death. We didn't come here because we felt we were ready for death. We came because we believed in something. And when you believe in something you're never ready for death, but you're willing to risk death to fight for it."

"Canadian, aren't you? Good fighters, the Canadians. Want a drink? I've got two bottles of English whisky left."

He went to a drawer and came back with a half-filled bottle. He filled two glasses.

"To the youth," he said.

"To victory," I said.

We drank.

"Here's a note to Comandante Motril. You'll have to stay over at least a week. Probably nothing will happen, but we can't take any chances. Good thing it's your left arm. Motril will probably be able to use you in his office. Can you work a typewriter?"

"Yes. But I came to work a gun."

"Anxious, aren't you? Anxious to get there."

"It isn't that." I poured myself another drink. "It isn't that. It's me staying over and all the other guys going to the front."

"Bosh! You'll join them soon enough. Don't let that worry you."

"That's good stuff. I feel drunk already."

"You'd better lie down. It shows you haven't got a fever. If you had, the whisky wouldn't bother you."

I walked out of the doctor's room with the note in my hand. When I came back to the dormitory I flopped down on my cot. Milty was there.

"Where you been?" he asked.

"Doc Woods."

"What'd he say?"

"I've got to stay over for a week. He says the arm is infected."

"Hope it's nothing bad."

"He says the guys are leaving here to-morrow morning."

"To-morrow? Sure?"

"That's what he said. Where are the other guys?"

"I don't know. Around somewhere. To-morrow, eh? That's the twenty-sixth."

"Well, I can write home that I've been wounded already. Never saw a gun. Never saw a fascist. But wounded."

Harry and Alan walked into the dormitory.

"How goes it?"

"I'm a hero," I said.

"What?"

"Woods says my arm's infected."

"He also said we were leaving to-morrow morning," said Milty.

"How does he know?" asked Harry.

"That's what he said. Also said I'd have to stay over for a week. So I don't get into action for a week."

"Nice life," said Alan.

"Funny goddamned world," I said.

"How bad is it?" asked Harry.

"What?"

"The arm."

"If you ask me, there's nothing the matter with it. Woods probably wants a patient who can speak English. Probably tired of Spanish patients."

"Come and see us sometimes," said Alan.

"Sure. Sure will. I like those shoes of yours, Alan. How about them?"

"The black ones?"

"Uh-huh."

"Okay. I hope they bomb this place the day after we're gone, and you get a piece of shrapnel in the head."

"I hope the Moors pull your nuts off."

"Come on, there's the dinner-bell," said Harry.

After dinner Doc Woods took me to the International Brigade hospital and a pretty Spanish nurse injected anti-tetanus into my arm.

Motril seemed pleased that I was staying over. "Will you be able to handle a typewriter?" he asked.

"Yes."

"Good. If your arm isn't too bad, I've got some work for you."

At five in the morning Alan woke me up.

"So long, kaker," he said.

"So long?"

"We're going."

I jumped out of bed. The five of them were standing in front of me. The other boys were marching out of the dormitory.

"So long, kid, take care of yourself." Harry shook my hand.

"When you come up bring some cigarettes," said Milty. "Some American cigarettes are supposed to be coming any day."

"Bring me a writing-pad. I forgot to get one," said Alan.

"'Bye," boomed Doug.

"Au revoir," said Lucien.

"I'll be with you soon, guys," I said.

"Take care of that arm."

"I will. Are you going right now? Right this minute?"

"Yep. The trucks are outside. We're late. So long."

"Wait a minute," I said.

"What is it?" asked Harry.

"Nothing. Good luck. See that Alan keeps low. He's too damned tall for a trench. Take care of yourselves."

"We'll all be together again in a week," said Harry. "And for Christ's sake, good-bye. You'll have me crying in a minute."

They marched out of the dormitory. I heard the trucks start and rumble into the distance.

11

The barracks were empty. I could hear the sound of my feet echoing across the square. I moved my cot to the wing where Woods and Motril slept. Another contingent of Americans and Canadians was expected to arrive in two weeks. I ate my meals with Woods and Motril and listened to the gossip of the war.

Woods seemed to know everything and did most of the talking, while Motril listened most of the time with a detached tolerance.

"There are no reserves," said Woods at the table. "The Brigade will have to hold the Jarama sector, while Lister and Modesto and Campesino concentrate everything they have on the central front. The Aragon front is as good as dead. There's been no action there, and there won't be as long as the POUM is in control on that front. Caballero is planning to do away with the political commissars. And if that happens you know what the result will be."

Motril sighed. "Doc, you should have been a general."

"The only reason we've been able to hold them up to now is because of the political commissars," continued Woods, sipping some wine and smacking his lips. "An army with as little training as ours needs political commissars. Every army in the world should have them, assuming we'll always have armies. They are the ones that give an army its political consciousness. In some cases they're even more important than the officers. No, I shouldn't say that. Each is important; each is necessary."

"More wine, Doc?" I asked.

Motril smiled.

"Take our own kids," said Woods.

"No one is arguing with you," said Motril. "I agree. Political commissars are necessary. They are the backbone of the people's army. Okay."

"Are they elected?" I asked, trying to make conversation.

"Sometimes they're elected and sometimes they're appointed," answered Motril. "And some of them have been lousy, but most have been good, and what Doc Woods says is true. The political commissars are the mothers and fathers of the boys. They listen to their grievances. They help them. They give them advice and, when necessary, they lead them in battle."

"Take our own kids," continued Woods. "If it weren't for their high political level God knows what would have happened at Jarama after that mess yesterday."

"What mess?" I asked.

"Hmm, you would have been in that if I hadn't been afraid of your arm getting worse."

Motril glared at Woods. "The kids went over the top yesterday," Motril explained, "and the fact that they only had a couple of days' training could not be helped. The situation was too serious to allow time for training. But something went wrong somewhere. They went over the top without any artillery preparation."

"What about our guys?" I asked.

"That's the point. If it weren't for the high political level..." Woods started to say again.

"But the guys who were with me. Were they—did anything happen to them?"

"We don't know yet. The casualty-list hasn't come in yet," said Motril.

"That's war, boy," said Woods.

"How the hell can you sit there sipping wine talking like that!" I rose from the table.

"Take it easy, kid," said Motril. "That's what war is. We've got to understand all of it if we want to see it through. Especially a war like this, with inexperienced officers, insufficient ammunition, espionage."

"But those friends of mine. You say they were in that mess yesterday?"

"I suppose so," said Woods.

I couldn't finish my meal.

That afternoon I walked through the city. Life had become normal again. Shops were open. The market-square teemed with people. The debris was still being cleaned away. There was a mass funeral for the dead who could be lowered into graves. Everything else was cremated. A brass band played a funeral dirge. The townsfolk lined the sidewalks, some of them with their fists clenched, others just staring silently.

I came back to the barracks and flung myself on the cot.

12

Three days passed, boring, tiresome days.

I was sitting in Motril's office writing out the names of the volunteers who had passed through the barracks.

"Any news about our guys yet?" I asked.

"When there's news I said I would tell you. We won't get a casualty-list for another couple of weeks yet." He turned to me. "Your arm's better now, isn't it?"

"Hell, yes."

He was reading something. He looked up. "Did you ever do any radio work back home?" he asked suddenly.

"Radio work?"

"Yes. I just got a letter from the political department in Madrid asking for someone suitable to undertake a series of regular broadcasts to North America."

I listened.

"You'd be a good man for the job."

"What makes you say that?"

"Well, I understand you were a reporter back home. You could at least write the news. And your voice sounds good enough to me."

"There was a guy in our gang, Milton Schwartz, who was dying to be a radio announcer."

"But he isn't here and you are."

"Thanks. It's tempting. But I wouldn't be able to look the guys in the face."

"Why not?"

"I just wouldn't, that's all. You know why not. You know what they'd think of me."

"Don't be an idiot. You have to look at this from the point of view of where you can be most useful."

"But I came to fight, not to talk about the war."

"This job happens to be an important part of the war. Telling the American people the truth about the war will help us win the war. The job is important or the political department wouldn't have sent me a special letter on it. Take my advice and accept it."

"Why?"

"I just told you. And on top of everything else, I think you'd be more useful doing that than you would be in a trench. Doc Woods tells me your nerves are shot to hell."

"Doc Woods is a nervous wreck himself."

"That may be. But he knows what he's talking about."

"And that's why you think I should take the job because I'd be a flop in the trenches?"

"That's not the reason I think you should take the job. If you were a crack machine-gunner or came from West Point I wouldn't even give the matter a second thought. But here's an important job that has to be done. Someone has to do it. You aren't being taken away from anything. I think you're the man for the job, and I think you should accept it and not make such a fuss about it."

"If I do I'll never be able to look those guys in the face again."

"You'll stop feeling that way once you've got down to the job. You will be doing your job and they will be doing theirs."

"Yeah," I said.

"I'm arranging for your transfer immediately."

"I'm telling you you're making a mistake."

"Let me worry about that," said Motril. "You worry about doing a good job in Madrid. I'm telling the political department that you are reliable in all ways. And drop me a line occasionally on how you are getting on. If I ever happen to come to Madrid I'll look you up. Get your civilian clothes. You leave to-night."

13

The train to Madrid left Albacete late at night. I tried to sleep, but the wheels kept drumming in my head. My nerves were still jittery from the bombardment. Jittery was the only word I could think of. Even the sound of the train bothered me. I tried to compare the sounds. What could you compare the sound of bombs to? A subway train rushing through a station? And then crashing into another train? It was worse than that.

What will the guys think?

But it is an important job.

I shouldn't have agreed. But Motril said I should, that I could be more help that way.

If I hadn't hurt my hand. If that letter to Motril had come a few days later. If Motril were a different kind of a guy. If I were a different kind of a guy. If. If.

The train didn't go all the way to Madrid. It stopped at a small village where a bus took you the rest of the way.

There were about a hundred people waiting to get seats in the bus. A guard stood watch by the door. I showed him my International Brigade Salvo Conducto.

"Ah, Internacionale, bueno, adelante camarada," he said, smiling.

He pushed back some of the crowd. "Internacionale!" he barked.

"Viva!" some began shouting. They crowded closer to see me.

"Oh, hell!"

"Qué camarada?"

"Nothing. Let the others go first. I'm not an International, I'm a radio announcer."

"Sí, sí, camarada, sí, sí, No Pasarán. Viva Democracia."

The people began shouting excitedly: "Viva Brigada Internacionale!"

I turned slowly and quietly answered: "Viva Democracia." Then I went in and took a seat.

The bus filled quickly. As they passed me they smiled. A few militiamen, some families with baskets of food, a few nurses, and fathers and mothers on their way, I supposed, to see sons recuperating in Madrid hospitals.

A young Spanish woman sat beside me. She was a nurse from Barcelona on her way to the Catalonian Hospital in Madrid, formerly the Hôtel Ritz. She spoke a little French. "Un petit, petit peu," she said.

"Moi aussi," I answered. She smiled. Her name was Juanita.

"Battalion Ab-bra-ham Leencohn?" she asked.

"No, maintenant je vais à Madrid pour travailler, eh, well, la radio."

"Radio? Ah, muy bueno, pour Norte Amérique?"

"Oui."

She didn't seem disappointed. She turned round and announced it to the rest. A man behind us leaned over. "Ruso?" he asked confidentially.

"No," I answered, "Canadiense."

"Huh?" he grunted.

"Canada," I repeated.

He seemed never to have heard of the place.

"Norteamericano," Juanita explained.

"Ah sí, Norteamericano."

"Norteamericano, sí," I insisted, "pero Canadiense."

He shook his head. Juanita turned round and explained that Canada was a country north of Estados Unidos. He was very surprised to hear about it.

"A farmer," Juanita explained, "not much education, before war, he does not know much about geography."

The bus got under way. The Spaniards began singing songs. They passed around their food. One woman offered me a hunk of soft white bread filled with two fried eggs. I said, "No, gracias," but Juanita urged me to take it. When I did the woman smiled happily and someone else offered me his wine-pouch. They laughed when I spilled some of the wine down my neck. Someone else passed me grapes. Still another figs. Juanita had a basket of fruit and she shared that with me. When I could eat no more, she made me put two oranges in my pocket.

Then the bus-driver began waving his head and started to sing a song. It was a strange song. At first it sounded like an oriental form of yodelling.

"Flamenco," Juanita explained.

It was my turn to say "Huh?"

Struggling with her French, she explained that Flamenco was a type of Spanish folk-song which had a Moorish origin. The bus-driver was improvising as he sang. The people in the bus clapped their hands in time. When the bus-driver reached a high note, kept it, made it trill, brought it down, then up again and down and up again, they held their breath and then shouted "Olé!"

A bus-driver
Drives a lot.
Fascist planes come
And bomb the roads,
And the cities,
And the bus-driver wonders
About his novia in the city,
But he still drives,
And drives,
And drives.

"Olé!" they shouted.

We settled down to the monotony of the drive. I had bought a little Spanish dictionary in Albacete and I kept turning the pages to get the right words.

"Dónde el frente Jarama?" I asked Juanita.

"There," she pointed to the left.

I looked and saw nothing but fields.

"But where?"

"There, beyond…there is the front and there is fascist territory."

"And Madrid. Is it far yet?"

"No. Two hours more."

One of the militiamen in the back started to sing a song. Juanita brightened. "It is a wonderful song. An old folk song with new words."

Before long everyone in the bus had joined in. I made Juanita write out the words.

Los cuatro generales
Los cuatro generales
Los cuatro generales, mamita mia,
Que se han alzado
Que se han alzado.

Quieren pasar los Moros,
Quieren pasar los Moros,
Quieren pasar los Moros, mamita mia,
No pasa nadie,
No pasa nadie.

"Mira!" Juanita pointed. "Telefonica."

I looked and saw the top of a building in the distance. Madrid's only skyscraper, the Telephone Building.

It was getting dark.

Soon we approached the stone barricades that guarded every entrance of the city. I saw trams filled with people. There were no lights in the city. I stared out. Stores, apartment-houses...it looked like any street back home.

The bus let me off in front of Brigade headquarters on Velásquez Street. I said good-bye to Juanita and waved to the others, but not before one motherly-looking woman slipped me two raw eggs. I stared at the eggs and said gracias. Juanita was smiling.

An armed guard at the gate asked for my credentials. I entered a small courtyard and then walked up a flight of stairs. Down a corridor to a sign, "Political Department," on a door.

I placed the eggs on the desk of the man in front of me.

"Vas ist das?" he asked.

"Eggs," I answered.

He called someone into his office, an Englishman. "How do you do?" he said.

"Hello. Someone on the bus gave me two eggs."

He laughed. "Fine. We'll have them for breakfast."

"I'm Bob Curtis." I gave him Motril's letter.

"Oh yes. We've been expecting someone for some time. Have you eaten?"

"All day. The people on the bus kept me well fed." I pulled out the two oranges from my pocket.

"There are enough of those around here. Eggs are a scarcity, though."

"I'd like to get washed. I'm dirty."

"Of course," said the Englishman. He led me to a room upstairs, carrying my valise. "Just thought of it," he said, "there are no extra rooms here. You can use this one to wash up and change, but you'll probably have to get a room in one of the hotels. Lucky. The rooms in the hotels are much better than these."

"I didn't get your name," I said.

"Smith," he answered. "Believe it or not, John Smith."

I smiled: "I believe it."

"Thanks; no one else around here does. Anyway, if you need any help at the beginning, I'll be glad to give you all I can. I help Patterson on the Brigade paper. I usually have lots of time on my hands. But I suppose you'll manage. I'll take you down later to the radio station and you can get acquainted. It isn't far from here."

After washing I was taken to the Hôtel Nacional in one of the Brigade cars. A room on the tenth floor had already been reserved for me by the time I arrived. It looked over a wide boulevard with trees. Smith told me not to worry about any strange feelings I had the first couple of weeks. "Everyone has it when they first arrive here," he said. "But you get used to things in time." Then he took me to the radio station in the car. It was in a cellar.

A thin Spaniard threw his arms around me. "At las', at las', at long, long las', they have given over to me someone who speak American like American should be speak. Can you think of me with my accent having to deliver via radio announcements in American to your country? Can you think of it? At las' we have real American broadcasts and announcements. Not English. Not Spanish. But real okay American. Surely we must drink to celebrate." He pulled out a wine decanter from a shelf and poured three drinks.

"But I'm Canadian," I said.

His face dropped. "Is there, is there much radical difference in delivery of accent?"

"Nope. I fling it across like a real okay American."

He was impressed. "Bueno hombre." He heaved a loud sigh. "My name is Miguel José Gonzales, but everyone call me Pepe."

"Bob's my name."

"Bobs?"

"Just Bob, without the 's'."

"Bobs...bueno. Bobs and Pepe," he repeated. "How soon can you start your delivery?"

Smith was chuckling.

"As soon as we can," I said.

"Bueno. To-night you get some sleep. To-morrow night we start. How do you like Madrid? But, of course, naturally you do not know yet you have just arrived, yes? Ah, you should have seen Madrid: just like your Broadway it was, the Gran Via with electric lights that shone and shone all through the night and night clubs. But you are not American. I forgot. Still it was wonderful. My English is not bad, eh? I learn it all from American dancer some years back. She was what they call hot stuff. *Mucho calor.* Hmm sí." He flipped his wrist three times for emphasis. "But she has gone. Yes, you get some sleep now."

Smith started for the door.

"He's harmless," said Smith.

"And he was broadcasting to the States?"

"Just for a short time and, anyhow, someone wrote the announcements for him."

I told the desk clerk at the hotel to wake me at noon next day. I'll write the guys a long letter, I said to myself. The feel of the sheets against my skin was soothing.

They're sleeping in dug-outs to-night. And me. Soft. Sheets. Good mattress. Hotel. A radio announcer. My God! I must stop sweating. Maybe they're not sleeping at all. Maybe they're all dead. No. They're all right. Sure they're all right. Motril said I'd be more valuable...that's rot....I'm a fake. No. Sleep. Go to sleep. Stop thinking. Count. Onetwothreefourfivesixseven. Twentyseventh over the top. Planes are lousy. They scare the guts out of you. Digging those kids out was awful. God!...we'll win. We'-ve got to win. A radio announcer. Me a radio announcer and them in the trenches....God! I must stop sweating. I must stop thinking. Sing myself to sleep...that's the only way now....I'll see them soon....I must stop sweating....

This Time a Better Earth
PART II

14

Next day a new kind of life began for me. Pepe showed me what I had to do and told me what was expected. We were sitting in the little cellar room now transformed into a radio studio.

"You will deliver general news such as the war and in subsequence, the life of our city, which is the tomb of fascism, is it not? From the censor, Rosa, a wonderful woman, an Austrian, she is the censor, you will receive communiqués. You will say *allo, allo, esta estación*, pardon me, this is Station E.A.R. the Voice of Republican Spain delivered over wave-lengths of thirty-two kilocycles. In afternoons and evenings. Is it not simple? *Claro?*"

"Claro. Very claro. Better write it out and I'll try and put it in good English."

"American," corrected Pepe.

"Right."

"And you will perform records so. Observe." He placed a gramophone record on one of the three disks and turned a switch. He lifted the ear-phones to my ears. "Himno de Riego," he said. "Now we will go meet Rosa."

We walked out of the cellar to the street.

"Isn't it dangerous for the trams to be running?" I asked.

"Dangerous? Sí, hombre. It would seem apparently. But Madrileños say life must go on."

We walked up the wide Alcala, in the centre of which was a boulevard bordered by trees. The trams ran on each side of the boulevard. People strolled leisurely. Some sat on benches reading newspapers. A few women were knitting.

We turned the corner. A hardware store on one side and a book store.

"This is the Gran Via," announced Pepe like a tourist guide. "On this street is theatres and famous cafés. Observe the unbeautiful results of *obuses*—pardon, shells. If you will follow the Gran Via and turn there by the barricades a walk of fifteen minutes arrives you at the trenches. You can arrive at trenches by tram or by subway. Trenches run through the streets. Amazing? Amazing," Pepe answered himself. "But life goes on."

"You should be a tourist guide, Pepe."

"Tourist guide? Ah, yes. You mean I should say, señores y señoritas, here real trenches, real men fighting, shooting real bullets, all for ten centimos by subway and by tram."

"That's right."

"You have good sense humour," said Pepe. He laughed to show me he appreciated it.

The left side of the Gran Via had suffered badly from shells.

"Why do people walk on that side of the street?"

"What matters? Camarada Bobs, life in Madrid continually dangerous with death flying everywhere like birds…no, unlike birds…with death…I can say it better in Spanish. What matters which side?" he went on. "What matters here or there? Shells fall here. Shells fall there. Death everywhere. Matters not which side or where. Would you like some café con leche?"

"No, thanks. I had some coffee in the hotel."

The censor's office was on the fourth floor of the Telefonica. My eyes roamed over the street, the cars, the people, the stores.

"Soon you will get use to everything," said Pepe.

News-boys shouted out headlines. Trams clanged. Cars swept by swiftly.

"Where are the policemen?" I asked.

"We do not need policemen," answered Pepe. "Mira!" he pointed to the Telefonica. "Observe the shell-holes. Like yawns of death. You like my English?" and went on without waiting for an answer. "It has been hit and hit perhaps sixty times, but it still stands. Life goes on. It is like Spain. They tear it and wound it, but it still stands.…Yawns of death," repeated Pepe, "I speak good English, have I not?"

"Yes.…"

Pepe knew everyone. "Salud. Salud. Cómo está?"

Uniformed soldiers walked in and out. People came out of elevators. Armed guards patrolled the entrance. A sign pointed to the Workers' Committee in charge of administration. War posters were plastered over the walls. "Vigilance in the rear." "Unified command." "Unification of the political parties." "Build a war industry." "Madrid will be the tomb of fascism." One poster advertised Juanita Crawford in a sensacionale, excepcionale cinema.

We got into the elevator. "Rosa is fine woman. She will give you everything according to your desire."

"Really?"

"Everything," emphasised Pepe.

The censor's room was next to the press-room. It was a large well-lighted office. There were two desks. At one desk sat a plump, short woman with a boyish bob. She turned as we entered. "Salud, Pepe." She had a pleasant smile.

Pepe beamed. "Salud. Salud. Cómo está?" They shook hands. "Here is the fine radio broadcaster they have sent us from Los Brigadas Internacionales. Camarada Bobs Curtis."

"Bob," I corrected.

Rosa smiled. She rose from her chair and we shook hands. "Welcome to Madrid. It's about time someone arrived to do this work. It's been neglected. I'm glad you've come."

Pepe sat down. "We must get him Salvos Conductos. For day and for night."

"Have you worked out a schedule yet?" Rosa asked.

"Not yet," I answered. "Pepe and I will work on it this afternoon."

"I'll be glad to give you any help with it if you like."

"Thanks. We'll probably need help."

"You have to get all the war communiqués from this office. Do you know Spanish?"

"No. But I'll teach Pepe English and he'll teach me Spanish."

"I shall be happy to teach you Spanish," said Pepe, a little offended.

"Everything must be checked before going over the air," said Rosa.

"I have delivered to him those instructions not one hour ago," said Pepe.

"Good. Now, are you comfortable? You have a room?"

"I'm in the Nacional."

"I'll get you a pass to eat at the Gran Via. The food is better here. If there's anything you want, ask me."

"There is something..."

"Yes?"

"It's about some friends of mine in the Lincoln Battalion. They were in that attack on February twenty-seventh and I haven't heard a word from any of them. So if you..."

"That's going to be difficult to find out now. There are no casualty-lists being issued on the Internationals now."

"But isn't there any way of finding out? There must be some way?"

"I'll do what I can," she said sympathetically.

"It's very important to me. I'll write down their names. There are five of them."

"All I can do is send the names to Brigade headquarters in Albacete. But it might take weeks before we get an answer."

"And there's no way...?"

"Only by going up to Jarama."

"Then I'll go to Jarama."

"How will you get away? You'll be working most of the day. After you've been on the job for some time perhaps you could get someone to take over for a few days. But I'll do my best."

"You see, I was supposed to go up with them and I was transferred to this job, and..."

"I understand," she said. "I'll do what I can. And remember, if you need anything don't be afraid to ask for it. I remember how I felt when I first arrived."

Pepe and I went back to the radio station.

"Soon you will know everything," said Pepe.

"Why does mail take so long to get anywhere?"

"Esta la guerra. Do not worry. Soon you will get use to everything."

15

"Hello, North America. Hello, North America. This is Station E.A.R., the Voice of Republican Spain, coming to you over a wave-length of 32 kilocycles every afternoon at one p.m. and evenings at nine p.m. Eastern Daylight Saving Time. We bring you the last-minute war news and descriptions of life behind the lines. This evening..."

I began to recite the introduction to the broadcasts in my sleep. I sat in front of that microphone in the little cellar on the corner of the Alcala and the Gran Via and read the latest war communiqués or described how a city lived under siege.

My pay was three hundred pesetas a month. For two centimos I could buy a newspaper. For one peseta I could buy coffee, and for ten centimos more, a bun. Dinner could be bought for four to six pesetas. One of the waiters at the Gran Via did a good business in contraband American cigarettes, selling a packet at any price from ten to fifteen pesetas, depending on the supply and the look on your face.

His name was Ricardo, and you weren't supposed to mention the word "cigarette." You said: "Salud, hombre, cómo está?" And he would answer: "Bueno, y tu?" and you would answer back: "Muy bueno," and sigh and put two fingers close to your lips as if you were holding a cigarette, and he would either nod, blinking his eyes, or would pay no attention. When he nodded you followed him into the kitchen. There the transaction took place. We had to go through this elaborate ceremony every time we wanted cigarettes. Then the price went up. When he first sold me a packet, he asked only ten pesetas, but a week later he told me that it was going to be difficult to get the cigarettes and that he himself was paying a higher price. It cost me fifteen after that. Of course, he should have been reported for profiteering, but then we wouldn't have been able to get cigarettes... and he wasn't making a terrific profit, anyway.

Most of the reporters ate at the Gran Via. Everyone of them smoked cigarettes, and it was small wonder that his supply was running low. It was remarkable that he didn't ask more for each packet.

I became friendly with two of the reporters: Kenneth, who was in Spain for a New York newspaper, and Blorio, the correspondent for L'Humanité, the French Communist newspaper.

We were together one afternoon in the press-room. It was the week-end of the first week in March. A Government communiqué had just been issued announcing large concentrations of Italian troops north of Madrid in the Guadalajara Province. The communiqué reported that Government troops were retreating in orderly fashion.

Kenneth looked at the map on the wall. "There, see? Two days ago they were at kilometre 100. To-day they're at kilometre 60. That's forty kilometres in two days. It looks bad."

Just then the building shook.

We looked up. "Hit again," Kenneth announced, as if he were announcing rain. "That's the tenth time this week."

"I didn't even hear it come this time," Blorio said.

Blorio was still looking at the map. The shell had hit the other side of the building. He had not even moved.

"I shall go up there to-morrow," he announced.

"I'll go with you," said Kenneth.

I couldn't go. I had to be at the radio station at five o'clock in the afternoon and at one in the morning.

Rosa walked from the censor's office.

"Well, how do things look to you?" Kenneth asked.

"Bad," she answered.

"What do you know? Anything new?"

She didn't answer.

"Did you hear anything to-day?" Blorio asked.

"No. I just know things look bad." She was worried.

Later, alone with her in the censor's room, she told me: "The Italians are advancing like a steam-roller. We can't stop them. It looks very bad."

I stared at her, not believing. "But it's impossible."

She shrugged. "Not this time, I'm afraid. They are going to cut the highway from the north and they are advancing at a very fast rate."

That night my broadcast was very brief. I could only report heavy concentrations of Italian troops north-west of Madrid.

16

When I awoke next morning I went to the press-room immediately to get the latest news from the front. Rosa had been up most of the night.

"Better announce a retreat to-night. Prepare for the worst," she said.

Blorio and Kenneth had gone up to the front, or as near as they could get to it.

The press-room was in a gloom. Everyone was quiet at lunch. Ricardo scowled and the food was even worse than usual. Rice and beans, but this time the oil seemed more rancid than usual.

The agency men, Powers and Alexanders, were very glum, and Powers was predicting the end.

"It's all over," said Powers.

"Wait. I was here in November," said Alexanders, "and everybody was saying the same thing then."

"But they weren't Italian troops then," said Powers.

"That's true."

The dining-room was full as always. Officers mostly with their girl friends or tarts.

"There's Mercédès," said Powers, grinning.

Mercédès was a Moorish prostitute who had bitten Wellington's leg. He was a correspondent for an English daily and wasn't around this evening.

"Buenos días," said Mercédès.

"Sit down," invited Powers.

"Thank you."

"How's Wellington?" Alexanders asked her.

"What I care? You care a goddamn?" Her blonde-streaked hair waved.

"God, no."

She was satisfied.

"How did the whole thing happen?" I asked casually.

"Everybody make too much of whole goddamn business," said Mercédès. "Ricardo! Food!"

Ricardo slapped down a plate of rice.

"Ugh," said Mercédès.

Alexanders smoked his cigarette. "Wellington insists she bit off about a half-pound of flesh."

"He can afford it," said Powers.

"He-he!" giggled Mercédès. "Yes, he has plenty. He should not try to cheat me. How is the war going, gentlemen?"

"Lousy," said Powers.

"I am not busy this afternoon," said Mercédès.

"I'll take the afternoon off, too," said Powers. "But promise not to bite me."

"Everybody make too much of the whole business," said Mercédès. "I will eat first and then we discuss the war."

"Fine," said Powers.

"I hope you get hydrophobia," said Alexanders.

17

That night after the broadcast I went to Blorio's hotel. He would know exactly what was what. He'd been at the front. His hotel was near the Puerta del Sol. The streets were pitch-dark. I stumbled twice over shell-holes. The concierge at the hotel sleepily took me up in the elevator. I knocked at Blorio's door.

"Entrez."

I walked in. He was sitting at his typewriter.

"How goes it?" I asked.

He filled two glasses of whisky, sat down on his bed and sighed.

"Better get a car ready." He took a gulp.

"It's really that bad?"

"Madrid is going to be cut off....The Italians are coming down like a storm. It was terrible. Our soldiers are coming one way...backward."

"But did it look orderly? Were they in a panic?"

"They were orderly. So what? But we're retreating. I am writing an article preparing my paper for the worst. Only a miracle can stop them now....Get a car ready if you can and I will phone you if anything happens....We'll have to go to Valencia. And the Fifth Column is getting active again. There's been shooting in the streets again. Ah——" He brushed his hair back. "I will phone you and let you know."

"Phone me," I said. "But I work under orders of the Brigade. If I'm told to leave, I will. But phone me, anyway...."

We said good night and I gulped down another whisky.

It's impossible. After these months. After November. The fighting in University City. The stand at Jarama. It's impossible, I said to myself.

My flashlight batteries were going dead. I walked for a few blocks and realised that I had lost my way.

And if Madrid is cut off? The war wouldn't be over yet by a long shot...but better not think about it.

Where the hell am I? I've never been on this street before. A Fifth Column sniper could pick me off as easy as anything, and who the hell would know what happened? It can't be as bad as Blorio says. I'll stay on. That's the least I can do. I'll stay in Madrid till the end. But if it were as bad as they say, the Brigade would have begun making preparations to move.... Smith didn't say anything about the Brigade being moved...it can't possibly be as bad as they say....I could hear the occasional chatter of machine-gun fire in University City, and, at longer intervals, a trench-mortar exploding.

And then, out of the night: "Alto!"

I froze and stopped dead.

A flashlight burst in my face. Two armed militiamen peered at me.

One said something.

It can't be the password, I said to myself. You only have to know the password if you're in a car.

"Yo Norteamericano. Camarada, camarada," I stuttered.

I took a step backward and was about to put my hand in my pocket to get my night pass when I felt a bayonet-point in my back. My arms rose over my head.

"What the hell is this? I'm a comrade. Anti-fascista. Sure. What's the big idea?"

They said something again. I heard one of them mutter under his breath. He took a step forward. The other held the flashlight.

"Qué pasa, hombre?" he said. He pointed to my uplifted hands. "Por qué?"

I turned round slowly. The bayonet-point turned out to be an awning bar jutting out from the side of a wall.

I pointed at it, feeling foolish.

The militiaman grunted. The other smiled.

I swallowed and showed them my night pass. They glanced at it and walked away. I heard "loco Norteamericano" in their muffled conversation.

I suddenly remembered I was lost. "Hey, camarada!" I shouted. It echoed like a rifle-shot through the streets. They stopped, then came toward me slowly. I walked toward them. "Hôtel Nacional," I mumbled. I hadn't realised how much the whisky had affected me.

One of them cursed under his breath.

"Hôtel Nacional. Me. No. Lost. Dónde Hôtel Nacional, camarada, por favor, muchas gracias?"

They took me by the arm without a word and led me across the street. We walked one block, not uttering a sound. We turned a corner and there was the hotel.

"Well! Just round the corner. Well..."

They walked in with me and spoke to the night clerk, Diego. Diego's English was a little better than Pepe's.

"They say it seems you drank a little too much."

"That may be so. Only two glasses. Thank them very much."

"They want me to explain that it is their duty to stop anyone on the street after ten o'clock. The Fifth Column is getting active again."

"A misunderstanding. I'm terribly sorry. I'll never hold my arms up again."

The militiamen said "Salud," and marched out.

Diego took me up in the elevator.

"The food situation is getting worse and worse," he said.

"I know. We had rice and oil again to-day."

"They eat well in Valencia and Barcelona, I hear."

"I'd rather be in Madrid."

"Naturally. How can anyone compare Madrid to Valencia? But they eat better there."

The elevator made me dizzy.

"You are feeling ill, perhaps?"

"No. I'm all right....What do the newspapers say about Guadalajara?" I asked.

"Guadalajara? We have retreated. But that means nothing very much. We will attack soon and push them back."

"Simple."

"Good night, Señor Coortees."

"Good night, Comrade Diego. My name's Bob, call me Comrade Bob, not Bobs, but Bob...I'm sleepy as hell..."

18

We were sitting in the press-room next day burying Madrid and the war and the English Tories and the democracies and the world.

"Only a miracle can stop them," said Kenneth. "Mechanised equipment... finest material any modern army can boast of...two complete Italian divisions. I've seen them mop up in Ethiopia...."

"But the Spaniards aren't Ethiopians," I said. "We have some arms..."

Everyone sighed....

"The people in the streets don't seem to be disheartened," I said.

"That's because they don't know what's happening."

Blorio was staring out of the window. He shrugged his shoulders.

"I say nothing now...nothing...we better shut up and wait and see...."

The door of the press-room opened. All of us turned. My mouth dropped. A woman...a camera hanging at a strap around her neck...Lisa Kammerer.

The conversation died. The gloom evaporated.

Blorio made a clucking noise with his tongue.

"This *is* the press-room?" Lisa asked, a little unsure, staring at the gentlemen of the Press who were gaping.

"Mais oui," Blorio said eagerly. "But come in. Just arrived, yes? Photographer?"

"Yes..." She looked around.

Blorio was bubbling over. "Sit down. You must be tired. Parlez-vous français, peut-être?"

"Non. Mon français est très mal. Allemand et anglais."

"Well then," said Blorio, "I speak English."

"What is the matter?" asked Lisa.

"What is the matter?"

"Why does everyone stare so?"

"Oh..." Blorio laughed. "It's not every day that a pretty blonde woman enters our press-room."

Lisa turned and looked at each of us. Not a sign of recognition. Maybe it's because I need a shave, I said to myself a little sourly.

Blorio introduced us. Lisa didn't move from her seat. She nodded and smiled to each of us.

"You must join us for dinner," said Blorio.

"I want to get done with some things very fast," said Lisa. "First I want a room. Second, I want to wash. Third, I want to get up to Guadalajara."

"Let's see...a room. You will have to see Rosa, the censor, about getting front passes. Now a room..."

"I think you can get a room in the Hôtel Nacional," I said.

"The Florida might have a room," said Kenneth.

"I'm sure about the Nacional," I said.

"Is there any hot water there?" Blorio asked. "Maybe the Palace has a room."

"There's hot water once a week," I said. "Do you take a bath more than once a week?"

She looked a little weary. "Is it far from here?" she asked curtly.

"The Hôtel Nacional? A fifteen-minute walk."

"I have a car downstairs."

"I can go along and see that everything is arranged," said Blorio.

"That's okay; Diego speaks English. I'll be able to attend to everything."

Blorio gave me a look that said he would attend to me later. Kenneth was smiling. Lisa got up.

"See you later," I said.

I closed the door very softly behind Lisa.

In the elevator I asked her: "Don't you remember me?"

"You look familiar…but…"

"The fort. Figueras…Comandante Kuller's office. You were waiting for a car to go to Valencia…"

"But of course." She laughed. A low, throaty laugh.

"And the name's Bob Curtis…" I added.

"I remember now. But you've changed so…."

"Changed? It's only a few weeks…"

"You look much older. I would never have recognised you. I remember now. You were the one who asked me if I were married. I even gave you my address. Of course I remember. Were you not in the Brigade?"

"Yes…but I was transferred to do radio work."

"It must be very interesting."

"Very."

We walked out of the building. Her car was parked by the kerb.

"This is a bad place to park a car," I said. "The shells fall on this side."

"Then we will get away very soon."

We settled in the back seat. I told the chauffeur to drive straight ahead to the first boulevard with trees and then turn right.

We were silent for a while. I didn't know what to say.

"Have you been getting good pictures?" I asked.

"Yes and no. I want to get some good action pictures. I heard in Valencia that there was fighting in the Guadalajara Province."

"We're retreating."

"But they didn't sound pessimistic about it in Valencia."

"They don't know what's happening."

"I am glad I am here. I hate Valencia. I have wanted to get to Madrid for so long…."

She looked out of the window.

"Are you going to stay here long?"

"That depends on the situation. If I can get good pictures."

It felt unreal, her sitting beside me and our talking so casually.

"Are you sure there are rooms?" she asked.

"Oh, yes, sure." I turned to her. "I was just wondering about the guys I came with. I haven't heard from them since they went to the front…seeing you made me think of them."

We got out of the car and Diego shook his head. "There are no rooms, camarada."

I took him aside and told him she was all right and that she was a childhood friend. Then it dawned on me that I didn't really know if she was all right…

maybe...be a fine romantic angle if she turned out to be a spy....I walked back to her.

"Have you credentials of any kind?"

"Of course." She opened her purse. There was a letter of introduction from the Ambassador in Paris and another letter from the Press Department in Valencia, and her press-card.

I walked back to Diego, who had taken his place behind the counter.

"She's a childhood friend," I started over again, "and she and I are going to get married."

"Oh...well, then maybe I can find a room." He smiled benignly. "There is one on the floor below yours. Will that be satisfactory?"

"Swell."

"Is he convinced that I am all right?" she asked.

"Perfectly. He doesn't usually ask, but most of the people who come here are recommended by the Brigade. I told him you and I were childhood friends. That clinched it. I also told him you were my fiancée. That clinched it double."

"Fiancée? Did you have to tell him that?"

"No. But you've got a room."

I helped her with her baggage. Her room was large and, like mine, overlooked the boulevard.

"Those reporters," she said, "what is the matter with them? Have they never seen a woman?"

"Not a natural blonde for a long time. The peroxide has run out in the city and the blondes here have long streaks of black in their hair. You're the first bona fide blonde they've seen since they've come to Spain."

She sat on the bed shaking her head. "I hope there is hot water."

"I'll see." I went into the bathroom, turned the tap and put my hand under it. Ice-cold.

"No hot water," I answered. "I have an electric plate. You could heat a little water, enough to wash your face and hands. I'll get it."

I rushed up to my room and back again.

"Thank you," she said. "Will you call for me in about fifteen minutes?"

I paced my room, my excitement growing as I thought of it—she in Madrid—in the same hotel——

I kept looking at my watch. Twenty-five to seven. Twenty minutes had passed. I walked down the flight of stairs to call for her. She was combing her hair. Her face was radiant.

"A good wash makes you feel like a new person. That electric plate is wonderful. I must buy one. Look what I have! We will share it."

She went to the cupboard and opened the door. About a dozen cans of assorted foodstuffs were on the shelf.

"Good?" she asked, her eyes shining.

"Good? Wonderful!"

She looked up at me. "You and I are going to be good friends, yes?"

"I hope so."

"Yes—we will be. We will share my food. We will share everything, yes?"

"I haven't much to share."

"You have—in Madrid everyone must have something to share. Do you know what it means for me to be in Madrid? You do not think I am too—too——" she waved her hands—"too excited?"

"Why do you say that?"

"I do not know. I am so excited. To-morrow you will see...I will be so good and just like a lady. You will see. Tell me, you are very young, yes?"

"I feel very old."

"How old. Twenty-six, twenty-seven?"

"Twenty-one."

"No! Twenty-one? But you look so much older!"

"I feel older—but twenty-one, that's the age."

"I'm twenty-three. Do I look twenty-three?"

"No—you look about nineteen."

She laughed: "Nineteen? You should have known me when I was nineteen. Before I became a photographer. I was going to be an artist. Why do I talk to you like this?"

I had been standing near the door watching her. She had been standing by the bed. She walked toward me, her eyes looking into mine.

"We'll be late for dinner," I said.

"I am not always like this. But you make me want to talk. I like you. I'm so glad we have met again....Why are you unhappy?"

"It's a long story."

"Tell me."

"Not now—there isn't much to tell, but not now. And now I'm not unhappy. I'm happier now than I've been in a long time."

"Bob."

"Yes."

"It's a good feeling. You and I are going to be good friends....A month ago I would never have talked this way to anyone. Spain is doing something to me— do you feel as good as I feel? Don't look at me that way. Believe me."

"I do," I said.

"Your eyes. It is your eyes. They remind me of something—Bob? Canadian? Twenty-one? So old—and so young. But, shh! to-morrow you will see, I will be a lady. So——" She pulled in her chin and held her shoulders back and smiled, nodding her head.

"Don't be a lady—God! I'm glad you came. I knew you'd be like this. When I first saw you I knew it."

We stood there smiling at one another, not saying a word. Then she took my arm and hugged it.

"Only in Madrid could such things happen——" she said.

We walked out of her room to the elevator.

19

Dinner was wonderful that night. Everyone ate with relish and there were no cracks made about mule meat or monkey meat or dog meat. We were served steak, mule steak, but everyone ate silently, apparently enjoying it.

Blorio ordered wine for everyone and Powers ordered liqueurs.

Mercédès stared at her rival a little resentfully at first, but Lisa paid no attention to Powers, and after a while Mercédès began to smile.

Wellington, the bitten one, who was always very cheerful, even during his convalescence, was especially cheerful this evening. Ignoring Mercédès completely, he told Lisa that his hobby was photography, and they both discussed various types of cameras and films.

Blorio leaned toward me and whispered: "Madrid may be cut off—but does that matter? No! A blonde has arrived." He was scornful.

Blorio skilfully brought the conversation round to Guadalajara.

"What do you think will happen?" he asked Wellington innocently.

"Eh? Well, hang it all, chappie, you know the situation as well as I. Perhaps better." Turning to Lisa again. "Yes, I shall be glad to show you around. Take you to University City and the other places of interest..."

I was listening.

"Thank you very much," said Lisa. "But Mr. Curtis and I have arranged to go together."

"Oh...Curtis? Oh yes..." He looked at me and I smiled, nodding.

"Well, I am getting a car ready to leave at any moment," said Blorio quietly.

"What?" asked Wellington. "Surely it's not as serious as all that?"

"You don't have to worry," said Blorio teasing him, "when Franco marches into Madrid, you'll be all right. But think of those of us from the Left-wing press."

"You really believe Madrid is going to fall?" Lisa asked Blorio.

"No, I don't. But I know that the situation is very serious."

He spoiled the dinner.

I had to leave to get to the radio station on time.

"I'd like to see the radio station, if it's all right to go," asked Lisa.

"All right? It's wonderful. Come on."

We said good-bye to our dinner companions.

"That fat man made me sick," she said, in the car.

"He's harmless." I told her about Mercédès and Wellington.

She laughed. "That is funny."

Pepe was very gracious. "How do you do, please? The honour bestowed is welcome to our greatest extent. Please seat yourself upon the chair, so."

Lisa sat down, a trifle bewildered.

I gave my fifteen-minute broadcast and Lisa listened.

"It was a good broadcast....Have you received any letters from America yet?"

"It's too early yet. We just started a couple of weeks ago. But I hope they start coming in."

Pepe shook hands and told Lisa to come any time she wanted.

"His English? What kind is it?"

"A special Spanish, Pepe kind."

Back in the hotel, I remembered what she had told Wellington. "I understand you and I have a date."

"If you want to....I didn't want to go with him."

"It's a pleasure. I'm free in the afternoons. We can go to University City to-morrow. Unless you want to get up to Guadalajara first."

"It depends on what happens. We will see to-morrow. I'm happy about our being in the same hotel....Do you feel sleepy? Perhaps we can go for a walk."

"Swell."

We decided to walk down the stairs instead of taking the elevator.

"Good evening, Diego. How are things?"

"Things? Things are as always. I have read to-day in the papers that the railway to Madrid is about completed. Perhaps we shall get more food now."

"I hope so. Good night, we're going for a walk."

"Remember not to raise your hands," said Diego.

I told Lisa about the episode with the guards.

"Do you think there are still members of the Fifth Column around?" she asked.

"Of course. But they're not doing any sniping these days. Have you your night-pass?"

"Yes."

"Let's sit on one of the benches," I suggested.

We sat on a bench and listened to the sounds of the night.

"What is that?" she asked.

"Trench-mortar...University City...hear? Machine-guns..."

Then quiet again.

"Do they shell at night?"

"Very often."

"A city looks dead at night without lights. The buildings are like ghosts. I feel as if I were in some ancient city. Perhaps it is the effect of the darkness...do you feel like that?" she asked.

"Sometimes, at night. During the day it is more alive than any city I've seen—the few I have seen."

"But this darkness and the streets and the building...and the sound of guns... Once in Berlin when I was a little girl the lights went out on our block. I was so afraid. I looked out of the window and watched the blackness and heard the footsteps on the pavement and I thought the blackness had come and I was to be taken away...I ran to my mother...I was shivering with fright...I had forgotten about it. Now I see it as if it had happened yesterday."

I could distinguish her face in the darkness, the chiselled beauty of her cheeks and chin, a high cheekbone and full lips. Her voice was low, almost a whisper.

"Let us go back now. I am getting cold," she said.

We walked slowly, listening to the echo of our feet on the pavement. We were alone on the street. We held hands and said nothing.

In front of her door we said good night and she said: "Shall we have breakfast together?"

"Yes..."

"Good night. It was nice..." She stood on her toes and kissed me quickly on the cheek and closed the door.

I climbed the stairs to my room three at a time.

20

The phone in my room woke me up next morning. It was Blorio. At first I could not understand what he was saying. He was speaking very fast and was very excited.

"Speak slower. I can't hear a word you say. Speak closer to the phone."

"It's happened! It's happened!" he was shrieking.

"For God's sake, what's happened?"

"The Italians...a rout...they're running..."

"Who's running?"

"The Italians....I got a call from one of our officers. First our troops held them and then our planes put them into a panic....I'm going out there right away. I will call you when I get back. Maybe Lisa wants to go and get some pictures...."

"I'm sure she'll want to go. Call her."

"It happened at Brihuega....The Italians fell into a trap. We captured hundreds of prisoners...machine-guns, ammunition. They were completely demoralised by our planes. Oh-oh. I am so excited. Good-bye. I'll call her. Wake up, Lisa. No, never mind. I'll call her myself. I kiss you...oh...oh..." He hung up.

I ran down to Lisa's room. She was still in bed.

"Say that again..." She said sleepily.

"The Italians have been routed. Blorio just called. He's hysterical. He just got a call from one of the officers. It happened yesterday. Our planes bombed them and they became demoralised and started to run. Blorio wants to know if you want to go up there and get some pictures."

She reached for her dressing-gown and jumped out of bed. "Go?" She ran into the bathroom and from there shouted: "Can you come too?"

"No, I can't. I've got to give my broadcast at one o'clock....But phone me when you get back."

The telephone rang. It was Blorio.

"Yes, she's getting dressed....No...in the bathroom....Don't be a fool. You phoned me in my room, didn't you? Better lie down and take a rest, you sound half insane."

"Who is it?" she shouted.

"Blorio."

"Tell him I will call for him with the car in fifteen minutes."

"She will call for you in fifteen minutes. No, I can't come. My broadcast... Of course, I know what it means. A turning point in the war? A turning point in world history? Stop agitating me. I'm convinced."

Lisa streaked out of the bathroom. "I could kiss you...it is wonderful...."

"Go ahead..."

She smiled, walked to me and took my face in her hands and planted a loud kiss on my lips. "There, like a mother," she said.

"You can adopt me right away."

"Now, get out, please. I have to finish dressing."

"Okay....Hell, I wish I were going with you. I'll have to get someone to help with those damned broadcasts....Take care of yourself. We'll go to University City some other time."

I stared out of the window of my room and waited until I saw her leave. Then I sat down and wrote my long-postponed letter to the gang. I addressed the letter to Harry. After starting a few times and tearing up the paper, I finally wrote:

Hello, Guys:

It's about time that I wrote this letter to you. But now that I sit down to write it, I don't know how to start.

I'm doing radio work....After you guys left Albacete, Motril got a letter from the political department in Madrid asking for a suitable guy to conduct radio broadcasts to North America. Someone suitable meant someone handy, I suppose, and I was around and Motril suggested that in view of the fact that I was once a reporter, I take the job. I protested a little—not too much, it seems—and here I am.

There's so much I want to write, but we better hold it until we see each other, which I hope will be soon.

Do you get cigarettes? How's food at the front? It's rotten in Madrid.

I don't know why, but I sort of take it for granted that none of our gang got hurt. I heard about the February 27th business, but it seems unlikely that any of the guys would get hurt on the same day they arrived in the lines. That's silly, I suppose, but write me and let me know what's what.

You can write c/o Station E.A.R. Madrid or the Prensa department. God knows when the letter will arrive, if it ever does arrive. I understand mail takes about a month to get here from home. It seems to take the same length of time to get here from Albacete.

Tell Alan to keep low....I still think he's too tall for a trench. And I hope his hair has grown back to normal. Did Milty get his Soviet gun? And has Doug been mistaken for a Moor yet? I suppose Lucien is still batting his eyes around.

Madrid is all we've imagined it to be. They'll never take this place. By the time you get this letter (if you get it) the excitement about Guadalajara will probably have died down. But we just heard the news this morning and it'll probably be in all the morning papers.

Tell Alan that Lisa, the photographer we saw in Figueras, is in Madrid and in the same hotel I'm in. I'll preserve her until you guys get leave or try to bring her to Jarama as soon as I can get away. Please write, all of you.

Salud,
Bob.

I had to mail the letter in Rosa's office. I walked out into the street and took a tram. The conductor held out his leather pouch.

"Diez centimos," he said.

The loose change felt heavy in my pocket. I made a mental note to buy a purse from the street pedlar who displayed her wares outside the Gran Via Hotel.

On the streets the news-boys were shouting out the story of Guadalajara. "Victoria á Guadalajara!" The newspapers carried flaming red headlines. Everybody was buying papers. Some threw them into the air and let out loud whoops. Women giggled.

Guadalajara. Guadalajara. Guadalajara.

Everyone on the tram was laughing. At the next stop about ten people, laughing and making a lot of happy noises, heaved themselves to the platform. The tram was crowded. A woman with a basket of eggs kept telling the man beside her: "Hombre, you're breaking my eggs." He grunted and told her that eggs did not matter when they had just won a victory at Guadalajara.

There were excited conversations.

"The highway is safe."

"First Jarama and then Guadalajara."

"Now if they'll sell us arms we'll clean them up in a month."

"Hombre, wait till the world hears of this."

When I began pushing my way through the crowd, saying, "Pardones, pardones," they smiled good-naturedly, but one militiaman who had had his fill of onions that morning breathed straight into my face. I said "Whew!" and everyone laughed, including the militiaman. When I finally managed to squeeze through and bring my feet to the street, I found I was a block past my stop. I walked back slowly towards the Gran Via.

Workmen were building a cement casing around the statue of Neptune to protect him from the shells.

I hailed them. "Salud."

"Muchas obuses ahora," one of them said.

He went into a long explanation of why he thought the city would be punished by more shells than usual now because of the victory at Guadalajara.

This section of the city, the business section, had not been subjected to intensive shelling yet. The Cuatro Caminos district and the quarters near University City had suffered badly.

I turned up the Gran Via. Posters advertised American films and some dealt with the war. One called for a unified command. Another, vigilance in the rear. Another, unification of the working-class parties.

The cafés were crowded, as usual, with early-morning breakfasters. Life seemed leisurely. The windows were criss-crossed with papers to prevent shattering if a shell dropped close by. Some of the windows were protected with sandbags.

I heard the drone of planes. My heart started to pound at the sound. People stared up at the sky.

Then I heard shouts of "Chatos! Chatos! Nuestra! Nuestra!"

Ten snub-nosed Russian biplanes skimmed over the buildings. Probably an air-show to celebrate Guadalajara. The people on the streets cheered. Children held their mouths wide open and shrieked at the top of their lungs, their necks almost breaking as they followed the flight of the planes. After ten minutes of showing off, the planes flew away.

I lit a cigarette. It was a warm day. I noticed the way soldiers on leave said "Guapa!" when a pretty girl passed and the way the girls answered, "Gracias." It was good. When they thought a woman pretty in Spain, they let her know it. Next time I saw a pretty girl, I was going to say "guapa" too.

A fast-moving camion narrowly missed bumping into me as I crossed the street. "You should have been an aviator!" I shouted at him.

"Whee!" shrieked the chauffeur.

The theatres were showing some American films. Charlot Chaplin in *Modernos Tiempos* was coming to the Capitol.

The purse pedlar had not arrived yet. I pushed my way through the revolving doors leading to the café of the Gran Via Hotel. The place was crowded. There was no one there I knew. All the reporters had probably gone up to Guadalajara.

Ricardo brought me what he said was chocolate, and as I sipped the pasty brown stuff that was almost taste-less, I dreamed of one single solitary day in Paris or New York with Lisa, sipping malted milk.

I saw the fat little old woman arrange her leather wares on the sidewalk.

Then I heard a faint swishing sound and the chocolate stuck on my tongue. The swish got louder and I felt my stomach contract. There was an explosion and the shatter of heavy glass.

People cursed.

There was the swish again, but the shell exploded farther away.

Some of the people ran into the street, making the revolving doors turn and turn. I walked out as slowly as I could, but the doors were revolving too fast and I had to make a dash for it.

I saw the little old woman lying on the sidewalk with her purses all over the place and her dress over her head.

She had been hit in the stomach with heavy pieces of shrapnel. Two militiamen were staring silently. One woman kept whining: "Why do they shell here? Why here?"

Then the ambulance came, and when they lifted the old woman a part of her intestines fell to the street. I remembered I hadn't finished my chocolate.

"A bad business," Ricardo said, "a bad business."

"I'd like some water, please."

"Sí, camarada."

The people ebbed back into the café. Some newcomers came in and asked what had happened, and one young prostitute was a little hysterical and kept whimpering; "But she was my friend, she was my friend," and her soldier boy friend was telling her to please shut up.

Ricardo came back with the water. He poured himself a drink first and sat down beside me. "You are pale," he said, "better drink."

I sipped the water slowly.

"They think they can demoralise us that way. They are crazy. Perros!" Ricardo spat.

"You'll have to board the window," I said.

"Yes....Every day...every day...Ten killed. Fifteen killed. They're trying to kill us off one by one. Poor old woman. She has been coming here for five years now. She has two sons at the front. Wait till they hear of this."

"They should clean it up right away," I said.

"They will. Soon the street-cleaners will come and wash it away with their hoses. Ah, I have seen them washing the blood into the gutters for months now. I'm getting used to it. Perros!" He let out another foul oath.

I paid my bill and walked through the revolving doors. I didn't look at the sidewalk and ran up to Rosa's to mail my letter to the guys.

21

"We shall move the press-room from the telefonica. It's becoming too dangerous for the reporters to walk up the Gran Via," Rosa was saying.

I told her about the woman on the sidewalk.

"Oh," Rosa shuddered. "I have told her so many times to move from that place."

Again the whining shriek of a shell. We both waited. The building shook. "Hear? That's the sixth hit to-day. My nerves! I envy the reporters. They can get away."

The press-room was deserted. Everyone had gone up to Guadalajara.

Rosa read my letter to the guys and stamped it.

"You didn't hear anything yet, did you, about my friends?"

"No. I sent their names to Albacete. I haven't heard a word yet."

"I've got to get up and see them. I'll manage it some way."

"In a few weeks or so, maybe you'll be able to have someone take over for a day. I wish I could. I'd do it for you."

"I'll manage it somehow....When will the official casualty-list come in on the shellings?"

"Perhaps late to-night or to-morrow morning. Your nerves are bad, Bob. Better take things easy."

"I'm all right. It's getting tiresome, talking about shelling, shelling, shelling. Madrid was shelled again to-day. Fifty people killed. One hundred wounded. The people listening must be bored with it."

"Soon you'll be able to report some interesting political developments."

"Such as?"

"Well, I cannot say anything now. But there will probably be some Cabinet changes. Perhaps Caballero will find himself out in the cold."

"How soon will the fireworks start?"

"That I do not know. But things are coming to a head. The Poumists are allowed to fight the Government in the open. The inefficiency in the high command makes you ill when you hear about it. But after the Guadalajara victory the army and the political commissars will demand drastic and immediate changes, a unified command, a functioning war industry. The army still isn't strong enough to conduct an offensive. It cannot be until the rear is properly organised. The central command in Madrid has been opposing Caballero's policies. After the miracle at Guadalajara they will have an argument that will be hard to fight. And it's about time."

"Why do you call Guadalajara a miracle? It looks like a well-planned trap."

"It was. And the Italians fell right into it. That's the miracle. Remember me predicting the end? I honestly believed that everything was almost over—for Madrid, anyway. But I was at the War Ministry this morning and I learned that while we were all predicting the end, Miaja was laughing up his sleeve. The plan worked perfectly. There wasn't a leak anywhere, and usually the enemy knows about our plans almost before we do. I'm too tired to get too excited about it, but if you only realised what it means."

"Well, do you think the war will last long now?"

"Mussolini will send even more soldiers now. Prestige. Hitler and Mussolini are not going to give up after one defeat. Not while England is so obliging."

"It'll end in a world war...or they'll kill every Spaniard on this side," I said, staring out of the window.

"The people in England and France aren't dead yet. They can't allow things to go on as they are much longer...I hope," she smiled. "You get a feeling after a while that the only people that realise what it's all about are the Spaniards. But I suppose London and Paris will have to be bombed first before they wake up."

She began checking some communiqués that had come in.

"Did that girl photographer get a room?"
"Yes...in my hotel."
"She seems to be very nice."
"She is."

Rosa held out her hand and smiled. "Take care of yourself. They are still shelling."

"I'll run like hell all the way. Pepe must be composing a masterpiece on Guadalajara."

"Give my love to him if it so pleases him according to his desire," giggled Rosa.

22

Lisa had not returned when I got back to the hotel from the radio station. I picked up a copy of Keats and read it, waiting for her.

There was a knock on the door. She came in looking tired and pale.

"It was terrible," she said.

"Terrible?"

"I got good pictures...wonderful pictures...." She sat down on the bed. "You will see them. But, Bob, it was terrible. Their bodies strewn over the ground like garbage. A hand here. A head there. Wait till you see the pictures. They were being buried in heaps. They were so young, young Italian boys."

She pressed her temples. "I was sorry you were not there with me. Blorio is used to such things. He sounded inhuman. Without feeling. Ach! I suppose he felt it too, but he didn't want to show it, being a man. God! hundreds and hundreds of them. It smelled so bad. Hundreds of Italian trucks, machine-guns, hand-grenades, rifles, ammunition. They threw away everything when they ran. We spoke to some prisoners. They were so frightened. So young. Like you. The same age as you and your friends."

"Don't compare them to my friends."

"Oh no. I do not mean that way. But they look the same when they are dead. They look the same. I wanted to cry for them. The poor, poor fools."

"I'll get you a shot of whisky." I poured it. "Take it. It will do you good. Where is Blorio?"

"Thank you. It is good. It makes me feel warm. Blorio is telephoning his story. All the reporters were there. Kenneth kept saying: 'It's amazing. It's amazing.' He examined the equipment. The same kind they used in Ethiopia. He couldn't believe his eyes. He speaks Italian fluently and he spoke to some of the prisoners.

They told him they were glad they were prisoners. They didn't want to fight. He spoke to two Italian colonels. They tried to act so brave. Maybe they were brave. I hated them because they knew what they were doing and they were so proud of it."

"I'm sorry I wasn't there," I said.

"I will show you the pictures. There were documents showing that two complete Italian divisions were working under direct orders from Rome. I took pictures of them. I got a picture of a telegram Mussolini sent to his generals wishing them victory. It was some victory. He'll learn that he needs more than guns to have victories."

"Have we advanced far?"

"We chased them beyond Brihuega. We hold Brihuega."

Then looking at me in that serious way of hers, and talking half to herself, "How long can it go on?"

"Years, if they send more Italian troops....You're tired. Better try to sleep now."

She lay her head on the pillow and closed her eyes. I stared down at her. I bent down slowly and kissed her cheek. Her eyes opened.

"You are sweet," she said. "Remind me to tell you that I like your eyes when I wake up."

I bent down swiftly and kissed her lips and she put her arms around me. We didn't say anything. I held her close to me and she fell asleep in my arms.

Quietly I untangled her arms. I watched her for what seemed an eternity. Then I rose from the bed without making it creak too much and sat down by my desk. I wrote furiously for half an hour. It started out to be a broadcast on how the tempo of the war was changing the habits of the people, how the reality of machine-guns and planes and tanks and the threat of destruction were forcing the people, the Republicans, the Socialists, the Catholics, the Anarchists, the Communists, to unite their forces and merge their differences.

Then I looked at Lisa again and heard her mumble something in her sleep. I stared at the pencil in my hand.

What the hell do I really know about the habits of the Spanish people, and about the realities of the war and the forces underlying them?

Then I began writing about myself and stopped again when I realised that either I began with myself or ended with myself, and that everything I thought about revolved around myself.

I decided to boil some water. I had received my ration of minute coffee from Brigade headquarters. Lisa still had some crackers left. I listened to the water boiling and waited for her to wake.

"Hello," I said, smiling as she rubbed her tired eyes.

She yawned and curled up again.

I sat beside her. "Like some coffee?"

She opened her eyes. "Mmm, yes." She turned her head to one side and looked at me and then lifted her hand and touched my eye with her finger. "A man should not have such eyes."

"I'm very lucky."

"How many women have told you about your eyes?"

"All the little girls I knew back home."

"It made you conceited, didn't it?"

"I suppose so."

She sat up. "Is the coffee ready?"

"In about a minute."

"Why did you come to Spain?" She asked it casually and reached for her purse and took out a comb.

I went to look at the water. It was boiling. I poured it into two cups and brought one to the bed. "I have no sugar."

"Any milk?"

"No."

"It is bitter without sugar or milk...it is hot....Do you get afraid at night alone when they begin to shell?" she asked.

"Not now. I used to at the beginning."

"You have not answered my question."

"I came for the same reason most of the guys came. I came because I thought I could do something in the world beside talk. So I'm still talking....I probably came, too, to understand myself a little more."

"Do you like doing radio work?"

"No, not very much..." I sipped my coffee. "And why did you come, outside of the apparent reason?"

She stood up and placed the cup on the chair. "I came, too, because I wanted to do something in this world beside talk. But I want to find out about you... what did you do in America? What kind of a life did you have? Were you happy? No, that is silly. You could not have been very happy. But——" she shrugged— "you know what I mean. What kind of a person were you? What did you think about? What did you want to do? What were you like when you were a little boy?"

"I belonged to a gang. We raided fruit-stores and stole apples and bananas, mostly apples. I wanted to be an aviator. Then I wanted to be an archæologist. Then I wanted to be a doctor. I was a Boy Scout and then became a cadet and then

I wanted to be Prime Minister of Canada. My family was poor. I used to work during the summers. I was a bus-boy in a summer hotel. I was a caddie."

"Caddie?"

"The boys who carry the bags for the people who play golf. Then I worked in a printing factory. I sold magazines from house to house. I sold vacuum-cleaners, electric light bulbs, scales, coffee-grinders, and one time I sold meat-cutters. In high school I became interested in politics. When I got out of high school it seems there was a depression. Couldn't get a job. Then I landed something on a paper. I was very excited about being a reporter until the glamour wore off. It took three weeks for the glamour to wear off. When I was seventeen I read a lot. Russian writers, Gorki, Dostoievsky, Tolstoi, Turgenev, Chekov, Pushkin. Read everything very fast and forgot what I read a week after I read it. Someone I knew gave me some pamphlets on political economy. They seemed logical. I became convinced that capitalism had to go, that only Socialism was the way out, for me, for the world. I read more and more. Lenin, Marx, Engels, Stalin. I became very active. Study groups, demonstrations, picket lines. I was a good speaker. Most of my friends were going through the same thing, more or less. They read very fast and forgot very fast. Some became Communists, others didn't give a damn. My so-called youth is almost a general biography of the youth of America—my background, that is. I did sell a few stories to some magazines, and slowly but surely concentrated on nothing else but the movement. The thousands of other guys my age were living the same way I was, perhaps not thinking the same way, but seeking a way out the same way I was. I found it. They didn't. Some day they will. Now I am in Spain. And I still haven't settled one thing, but most of the guys who came, have."

"And that is...?"

"Is the world really as important to me as I said it was? It boils down to that."

"It is good," she said. "I mean it is good that you are able to sit back a little and watch. I do not think it is wrong. You are so young yet. Give yourself a chance. If some of the other boys found themselves in your position they would be thinking the same way you are. It is good that you are honest with yourself."

"I can content myself with that. But for how long? I've got to make a move, one way or the other. A man can be very honest with himself the same way I am and end up a complete fake. I've seen them. But it's not going to happen to me. At least, I hope not."

"And me. My childhood was so different. Is there more of this bitter coffee?"

I poured more hot water into her cup.

"My family was wealthy. My father was a rich merchant in Berlin. I was the only child. You did not tell me how many in your family."

"One older sister. Two younger brothers. One brother is becoming a good salesman, and I understand from my mother's letters that he is still interested in one thing, how to make money. My older sister just got married. To a doctor. She was his secretary. My other brother just entered high school. He's a good student. Won a scholarship."

She chuckled, remembering something. "I was going to be a nurse. I went to college. Then I became engaged. I was nineteen. Life was so boring. I did not know how to do anything and my father wanted me to get married as soon as possible. That was the only thing he thought I could do. I went to Paris for a two-week vacation. Then it started. Life, I mean. In a strange way. My cousin was a photographer on one of the newspapers. He took me with him on his assignments. I bought a camera. Carl, my cousin, told me I was dumb. I was beautiful but dumb. He said that if I didn't leave Berlin and my family, the same thing would happen to me that happened to Auntie Catherine. Auntie Catherine," Lisa smiled reminiscing, "was a brilliant chemist. Then she got married. She has four children and she has become fat and she does nothing. You would not understand. Catherine was our god. She was my mother's youngest sister. I was unhappy in Berlin. I was engaged to a boor of a man. A good-natured idiot whose father was a rich banker and who spoke about art the same way I have heard people speak about horses. Carl started to talk about politics to me and about the future of mankind. Carl was a Socialist. He introduced me to his friends, artists, journalists, photographers. I felt then that all my life I had been dead. I began to read, the same way you did, but I started later. I didn't go back to Berlin. I wrote my mother telling her I had a cold. I studied photography day and night. Carl got me a job on his paper. My mother and father came to Paris to take me home. I was living alone then, and I told them I was staying in Paris or anywhere I felt like staying. My father threatened to disown me. My mother cried. I weakened a little. But very little. They went back to Berlin. That was four years ago....I worked very hard during those four years. I tried to make up for all the time I had lost. I became a good photographer, and when the war started in Spain I knew that I was going to come here whether my paper sent me or not. I made the editor's life miserable. First he said a woman should not be sent to a war. When I reminded him how much better the pictures would be if a woman took them, he listened. Then when I told him I would go anyway, and give the pictures to another paper, he sent me to Spain. Now I am here."

"Both of us...but there's so much you haven't told me."

"Soon we will know each other. I feel it," she answered quietly. "You and I are going to be good friends." She looked at me and then: "Don't you feel that too?" she asked.

"I do," I answered. "I do, very much."

23

The last days of March passed swiftly. Blorio twitted me about a new light in my eye.

"In love?" he asked me.

"How's your stomach?" I answered.

"She is very beautiful. Ah...how a woman could choose you with me around I do not know. The way you managed to get her to your hotel. Such finesse."

"How's your stomach?" I asked. "I understand you had diarrhœa yesterday."

"Ah, she is so lovely...and I did not have diarrhœa. I had cramps. Tell me, does she really like you very much?" He was having fun.

Lisa bounced in and out of the press-room with her cameras, took pictures of everything, visited the nurseries and the factories, and studied Spanish.

We were in my room one afternoon during the last week of March.

I looked up from the paper and stared at her.

"And what are you looking at?" she asked.

"You. I can't believe it."

"Do not try to tell yourself it is love," she said. "It's the war. You need a woman. I need a man. There aren't any women who speak English, but there are plenty of men, and why I chose you..."

"It was convenient. We're both in the same hotel."

"Yes...if you had met another woman first you would have said you loved her."

"Maybe... if she were like you. If she looked like you. If she had your hair, your lips, your breasts and your German accent."

"So? You love me because I have hair and lips and breasts and a German accent! That is very fine!"

"But such hair and lips and breasts and *such* an accent."

"I hate you. I really do not like you at all." She looked at me tenderly. "It is a maternal complex. I feel like a mother to you."

"That's fine...but remember there are a few other women around now. There's that blonde dame who came here for one of the American magazines. She's not bad-looking at all. And there's that American brunette, who looks like a magazine cover."

"They have their men. I like the man that belongs to the blonde and he is really a good writer. I think I will take a picture of him. He will be flattered."

"Okay...we'll make an exchange...."

"Do you really think it is love?" she asked. "Do you honestly think you are in love with me?"

"What then? I want to marry you. That's proof enough for me."

"And you think you would want me after the war is over?"

"Goddamn it, I love you. I can't help that."

"Come here, Kindchen. I must love you or I wouldn't want to eat you up when your eyes start getting so big and you get so, so dramatic. Darling..." She pushed me away gently. "Darling, what should happen if I got a baby?"

"What?"

"No. Do not be foolish. I am not going to have one. I am asking what should happen *if* I were going to get one?"

"I forgot about people getting babies. I don't know. You'd probably go to Paris and wait there for me. But why think of it?"

"I do not know why I think of such things." She sighed and shrugged her shoulders. "Tell me, are you very happy?"

The question brought me out of my dreams.

I didn't answer.

"What is the matter?"

"Oh, nothing...." I went to the cabinet and poured myself a drink.

"Please do not drink it. Come here and talk to me."

I let the glass stand.

"I thought you had forgotten all about that...I thought you were satisfied with your work," she said.

"Let's not talk about it. I have...I've forgotten all about everything."

She kissed me. "Come here and love me. Promise me you will not do anything foolish. You are doing important work. Promise me...."

"Let's not talk about it, please," I said.

"Kindchen, I love you. Does not that make you happy? I love you, do you hear?"

"I hear. You're not telling the truth. How the hell can you love me when I'm so damned weak?"

"Weak? Hug me like that again. You call that weak?"

I was about to speak, but she closed my lips with hers, and closed my eyes with the tips of her cool fingers.

24

"Goddamn it, the only damn time we're alone together is at night."

"Well! Is there a better time to be together?"

"You know what I mean," I said.

"I know...." she sighed. "But to-day we will go and see the city and be alone. No reporters. No censors. No soldiers. No war. Nothing but you and me."

"I've got to be at the radio station at five o'clock. Then I've got to leave you at night and broadcast at one o'clock. Then I've got to take time off in the afternoon and write the broadcasts."

"I suppose it is the best possible honeymoon two people can have during a war," she said sadly. "Some day I'll cook you good dinners and…"

"Yeah…"

I got out of bed. There was a strong sun. The blind went up with a snap.

"Some day, soon, both of us will get a leave of absence," she said, "and we will have a real honeymoon."

I walked back to the bed and sat down and pulled her to me violently.

"You are breaking my bones," she said.

"Do you love me?" I asked her.

"I think so."

"Say yes or no."

"Yes…you know I do."

"Do you know that I have never loved anyone in my life before as I do you. Do you realise that?"

"Why didn't you speak like this last night instead of going right to sleep?"

"I was tired."

She was smiling.

"I am afraid that you are my first love too. A Canadian boy. A baby. Who hasn't found himself. Carl would laugh."

"What's funny?"

"Nothing…." She kissed my cheek and bit at my ear.

"You don't love me as much as I love you," I said. "Things don't bother you the same way they bother me. You're becoming the most important thing in the world to me, and I'm getting frightened by it. I'm getting frightened because if I lose you I'll die."

"You will make up your mind to go into the trenches soon and then where will I be?"

I stood up quickly.

She put out her hand, "No…I did not mean to say that."

"Okay…let it pass….I wish I didn't love you. I wish to hell you had never come to Madrid. Why the hell didn't you stay in Valencia?"

"I didn't like Valencia. Bob, stop being so nervous. You and I will have to get away. We must. Your nerves are cracking. Put your head here."

"Go to hell," I said.

She didn't answer.

"I said go to hell!"

"I heard you."

She got out of bed and began to dress. I stared out of the window at the cars and trams below.

"I'm sorry," I said.

She came to me. "I love you very much," she said.

I kissed her.

We walked slowly along the Alcalá....Lisa's camera swung by her side.

"Want me to hold it?"

"Mm," she shook her head.

It was a pleasant morning with the smell of spring in the air. Uniformed soldiers on leave walked along breathing the clean air. Some peasant boys, obviously in the big city for the first time, gaped at the ten-storey buildings. We saw new recruits, mostly young men, learning how to march, swinging their arms in front of them instead of on the side as American and French soldiers do. It made it look more amateurish. They drilled without guns. One soldier with a drum kept time. Some children stopped to watch them, but marching men aren't much to look at without a band, after nine months of war.

"Do you know any good American songs?" Lisa asked.

"Some negro songs. There's one that Doug used to sing."

"Sing it."

I sang it. *Religion is somethin' for de soul....*

Lisa made me sing it over a few times until she learned it. Then in her German accent she tried to sing the song in negro dialect.

"And why do you laugh?" she asked.

"I'm sorry none of the guys are around to hear it, that's all."

"When will Ricardo get more cigarettes?"

"God knows. Let's not go to the Gran Via to-night. The people make me sick. Let's invite Blorio and Kenneth and have a little party in our room."

"Okay...." said Lisa. "I like saying okay. Okay. Okay."

"Okay..." I said.

"Religion ees somethin' for de soul," sang Lisa.

"Better sing a German song."

"Maybe I better whistle."

"That's an idea."

"Happy?"

"Yep...you?"

"Yes...."

We stopped at a food queue. About three hundred women were standing in line. Some held babies in their arms. Lisa focused her camera and took a few shots.

"It is the faces, the faces," said Lisa. A woman smiled. Her quiet, wrinkled face was patient and her thin lips smiled. A little baby began to reach for the camera with its chubby hands. Lisa asked the mother if she could hold the baby. I held the camera while Lisa hugged the baby.

She sat down on the kerb with the baby in her lap. The baby's face was a soft brown.

"A boy or a girl?" Lisa asked in Spanish.

"Girl," answered the proud mother. "Teofila."

Teofila was interested in Lisa's blonde hair. She pulled at it, first very solemnly, and then chortling.

Lisa looked up at me. I raised the camera to my eye and clicked it.

"I want a baby," said Lisa.

"Better give it back."

She enfolded the child in her arms and rubbed her cheek against its face.

"Let me hold her a little." I sat down beside Lisa on the kerb and took Teofila. Her mother watched us with an amused smile.

"Married?" she asked.

"Yes," I answered, not looking up.

Shweeeeeee—shu-shu-shu-shu-eeeeee!

I ran to the wall. The mother tore the baby from my arms.

"Virgin Mother!"

"Do not be afraid."

Crash!

The shell exploded on the far end of the street. The women hadn't moved out of the line. They weren't going to lose their places. They huddled closer to the wall. Teofila heard the noise of the shell and saw the frightened face of her mother and began to cry.

"Shh, baby. Shh, little one. Shh...shh...."

And the thunder broke again and another shell came and then another and another and the street was hidden from us because of the smoke and dust and the women coughed, and in front someone had been hit and blood was colouring the dirt on the sidewalk.

Two women and a child. Dead.

Teofila's mother placed her hand over her child's head and cursed.

"No—I do not want a baby—no—no," said Lisa.

"Come, let's get away from here."

Lisa was biting her lip. "I will take a picture. Look at it....I will take a picture...."

"Come, darling," I said.

25

April came and with it a mad burst of shelling. General Miaja issued an order warning citizens to keep away from the down-town sections of the city. The Gran Via was deserted. It was debris-littered now and only one or two of the shops were open. The press-room had been moved from the Telephone Building to the old Ministry of War building off the Puerto del Sol, which had a deep cellar, to which you could run during a shelling or bombardment.

Day after day it kept up. Sometimes during the morning. Sometimes during the afternoon and sometimes right straight through an entire day into the night. Sometimes it began at night.

We used to stand in front of the Ministry of War building and listen to the shells coming over our heads as they poured into the centre of the city. First you could see a flash in the sky, then you counted one-two-three-four-five and then you heard it. The shu-shu-shu-shu-sheeeeeee and you waited....It passed over your head and you counted again one-two-three-four and then the explosion. Sometimes they came so fast that there was no time to count.

You either got used to it or you didn't. Lisa and I became used to it. We could stand it as long as we didn't have to see the results, or the blood being washed off the streets.

For days it seemed that no one moved in the city except the reporters, who had to file their stories. But in spite of the shellings the trams still functioned, the subways ran, the factories were open, and life went on as usual.

There was no panic. Sometimes people ran into subway entrances when the shelling started, but more often they ran to the other side of the street and continued on their way.

The Madrileños accepted it as they did rain, and as they did the food rations which found the women standing in line day after day waiting for their small share of milk or bread or fish or firewood.

And in all this time I had heard nothing from the guys. Rosa had had no news. All that we knew was that the Americans had suffered heavy casualties on the Jarama sector.

It was on an afternoon during the first week of April that I walked into Brigade headquarters to see Carlson, the Political Commissar, about getting time off to go to Jarama.

After inquiring about my work, he asked the reason for the visit.

I began: "My North American broadcasts are all very well, but the people back home would like to hear news about the Canadian and American volunteers."

"So they would," said Carlson; "then give it to them."

"But I cannot, for the simple reason that I don't know what to tell them. I would suggest that I be given a few days off so that I may take a trip to Jarama and see the boys."

"I can see no objection to that, but who will give the broadcasts while you are away?"

"That's just the problem. I hoped that you might suggest someone."

Carlson thought a while. "Perhaps one of the Englishmen working on the *Volunteer for Liberty*. But you will have to see Patterson about that. He would know whom he could spare from the paper for a few days."

Carlson wrote a note to Patterson. I went to his office. He was poring over some proofs. I coughed and he looked up.

"Yes?"

I presented Carlson's note.

"Well, who?" Patterson asked.

"How about Smith?" I suggested.

"For three days...I don't know if we can spare him for three days. But, of course, he could still do some work on the paper during that time. I'll call him."

Smith entered and Patterson presented the problem to him.

"I'll be glad to. But only for three days, mind you. The boys want their paper out on time. The real reason I'm doing it, though, is to give you a short rest away from the shelling. That is, if Patterson doesn't object."

"No, I don't object. The only thing I object to is finding ten mistakes in one galley-proof. Maybe a vacation wouldn't do you any harm either, Smith."

"Ten mistakes? I must be slipping," said Smith.

"You *must* be?" inquired Patterson.

"Swell," I said. "Sorry about the mistakes. Don't stutter over the radio. I can arrange my own transportation. I'd appreciate a Salvo Conducto from the Brigade. That'll make it easier for me to get around. I'll take Smith to the radio station this evening and show him what's being done."

"Remember," said Patterson, "only three days."

"I'll be back in three days, dead or alive."

"If it's the latter save yourself the trouble," he answered.

"Fine."

We shook hands. "Incidentally, your broadcasts are fine. I listened in last night. They're much better now than they were at first. More objective." Patterson smiled and offered me one of his English cigarettes.

We shook hands again and I ran back to the hotel as fast as I could to tell Lisa the news.

She was excited. "I'll tell Sanché to be ready to-morrow."

"Wait till you see them…Alan and his pipe. He'll probably go to work on you with Shakespeare. He's handsome. Tall and handsome. I hope you don't fall for him. And Milty, you'll die laughing. They're the swellest bunch of guys I've ever known."

"Fine…fine…I'll love them. We'll start early in the morning and get there by the afternoon. We have to go to Morata de Tajuna."

"Yes…I've got to buy a writing-pad for Alan…he probably has one by now… and cigarettes. I wonder if Ricardo has a good supply."

"He hasn't. I tried to buy some this morning. He's all out of them."

"Hell, I can't go up there without cigarettes."

"I still have two packets left. You can give them mine."

"You're a honey…" I hugged her.

"I'll tell Sanché to be ready at seven o'clock. Is that fine?"

"Swell."

This Time a Better Earth
PART III

26

Morata de Tajuna was a smelly, dirty village. We saw the inevitable church spire as we drove up the main street, the only paved road in the entire village. There were no stores open. The village inhabitants had been evacuated long ago. Some of the two-storey huts that were still standing now quartered the soldiers of the People's Army.

We passed piles of wreckage, results of shellings and aerial bombardments. The streets were thick with flies. Stray dogs and cats were sunning themselves and rose lazily to get out of the way of the approaching car. In the centre of the village was a square. On one side was a tavern, on the other a three-storey building on which a crudely written sign, "Intendencia," was hung.

We walked into the Intendencia. A tall, lanky Canadian by the name of Dickson greeted us and gave Lisa a great big smile. When we told him we both wanted to get up to the trenches, the smile left his face.

"I'm awfully sorry, but the lady can't go up now. We had a bit of action this morning. To-morrow maybe she can go, but not to-day."

"I'm a photographer, not a lady," said Lisa.

"Orders are orders. We had a few women reporters come and visit us a couple of days ago. Now the colonel says no dames unless it's absolutely quiet. You can go up, but I'm sorry about the lady comrade."

"Please stop calling me a lady comrade. Call me comrade. That is enough."

"Okay, comrade, but maybe to-morrow."

"All right," said Lisa, "I'll wait here for you. You go up and see your friends."

Dickson told her she could have a room in the back all to herself. "You'll have to go up to H.Q.," said Dickson to me. "Get a trench pass."

I walked into the room with Lisa. "I'm sorry you can't go up with me. I did want you to see them, and they you."

"It's all right. I told Sanché to put the car in a good place. I'll wait here for you. Maybe I'll get some pictures of the village. Don't be too long."

Dickson was waiting for me on the sidewalk.

"Excuse the flies....We're going to clean this place up any day now. There's an ammunition-truck going up right now. Let's hop in."

We climbed in beside the driver.

"What part of Canada you from?" he asked.

"Toronto."

"I'm from Vancouver," Dickson informed me.

"Anybody hurt this morning?" I asked.

He looked at me. "What the hell do you expect? We went over the top this morning. That's the first time since February 27th. But this time our casualties were very light, considering."

"Considering what?"

"Considering everything. Boy, this time our artillery worked like a charm. Sweet. Everything worked in perfect order. The Spanish comrades went over first and we captured back a trench the fascists got from us last month. Say, maybe you've got a Canadian cigarette?"

"No. But I've got a few American ones."

"They'll do. Sweet-looking kid, that."

"Who?" I looked around expecting to see someone. The driver was the only one there, and he looked ahead, seemingly intent on nothing but his driving.

"That dame you came with," answered Dickson.

"Yes...she is."

"Girl friend?"

"Yes...."

"Lucky bastard. She's German, eh?"

"Yes....Tell me, are the lines far from here?"

"Nope. H.Q. is just around the bend. Then we walk a way, about two hundred yards, and there are the lines. H.Q.'s a swell dump. Former country home of some duke or something. I think the Duke of Alba, but I'm not sure. Anyway, whoever it was, he'd be happy to know how his villa is being used now....Lovely grounds, too. Lilac trees and all kinds of flowers. The Duke was a lover of nature. The lilacs are blooming now."

The truck coughed and spluttered up the dirt road.

"We built this road ourselves," Dickson said. "Dr. Tyke supervised. It's really for ambulances."

The driver hadn't opened his mouth once since we had got in beside him.

"How you doing?" Dickson asked him.

He nodded and closed his eyes and heaved a sigh.

"Gloomy Joe, we call him," said Dickson, referring to the driver. "Much ammunition come up to-day?" he asked.

"So-so," answered Gloomy Joe. "Got a cigarette?"

I offered him one.

"This is Bob Curtis. This is Gloomy Joe Lord."

Joe Lord nodded his head without saying a word. He lit the cigarette and let it dangle from the corner of his lips.

"How are things in Albacete?" Dickson asked.

"Same as always. It's a dump." Joe Lord looked bored as hell.

"Are you getting a transfer?" Dickson asked.

"I'm still waiting."

"To go into the lines?" I asked.

"Nope," said Joe Lord.

"He wants to get into artillery," explained Dickson.

"Don't like the trenches," drawled Joe Lord, "too close to the front."

"Christ! you look sour as hell," I said.

He turned very slowly. "Do I look sour?"

"Yes."

"That's how I always look."

"He's sick of driving a truck. No excitement," explained Dickson, smiling.

"It's a lousy truck," said Lord, "and it has nothing to do with excitement. I just want to get into artillery." He blew out the smoke from the corner of his mouth.

"Well, hope you get your transfer," I said.

"Yeah," said Lord.

We got out of the truck. H.Q. turned out to be a two-storey villa surrounded by a marble walk. Vines grew on the walls.

Dickson presented me to Colonel Dimitri, the Jugoslav commanding the 15th Brigade. He read Patterson's letter of introduction and the Salvo Conducto issued by Carlson. Dimitri wrote out a trench pass.

"You can go up to the lines," he said. "But you have come at a bad time. We expect some action to-night. Better get back within the hour. Dickson, you go with him and see that he gets back in an hour."

Dickson and I walked along a narrow path between a row of lilac trees.

"Ah!" He broke off some flowers. "Bring 'em to the boys. They can stick 'em on their bayonets." He sniffed at them and stuck them under my nose. I took a long breath.

It had rained that morning, and the earth was still damp and muddy in spots. You could hear it make a plop-plop sound when you walked over it. There was the beginning of a sun somewhere beyond a hill. So far there had been nothing to indicate that a war was going on. Now and then a uniformed soldier passed us, but the scene was pastoral and lovely, like hilly, green country back home.

"See that hill?" Dickson pointed.

I saw a small hill dotted with olive trees a few hundred yards in front.

"We call it Suicide Hill. Real name is Pingarron Hill. Lots of our guys got it there in early February. It's ours now."

"I wonder if you know any of my friends?" I asked, not able to keep it in any longer.

"What are their names?"

I reeled off their names.

"Nope. I don't seem to recall any of them. When did they get here?"

"February 26th...."

"They came on a good day, all right. I wouldn't know them. I was transferred to the Intendencia on the twenty-third. I hardly know any of the guys who came after that."

"What happened on the twenty-seventh?" I asked.

"Aw, there's a million versions of what happened that day."

"But what's the official version?"

We walked slowly. I expected suddenly to see trenches emerge in front of me. But there was an absolute stillness.

"We had to attack. We had just dug our trenches. The fascists had concentrated everything they had here for three weeks, but couldn't gain an inch. It's as Dimitri explains...we had to take the initiative and show them we had sufficient strength to attack. So we did. Only the attack went a little screwy because our artillery either forgot what it was supposed to do or because we didn't have any shells. I still haven't found out what it was. You can't go over the top without an artillery preparation. We did. Bango into strong machine-gun emplacements. So we had to come back. A lot of our guys got it. But the main object was fulfilled. We took the initiative and the fascist bastards haven't dared to come out of their trenches since. The highway is safe. We've got Moors facing us now. A number of deserters came over and told us."

"Are there many deserters?"

"A few a week. They trickle in. They tell us there'd be more only the Moors keep careful watch."

"It's very quiet," I said. "Nothing like I expected a front to be."

"It's like this most of the time. Gets boring as hell. But you should have been here this morning. Ever hear a barrage?"

"In Madrid we hear plenty."

"That must be something too. But, boy, when your artillery is going like hell and theirs is going like hell and the machine-guns are going like hell and hand-grenades and trench-mortars and anti-tank shells, boy, sweet music. You go stone deaf."

We came to the top of a little hill.

"Keep low here," he cautioned. "Lots of strays."

I heard rifle-shots...one, and then a long space of time before another. I crouched.

"See...there below...there's the dug-outs. See those bumps in front of the olive trees? Those are the dug-outs. See the sandbags?"

I grew tense. I heard the strange, almost soothing whistle of a stray as it passed over our heads. I ducked.

Dickson laughed. "When you've heard it it's okay. It's passing by then. It's when you don't hear it."

"The whole thing seems screwy...they're really trenches..."

"That's the same reaction I got at first," said Dickson. "I kept thinking I was seeing it all in a movie."

The dug-outs were situated in an olive field. On the left was a vineyard with gnarled grape-vines looking like bleached bones.

I shivered.

"What's biting you?"

I didn't answer.

Dickson was smelling the lilacs.

A small valley below. There were swellings at the foot of some olive trees. The trees were bare of leaves. I saw the sandbags.

"Where are the guys?" I asked.

"In their dug-outs or in the trenches."

We walked down a hill and came closer to the swellings.

The clouds had moved away from the sun and it was bright now. Up there, on the crest of the hill, were trenches. I heard a rifle-shot. Then quiet again.

"Guys taking pot-shots," explained Dickson.

I saw a head peer out of a dug-out.

"Bob!"

A man emerged and started to run toward me. I didn't recognise him until he got closer.

"Milty!"

He was grinning from ear to ear. We hugged. His beard rubbed against my face. "Ouch! Why the hell don't you take a shave?"

"Nobody shaves. We're all trying to look like Abe Lincoln...geez, it's good to see you. Lemme take a good look. Why the hell didn't you come before? What's happened? How's Madrid? Whataya hear from home? Boy, it's good seeing you!"

"Wait a minute...give me a chance." I stared at him.

"You've changed," I said. "You look different."

"I feel different. You look kind of changed yourself. All of us got changed. We got your letter. A radio announcer. Gee! How is it?"

"It's fine. Where are the guys?"

"Everybody's in the dug-outs or in the trench. Come on, Harry'll be dyin' to see you." His eyes were bright and he was excited. "And, boy, have I got a machine-gun. A Soviet Maxim." Then growing calmer: "Tough about Alan and Doug, eh? But these things...well, we've got used to it."

I stopped.

"What about Alan and Doug?"

He stopped with me. His face grew quiet. "Yuh mean you haven't heard?"

"No," I said quietly.

"Alan...he's dead...Doug's blind. Hand-grenade got him. Lucien's wounded, but not badly. Christ! we thought you knew. We figured you got the news by now."

"When?" I asked. Something stabbed at my temples.

"February 27th...."

I licked my lips. "Let's wait here a minute. I..."

"The colonel said that I got to bring him back in an hour, so you guys better hurry," said Dickson.

"Where's Harry?" I asked.

"In his dug-out. Geez, we thought you knew."

"And Doug and Lucien. What hospital are they in?"

"Lucien's in one down south, in Murcia. Doug's at the American hospital in Saelices."

I stared at the sandbags arranged criss-cross along the trench.

"Where is he?"

"I told you. In his dug-out."

"No...Alan. Where is Alan?"

Milty stared at me. He pointed slowly to beyond the sandbags, into the valley. "Harry'll be waiting. Come on."

I stared at the trench, then at Dickson, and then at Milty. I looked at the wet ground. The leaves of the olive trees were soaked into the earth.

"Since the twenty-seventh..."

"Come on, eh?" said Milty.

Dickson trailed behind. I followed Milty slowly. The lines ran through a vineyard and an olive field. The Jarama River was somewhere to the north. The highway was behind us. For some reason I kept thinking of the word "terrain." Terrain, terrain, this is a terrain. That is no-man's-land. I saw it in the movies. Terrain. Terrain. This is a terrain.

I saw Harry come out of a dug-out. His uniform was torn. He was clean-shaven. His eyes lit up. "Hello, fellah," he said. He gripped my hand and held my forearm with his other hand. He looked at my face a long while. "You don't look so hot for a guy who spends his time in Madrid. What's the matter, don't you eat?"

I winced.

"What the hell's the matter with you?"

"Nothing."

Milty was standing quietly beside us. "He didn't know about Alan and the guys," he said.

Harry let his hand drop. "Yep. Tough. Come into the dug-out. How you doing, Dickson? Here, give me some of that."

Dickson gave him a branch of lilacs. Harry sniffed.

"Come on and tell us what's the news from home," went on Harry. "How about the C.I.O. organisational drive? We haven't heard a word or got a newspaper in weeks."

We climbed into the dug-out. The roots of the olive tree now served as a towel-rack. "Nice, eh?" said Milty.

"I'll amble around and see some of the guys," said Dickson. "I'll be back for you in forty-five minutes."

Harry sat down on a blanket spread over the ground. "Sit down. Sit down. Stop looking like a bloody corpse. Sit down." He placed the lilacs between the roots. He smelled them again and closed his eyes.

"I brought some cigarettes...here. Here's the pad. I hope you get enough cigarettes. This is all I could bring."

"We never get enough cigarettes. Now spill it. What's news from home and how've you been doing since we last saw each other? You didn't say much in your letter. Just that you were doing radio work."

"I don't get very much more news than you do here. The papers that come to Madrid are weeks old."

"We haven't received a newspaper here for three weeks. Some woman, God bless her, sent one of the guys *The Ladies' Home Journal*. *The Ladies' Home Journal*—I've had to read that." He chuckled.

"Why didn't someone bring him in?" I asked quietly.

"Because you don't risk the life of a comrade for a dead man," Harry answered curtly.

"But out there, the rain...the sun..."

"That's how it is...if we'd get into such a state after every comrade of ours got it we wouldn't be able to stick around very long. Listen, boy, get this into your skull: there were many Alans and many Dougs. And there'll be more. I don't want to sound like an editorial, but there's no time for us to cry. We've got one job here. Fascism has to be stopped. Well, we've stopped it so far. Alan died doing it. Doug got blind. Lucien wounded. But when we've helped to stop them long enough to give Spain time to build a strong army, a strong disciplined fighting force, then our job will be done. Those of us left will go home. That's all we must think about. We've learned something here. All of us. You better learn it too. First, that there are such things as heroes. It's a hell of a word. I don't like it because I've always connected the word 'hero' with the word 'fool'. But not here. I've seen them. And another thing I've learned is that when you're fighting for something, the people you love don't die, even though the bastards we're fighting have killed them. Maybe that isn't too plain."

"That's how I feel," said Milty. "That's how I feel too."

"Alan's death..." Harry went on quietly. "It's not like death somehow. If you look at him alone, if you remember his laugh, the way he sang, how he spoke, then something inside you hurts—but that's not the way to look at him now. I know it isn't easy. But we've got work to do. Alan's work. All of them who died. His dying and the other kids' have only made me all the more determined to see this thing through to the end. And that's how most of us feel now. The guys in the Brigade and the Spanish comrades. It's a long speech, but I had to get it off my chest."

I lit a cigarette and inhaled deeply, thinking.

"You can't help feeling like you do right now," Harry went on. "You haven't seen it as often as we have. I remember that first shock." His eyes stared unseeing for a moment. "That look on their faces...youngsters...but..." He jerked his head. "There's another thing I'm hoping for. A Canadian battalion. Think of it, from our country with only eleven million people, sending a battalion to Spain. We've decided on the name. The French-Canadian comrades have discussed it with us. Mackenzie-Papineau, like it? After William Lyon Mackenzie and Louis Joseph Papineau."

"Yeah, but who's ever heard of those guys?" interrupted Milty. "Everybody's heard of Abe Lincoln and George Washington, but who the hell's heard of Mackenzie-Papineau?"

Harry laughed: "If the world has been late in hearing about the past of our dear old homeland, it'll hear about it now. Whenever they read of the Mackenzie-Papineau Battalion in Spain, people will ask, that is, people outside of Canada, who the hell is that? Then they'll have to find out. And then they'll know. Yes-sir, and then we'll show the Lincoln guys how to fight."

"Yeah," said Milty, "you'll show us. By the time youse guys get a battalion we'll win the war."

"I hope so. But I'm afraid it's going to last longer than any of us first imagined. I'd say another two to four years, and I think the International Brigade will be pulled out before another two years are up. But what about Madrid? Come on. Is it a big city?"

"As big as Montreal...but there isn't much to tell you."

Then I began slowly to tell them of Madrid, the cafés, the shells, the food queues, the reporters, radio work, the loneliness, and I told them about Lisa.

"Yeah, we read about it in your letter. When do we see her?" asked Milty.

"They wouldn't let her come up. I think they expect some action to-night. But maybe she'll be able to come to-morrow."

"Swell....Wanna see my radio mike?" asked Milty.

"Radio mike?"

"Sure. Come on."

We climbed out of the dug-out. There was a full sun dropping slowly now behind Suicide Hill. There was that occasional rifle-shot. Otherwise quiet.

"Doesn't look much like a war," I said.

"Not when it's quiet." Harry was looking up at the sky. "Two days ago a couple of birds came over. Real birds. Some of the guys said they were nightingales, but they sounded like sparrows to me. It was good hearing them sing though, sparrows or no sparrows. I hadn't seen a bird near here since we arrived. It must be the spring."

"Heard from your wife and kids?" I asked.

Harry's face broke into a grin. "Yep. A week ago. They still want me to bring home three fascists. Eddy and Jimmy have grown a foot, Martha writes. I wish it didn't take so long for letters to get here. She wrote it a month ago."

"Did anyone write Alan's wife?" I asked.

"No. She'll probably be notified through the usual channels, or, maybe you can write her?"

"I'd rather not. Somebody else can have the—yes, maybe I will. Or I could get one of the reporters to send his paper the story...they were only married a year...."

"Yeah....Say, take a look. Here it is," Milty said. It was his "mike."

The "mike" had once been the tin container of a gas-mask. Now it was perched on top of a bayonet. Beneath it hung a sign: "Station Jarama. Announcer, Milton Schwartz, through the courtesy of the Spanish War."

Milty stepped in front of the "mike." He bowed. "Ladies and gentlemen, this is Milton Schwartz comin' to yuh tru the kertesy of the Lincoln Exterminator Company. We exterminate rats, cooties, fascists, and other voimin. Remember our theme song——" He began to sing, "Mid pleasures and palaces tho-ho we may roam, be it ever so humble there's no place like a nice big shell-hole."

An audience had gathered meanwhile. We applauded.

"I think you should have my job," I said.

There were soldiers from all sections of the Brigade: Italians from the Garibaldi Battalion, Spaniards from La Pasionara Battalion, Germans from the Thaelmann, and Englishmen and Frenchmen from the English and Franco-Beige Battalions. All the foreigners had picked up enough Spanish to make themselves understood, and they chattered away and laughed at the crazy American who always made speeches through the gas-mask can.

Dickson walked over. "Time to go," he said.

"When you hear the gong it will be zero hour," finished off Milty.

"You look better," said Dickson.

"Better?"

"You should of seen yourself before. You were green in the face."

"Yeah—I feel better," I said.

Harry and Milty walked down with us as far as the road.

"Try and come up to-morrow. There's a lot you haven't seen yet. Our propaganda truck. We give speeches to the fascists every night and sing them to sleep through a loud-speaker."

We stopped at the foot of the hill. "I think we will come. Lisa will want to get some pictures. It's been swell seeing you guys. Hope you get leave soon and come up to Madrid. We'll get drunk."

"It's a date. Think you'll get up to see Doug? But anyway, we'll see you to-morrow. And remember what I told you before," said Harry.

"Yes."

"So long," said Milty. "We'll have the war won in a couple of weeks."

We grinned at each other.

"Take care of yourselves..." I said.

"Come on," said Dickson. "I'm getting hungry."

We waved to each other as Dickson and I climbed down the dirt road.

27

We were sitting on the bed in the back room. The afternoon was moving into evening. A truck rumbled by. Somewhere a dog barked. I kept smoking cigarette after cigarette.

"You should not smoke so much," Lisa said.

"Alan dead...Doug blind...Lucien wounded."

"Lie down. Dickson has gone for some food. Lie down till he comes back." She placed her hand on my forehead. "You are feverish." She pushed me back gently till my head touched the pillow.

The room was getting dark. The opening notes of the Abe Lincoln song kept running through my head.

Lisa caressed my cheek and lay beside me. I pulled her closer to me and buried my face in her hair. Something inside my chest was choking me. We held each other silently.

"It's good to have you," I said.

She smiled tenderly. "It is good to have you, too."

"I'd go crazy if you weren't here."

She placed her cheek next to mine. It was warm. I touched it.

There were words inside of me that couldn't come out. I opened my mouth to speak, but I could say nothing.

"To-morrow you will feel better. Try to forget now," she said. She stared at me and bit her lip. "I love you very much," she said.

I got up from the bed.

"What is it?" she asked.

"Nothing. Let's go and eat. Let's forget the whole business. Come."

We walked into Dickson's office. A table had been placed there, and on the table a huge bowl of steaming lamb stew. Dickson was smiling. "Voilà," he said. "When I told the cook we had a lady for dinner he piled on a few more helpings."

"Are ladies supposed to eat so much?" asked Lisa.

"No, but it's in your honour."

"Thank you. But there is enough to feed the army."

"Two more people are going to eat with us. Captain Brown and Feiglebaum. They're in charge of night patrol."

The door opened. The two men appeared. One tall, blond, English. The other short, stocky, Jewish-American. The short, stocky one glanced at his guests and his eyes stopped at Lisa. "Lamb stew and a blonde," he declared solemnly. And then, as if turning it on, his face broke into a grin. "Good evening."

The Englishman remained silent for a moment. Then, walking towards the table, he bowed from the waist. "Captain Brown," he said, clicking his heels. The stocky one followed and mockingly bowed too. "Lieutenant Feiglebaum," he mimicked.

Dickson introduced us.

"Will you excuse me, please?" said Captain Brown, and disappeared into a back room.

"A delegation to visit the boys?" Feiglebaum asked, looking at Lisa.

"I am a photographer," said Lisa. "He," pointing at me, "is the radio announcer at Madrid."

"Photographer. Say, I used to have a swell camera back home. What do you use?"

"A Leica," Lisa answered. "I boycott German goods, but I cannot help this. It is the only camera I can use."

Feiglebaum sat down beside her.

"Anything new?" Dickson asked.

Feiglebaum waved his hand. "Same old thing. But they're building new communication lines and new trenches. Probably preparing something. We saw three new machine-gun emplacements facing the Garibaldis. Staying around long?" he asked Lisa.

"To-morrow, and then we leave. I shall go up to the lines to-morrow to take some pictures. If there is going to be action I want to be around. I have my film camera with me, in my car. Oh..." she held her hand to her mouth.

"What is it?" I asked.

"Sanché. I forgot about Sanché. Where will he eat? He must eat here with us."

"Who's Sanché?" Dickson asked.

"Her chauffeur," I answered. "I'll go and see where he is." I rose to go out, but stopped dead when I saw Captain Brown. He was bowing again, but this time he was not wearing his uniform. He had changed into a dinner-suit.

Feiglebaum spat out some of the lamb stew he had been chewing. "What the——" he gasped.

"Good evening," said Captain Brown in an impeccable Oxford accent.

Lisa stared. "You brought a dinner-suit to Spain?"

Captain Brown smiled. He clicked his heels again and sat down by the table without answering. I was still standing. "Are you leaving us?" he asked politely.

"No," I half-grunted, "I'm going to look for Miss Kammerer's chauffeur."

"Christ! if the guys could only see you now," said Feiglebaum. His mouth was still open.

"Your mouth is slightly ajar," said Brown smoothly. "Close it." And then to Lisa: "It's really the only suit I have. I know it's funny."

Dickson was laughing quietly to himself. "Bloody Englishman. Evening clothes. Wait till the colonel hears about this one."

"May I take a picture of you with that suit holding a gun?" asked Lisa.

"Of course," smiled Brown. "But it's not quite the thing, you know, to hold a gun and be dressed for dinner."

I was about to open the door to look for Sanché, but someone opened it from the other side. A man appeared. He looked forlorn. He needed a shave and a new uniform.

"What the hell are you doing here?" Dickson shouted at him.

The man stared at us blankly. "I'm looking for Oscar," he answered uncertainly.

"You're looking for Oscar!" Dickson got to his feet shouting: "Get back into that cell!"

"Okay, but I'm looking for Oscar. I haven't eaten yet. If you see him, tell him to bring me my dinner, I'm hungry. And maybe you've got something to read?"

"Get-back-into-your-cell!" Dickson shouted.

The man looked at each of us, shrugged and turned around. "Okay, but if you see Oscar———"

When he closed the door, Dickson heaved a loud sigh and started to laugh. "What a jail! That's the prisoner out looking for the guard!"

Lisa burst into a laugh and then: "But he looks so lonely."

"What's he in for?" I asked.

"Drinking," answered Dickson. "He's a good egg when he isn't getting drunk. Oscar must have told him to take care of the jail. I think Oscar hates the damn place more than he does. Wonder where the hell Oscar is? We'll have to get another guard. Oscar's been squawking to get back to the lines. What a jail!"

I went out to look for Sanché. I found him in the tavern. He had eaten long ago with some of the soldiers quartered in one of the houses. He was drinking wine with a few soldiers when I found him. He had also got a place to sleep and seemed very happy. The man he was talking to turned out to be an old pal he had known in Madrid before the war.

When I came back Captain Brown was in the middle of a conversation. "And that is why I came to Spain. I'm a die-hard Tory of the old school. An Imperialist, if ever there was one. And that is precisely why I'm here—to protect England's Imperial interests, even though some of my Tory friends have forgotten our policy regarding the Peninsula."

"Yeah, he's all screwy politically," put in Feiglebaum, "but he hates the fascists."

"Quite," answered Brown. "I spent five years in India, in His Majesty's Cavalry, and then I began reading books I shouldn't have read. That," he took a gulp of wine, "was the beginning of my downfall and uplifting—books—I used to love Kipling and then I began to read, only out of sheer boredom, some books on British Imperialism, and that got me around to books on political economy, and finally I found myself disagreeing with my estimable government's policy on the Peninsula, so I upped and came to Spain." He took another drink.

"He's always giving speeches," said Feigy.

"Listen, what the hell's the difference in the long run, anyway?" said Dickson. "He's here and that's what matters, and he's fighting fascism, and he's here because he's protecting British Imperial interests, and Feigy's here, and I'm here because we believe in democracy, but we're here, and that's the point, isn't it?"

"Quite. We'll drink to that." Brown gulped down some more wine.

"Good wine," said Lisa.

"Like it? I got it from a peasant near Albacete. I offered to pay him, but he said, 'no, gracias; no, por Brigada Internacionale,' and so when I drink it I feel doubly warmed inside, by the wine and by the sentiment of that Spanish peasant." He began to eat and then looked at Lisa. "Do you like your work?" he asked.

"Very much. You seem to like yours."

"I do. Nothing like night patrols to soothe shattered nerves, I say. Feigy disagrees with me, but he hasn't lived right. There is something peaceful about a night between two lines of trenches. There is a loneliness that has nothing in common with the utter loneliness of going over the top. Then you are alone, painfully alone, even though there are men all around you. But at night, in no-man's-land, with the side you are fighting with on one side, and the enemy on the other, and you in between, alone, quiet, no crickets or birds singing, nothing but the sound of the wind and the sound of your own breathing, or if Feigy is near, the sound of Feigy's breathing—he has sinus trouble—that is being at peace with yourself. Don't ask me why. That is how I feel."

"You should write poetry," said Feigy.

"I do."

"Yes?" said Lisa. "May we see some of it?"

"No. Not my poetry. There is still something decadent about it, as there is about me. I had hoped that in Spain I would flourish again, but India sucked me dry. It is only at night now, on patrol work, or at a time like this, when there is a beautiful woman (and where would beauty be more appreciated?), that some withered leaf inside my soul becomes green again and little buds come out and something stirs inside of me and I talk like this. No, I will read you a poem. But it isn't mine. I found it on the body of one of the American boys lying in no-man's-land. He was in a bad spot, so I dragged him to a better one out of the range of the guns. I saw a piece of paper sticking out of his pocket. He may have written it that same morning before they went over the top. I will read that to you. I do not know the name of the boy. I say he was American because he was lying in front of the Lincoln trench. I will get the poem. It is unfinished, but I will read it if you want to hear it."

"Yes, I do," Lisa said quietly.

We waited silently till he came back. Lisa placed her hand in mine. Brown sat down with a slip of paper in his hand and began to read the poem.

"Not ours to ask you why, when we are done,
The little time we spent before the sun
Was bought so dearly, with such wealth of grief,
Such wasted hopes, such sad betrayed belief.

"Not ours to ask why you, who had the wealth
To waste a billion stars on empty space,
Could find but one cold world, one dying sun,
For those who might find meaning in your grace.

"Not ours to ask why, of endless time
You spent on tearing galaxies apart,
You gave but one short day, one bitter day,
To those who have your image in their heart.
It is not we shall ask. We shall be dumb,
Back in the nothing that you drew us from."

He finished the poem and then: "That is all. Our boys write poetry before going over the top." He sipped his wine. "But come, this is no night for sadness or for thought. Let us drink. Dickson, have you any of that anti-freeze left?"

"Yep," Dickson went to his desk and came back with a bottle of whisky.

"I use it for cuts," he said, "but it's whisky."

He poured us each a little.

"To victory," said Feigy.

"To victory and lasting peace," added Brown.

Lisa and I looked at each other and we all drank.

"I am going to bed," Brown said suddenly, taking another gulp of whisky. He took Lisa's hand. "I hope that I will see you again. Do you still want my picture in my dress-suit, holding a gun?"

"No," said Lisa, "I want your picture in your uniform."

"Thank you." He bowed a little wobbly. Then he went into his room.

"He is a good man," said Lisa.

"That poem," I said, "it is strange."

"I think he wrote it himself," Dickson said.

"No," said Feigy, "I was there when he got it. He took it out of the guy's pocket and read it there by the light of the moon, and said to me, 'Let us bury this poet under this tree.' So we buried him, what was left to be buried."

"I think we should go to bed now," said Lisa.

I stared ahead of me.

"Come," said Lisa.

"Was he out there long?" I asked.

"Who, Brown?" answered Feigy.

"No, the man who was dead."

"Oh, I think he must have been one of the guys who got it on the twenty-seventh."

"Come," said Lisa again.

28

I was awakened by what I thought was a nightmare. Lisa was up listening. It was no nightmare.

"Listen to it," she said, holding her ears.

It was an artillery barrage. The battery couldn't have been very far from the Intendencia. Later, we learned that it was situated in the valley just below H.Q. I understood then what Dickson was trying to say when he said, "Their batteries going like hell, ours going like hell, machine-guns, trench-mortars, hand-grenades, rifles," or whatever he had said. The shelling sounded like magnified machine-gunning and the air trembled. The shutters of the window rattled continually.

Lisa jumped out of bed. "It must be an attack. I've got to get some pictures." She dressed hurriedly.

I began dressing. "Dickson said, no women allowed."

"Do you think it was that that stopped me? I said nothing yesterday because I felt you wanted to see your friends alone. This is my job. I will get up there. Do not worry." She powdered her face, combed her hair, peered into the mirror. "There, I look fine, yes?"

"Going to a dance? You look beautiful. Wait for me."

"I am going to get Sanché." She left still combing her hair.

I finished dressing and walked into the office. Dickson was sitting with his feet on the desk.

There was another burst of shelling.

Dickson smiled. "We're attacking," he explained quietly. "Where'd your wife go? She flashed by me with a fast good morning and disappeared."

"She's getting the car. She's going up to get some pictures."

"She can't."

"She says she will. It's her job. She has a front pass."

"She'll have to see the colonel and he said no dames."

"Wait till the colonel sees her. He'll change his mind."

Lisa came back all smiles. "Everything is all right. I have enough film. Coming?"

"How about breakfast?" asked Dickson.

"No time."

"You won't be allowed to get very far."

"Do not worry. Will you take me up to H.Q.?"

"Okay…but I'll get hell."

"No, you won't. Come."

Sanché asked where to. Dickson pointed up the dirt road.

"But they are fighting now," said Sanché.

"That is why we are going," explained Lisa.

"For only two batteries we make a hell of a lot of noise," said Dickson.

An ambulance passed us on the way down.

There was no sun yet. Dawn had just broken. We stopped at the field-hospital half-way up the road. Stretchers were laid out waiting. First-aid men were rushing in the direction of the lines.

"Who's attacking?" Dickson shouted.

"The Garibaldis," someone shouted. A short, fair-haired doctor was issuing orders. "Dr. Tyke," introduced Dickson.

We would have to climb the rest of the way from here. There were lots of "strays." Lisa told Sanché to drive the car down to the end of the road and wait. I took her film camera.

"Better wait," cautioned Dr. Tyke.

"For what? Till it is all over?" asked Lisa.

"I'll take you to H.Q.," said Dickson, "but I'm going to get hell."

"You will not. Do not worry. You will not."

We arrived at the villa. The noise by this time had no rhythm or clarity. There was the burst of shells, the insane clatter of machine-guns, the burst of the trench-mortars. So far we had not seen a thing. We walked up to the second floor. Colonel Dimitri was at a telephone.

"Cover the advance. No, cover it. Get the Thaelmann Battalion. Fool! Get there immediately." He looked up from the telephone and said something quietly to a man beside him. The man rose and ran from the room. Dimitri paid no attention to us. We sat down on a sofa in one corner of the room.

Another officer was on another telephone. "Hermann, come here. Translate this into Italian. Hear? They go over in half an hour. Hear that? Half an hour. The tanks will be there. Tell him not to worry about it. The tanks will be there. In half an hour. Did he understand you? Good. Now get me the English. Hello. Hello. Hello. The line is dead. Hello…

"The English line is dead. Try the Lincoln. Hello....hello...Comrade Martin? Comrade Dimitri. Listen...I know....In half an hour. The English line is dead. Establish contact with them. They are to cover the advance. In half an hour. Get them to fix their telephone line—hello—hello—No...Schweine! I'm coming up myself...we'll get you more ammunition...." He began barking out orders. "More ammunition to the Garibaldis....What do you want?"

Lisa got up. "I am Lisa Kammerer...." She held out her camera. "I want to get pictures of the attack." She approached his desk and showed him her front pass. He looked at Dickson and Dickson held out his hands.

"All right. All right. Take her up to the hill. She can see the whole thing from there. Now, please...I've got a war on my hands..." He lifted the phone again. "What? Fine. Is it going according to plan? Fine. I am coming right up."

He rose from his desk, said something to the other officer at the other phone and walked briskly out of the room."

"Come," said Lisa.

Dimitri was walking swiftly up the road. Two officers were with him.

"I'm going to get hell for this," moaned Dickson. "But...it's important to get pictures. He'll forget all about it, I bet."

"Sure. He was not angry at all."

"I know a spot," said Dickson.

The shelling was dying down.

Dickson led us to the top of a hill. Below us were the trench systems. Lisa lifted the camera to her eye and it began to unroll. Shells kept whining over our heads.

"It is too far away. I will move close." She started to run down the hill.

"Damn fool!" shouted Dickson. We ran after her.

When we got to her she had crouched a short distance behind the Garibaldi trench.

"Oh for the life of a photographer," said Dickson. "At least a soldier can fight back."

We saw the tanks go into action. Machine-gun fire. Rifle fire.

Then we saw the men of the Garibaldi jump over the parapet one by one. One man advanced a little, then flopped to the ground, raised himself and advanced again. Each man did the same. Some ran behind the tanks.

Lisa crawled closer, her film camera taking the entire action.

Tanks wobbled clumsily, spitting out bullets. Men crouched, fell, rose, advanced.

I saw a man run, then stop, as if he had been hit in the solar plexus and then double up, his head diving to the ground. Another twirled, as if being spun around by an unseen hand, and then slowly fell to the ground. The noise was one mad screech by this time.

Lisa rose, jumped into the trench, over the parapet, and ran to the protection of a clump of trees.

"That dame has guts," muttered Dickson admiringly.

We followed and I heard the whistle of bullets all around me. There was no time to be frightened. We crouched behind the trees.

There was a shout. It was quick work. The Garibaldis had occupied the fascist trench on the left flank. It was as far as they could go. The trench had been abandoned and the fascists had placed a half-dozen machine-guns on the other side.

Scattered shots. Then quiet. As if the air were taking a rest. Then we heard shouts in English from the Lincoln Battalion. "Whee! Hooray. Fascist bastards! Come out and fight!"

Lisa smiled. She examined her camera and patted it. Dickson shook his head and looked at me. "What the hell are we two doing here?"

"You've got me. I'll describe it over the radio."

We crawled back to the Garibaldi trench. A few bullets winged their way over our heads.

"Lousy shots," grunted Dickson. "They aren't Moors. Moors are crack-shots."

"Thank God they aren't Moors."

We slid down the parapet and sat where we landed.

"Whew!" said Lisa, taking a deep breath. "That was something."

"Yeah."

"Let's go to the Lincoln trench," said Dickson.

We walked along the trench. It was a deep trench and well built. There were olive trees on the top of the parapet, or what had once been olive trees.

When Lisa entered the Lincoln trench there was a silence for a brief second and then: "Boys! Wo-ho! Mmmm."

Lisa was oblivious to it all.

I looked for Milty and Harry.

"Boys," announced Dickson, "this is Comrade Curtis and Comrade Lisa Kammerer."

"How do you do? Come to take our pictures?"

Lisa laughed. "Yes." She raised her camera to her eye and snapped the picture.

One boy ambled up. He was holding his rifle. "Say, take one of me. Wait, I'll get a good pose." He gripped his rifle, turned his head to one side, and stuck out his chin. "How's that?"

"Terrible," said Lisa. "Do not pose. Act natural."

"That's natural," someone said.

"All right." Lisa took his picture.

"The name is James O'Leary, of the Irish Company, if anybody wants to know," said the soldier. "And if you want, I'll get the whole damned Irish Company together and you can take a picture of us."

"Fine. That is a good idea."

While the soldier went off to find the Irish, I went to look for Milty and Harry. I found both of them resting farther along the trench.

"Hyah!" Milty shouted. "Just get here? Hear the music?"

"Yes. I was with Lisa. She filmed the entire attack."

Harry got up from the ledge. "We didn't have much to do. Just cover the advance. I don't think there were many casualties. It worked smoothly. They could pick off a few of us a day from that trench. It threatened our whole flank."

"Is she here?" Milty asked.

"Lisa? Yes. She's taking pictures. The Irish Company is getting its picture taken."

"Come on," said Milty, "let's get ours took, too." He turned towards the parapet. "Hey, fascist bastards! Call off the war for a couple of minutes. I'm going to have my picture took." Then, turning back to us, "Okay, come on."

Dickson was acting as Lisa's guide. She saw me coming and got a picture of Harry, Milty and myself as we turned the corner of the trench.

"She's nice," said Milty.

After the introductions and a few more pictures, the food came up. It was breakfast and it consisted of coffee and bread. All of us drank out of tin cups.

There was a rifle-shot. Men listened.

"Nothing. Some damn fool having fun."

"We'll probably not have a bit of action for months now."

"I think we should get behind them one night," said Dickson, "and give 'em the works. Brown and Feigy roam around there all night and nothing happens to them. We could take a couple of hundred men and wipe them out by attacking from behind."

"Simple as hell," said Harry, "but to undertake such a flanking attack would mean an offensive on the entire sector. From the looks of things, we'll have a stalemate on this front. If they attack they won't attack here again. They went to hell at Guadalajara and they went to hell at Jarama. They're going to try and clean up the north first and then they'll probably begin on the Aragon front. This sector will be dead. It'll just mean holding the lines. We're too strongly entrenched for them to try anything here first."

Milty jumped to his feet. "I forgot something. We're making a collection for Doug. You are going to see him, aren't you?"

I turned to Lisa.

"Yes," said Lisa, "we are going to the American hospital this afternoon."

Milty went along the trench and came back in ten minutes with two hundred pesetas. "There...that'll buy him something."

Comandante Martin passed. He stopped. "Are you the comrade taking pictures?"

"Yes," said Lisa.

"It's okay. But next time try not to demoralise the whole battalion." He was smiling. "If you'll let us know when you come next time, the boys will be shaven and clean for you. We'll even put on an attack if there's nothing doing."

"Thank you very much."

A soldier approached us. "Is he the guy going to see Doug?" he asked, nodding toward me.

"Yeah," said Milty.

"Well, you tell Doug that Mickey—he knows me, we both come from Chicago—tell Doug that I've knocked off a few with his machine-gun. And tell him we're all doin' fine. As soon as I get leave I'm going to get up to see him, tell him."

"Some of the guys want to know if you can mail some letters for us. It'll probably get there faster if it's mailed from Madrid."

"I'll be glad to."

"Before you go," said Milty to me, "lemme show you my gun."

We followed him a few yards. His gun was covered with canvas. He lifted the canvas. "See? A Soviet Maxim, just like I wanted. I call her Mother Bloor. She's a honey." He pressed his finger on the trigger to demonstrate. The bullets cracked out against the silence.

"Stop wasting ammunition," said Harry.

"I just wanted to show him."

We started to leave.

"Take care of that guy," said Harry to Lisa.

"I will. You take care of yourselves and come to see us in Madrid when you get leave."

"*When* we get leave," said Milty grimacing. "You mean, *if* we get leave. We'll probably get out of here in another year."

"No, as soon as there are reserves," corrected Harry.

Comandante Martin waved good-bye. "Hope you got good pictures."

"I did," answered Lisa, waving back.

"He was a private in the lines," said Dickson, "then he was made sergeant, then he became captain and now he's comandante and the swellest guy we've had for the job. He used to be a school-teacher in the States."

"The thing becomes more and more unreal," I said after a while. "The whole goddamn business. The olive trees. The sun. The vineyards. The attack. Men getting killed. Harry and Milty. You and me."

Lisa laughed. "It's real...you're not sitting in a movie."

We passed the field-hospital. Dr. Tyke was dressing a wound.

"Bad?" Dickson asked.

"No. Just a blighty."

The wounded man was an Italian. He lifted his good hand and saluted us.

"Malo?" Lisa asked.

"No, de nada," he answered.

"Many get it?" asked Dickson.

"About four wounded so far," answered Tyke. "A couple of bad wounds, but most of them flesh wounds."

Sanché was asleep.

"You slept through the entire thing?" Lisa asked him.

"No...in the middle of it I fell asleep. I am very sleepy."

"What if the fascists had advanced down the road?"

"I would have been warned...our soldiers would have run by first," he answered, laughing.

Sanché started the car. Again the fragrance of lilacs. A sun. Quiet.

We told Dickson to give our regards to Brown and Feigy.

Dickson got off at the Intendencia. "Try and send us some magazines or newspapers," he asked.

"I'll try."

Sanché waited patiently and then we drove through the dirty streets again on to the highway, away from the Jarama River sector.

29

Crickets chirped. We heard them above the hum of the motor and the sound of the tyres on the dirt road. We were on a detour off the main highway. It was a narrow road. A peasant herded his sheep to one side to let us pass. There was a slow flow of mule-carts bringing food to Madrid. The road detoured back to the highway at the village of Perales. It was slow going.

"Feel better now?" asked Lisa.

"I suppose so...I should have known that Harry would say what he did. Something's happened to them. They've lost something, but they've also found something. A certain sureness. Maturity, I don't know. And they've lost their youth. I'm afraid I've grown older too, but not old enough, and surer, but not sure enough."

"You can keep questioning yourself like that as long as you live. Anyone can do that," she answered. "But, Kindchen, I got good pictures. Is it not fine?"

"That's what you kept saying the first time I saw you—remember? Is it not fine? It was in Kuller's office. Whenever you feel good about something you say it."

"And what do you say when you feel good?" Her face became serious. "The trouble with you is that you do not feel good enough. I mean enough times. Always when you laugh you think of something to make you stop laughing. It is bad."

I looked out of the window and watched the wheat fields. Poppies grew by the wayside.

"I wonder what he thinks about? He hardly ever says anything."

"Sanché? His girl friend. The war—how long it will last. He doesn't worry about himself like you do. No one I have ever known has. He probably wonders when he will get married. He told me once he wanted to be a bull-fighter, but his bad leg makes it impossible. Now he is a good chauffeur. Let us ask him. 'Sanché, what are you thinking of?'"

Sanché turned round and smiled, "Qué?" he asked.

"What are you thinking of?" Lisa asked in Spanish.

"Well, right now I was thinking that we better get some petrol at Tarancón or we will not get as far as Saelices. But before I was thinking what a fine thing it was about the Internationals coming to Spain. I was thinking about that."

"Do you ever think of your girl friend?" asked Lisa.

"Mostly at nights. In the daytime I think of Spain. At night I think of María." He flashed a smile.

"Have you heard from your brother lately?"

"Last week. He has been made a sergeant. It makes me laugh. Pedro a sergeant! He is only eighteen. I brought him up. Now he is a sergeant. I brought him up as a good Anarchist and now he's gone and joined the Communists. I don't like that."

"Why?"

"Why? He is giving me orders now. He tried to explain the political situation to me in his letters. As if I were his younger, dumber brother. I wrote him back and told him to wash his diapers regularly. He wrote back that it was a good thing he wasn't an Anarchist, because he would leave the battalion when he felt like it and come and punch my nose. He belongs to the Listers. The reason they are good fighters, he writes, is because they are good Communists. I wrote the young fool and told him that the reason the rebels are good fighters is because they are good fascists." Sanché began to chuckle. "And then he wrote me a letter with one word, 'Guadalajara.'"

"What did you write him back?"

"Oh, then I wrote a long letter telling him not to under-estimate the bravery of our enemies and explained that it was a long, long fight, and there were many social issues involved, and it was not as simple as he would have it. So the fool wrote back and told me I was confusing the issues. He argues just like a Communist now. In the end, we wrote and said long live the Popular Front, and we are good friends again."

Lisa and I chuckled to ourselves.

"What do you think will happen after we win the war?" Lisa asked him.

"I don't know. I know we are fighting against fascism now. We will probably have a form of bourgeois democracy, but it will have to be more democratic and less bourgeois. What will happen? We shall have to let history take its course. But whatever happens, it will not be fascism. Whatever government it will be, it will be a government of the people. I do not worry about it. It would be a good thing if more people were like me and worried less about what was going to happen after, and worried more about what is happening now." Sanché was satisfied with himself.

He accelerated. Then turning round as a last shot: "But it is going to take a very, very long time. They are not going to let us win so easily…maybe it will take so long that our children will be fighting. It makes a man tired just thinking of it."

There was a petrol-station on the outskirts of Tarancón. A group of dirty-looking children gathered around the car. They were thin and looked undernourished. We gave them some centimos and they ran away.

While the garage man was turning the crank of the tank, a little girl about eight years old came out of the station-house. She was sucking at her forefinger. Her large black eyes stared at us. Lisa offered her a centimo, on condition that she take her finger out of her mouth. She refused, shaking her head. She seemed to be on the point of crying, but it was the effect of her lower lip pressed down by her finger.

"What is it?" Lisa bent down and asked her.

She said nothing.

"Qué pasa, muchacha?" Lisa asked.

The child said something in a tearful voice that could hardly be heard.

"Qué?" asked Sanché.

She repeated it. Had we perhaps seen a little black dog by the name of Pepe? she asked us.

The garage man turned from the crank. "Pepita, go back to the house," he said. Her face was quiet. Just a confused hurt. "Mi perro," she said again.

"Your daughter?" Lisa asked.

"No. She is an orphan. I am taking care of her till they take her to an orphanage. I knew her father. A good man. He was killed at the front. Her mother was killed during a bombardment. Some planes appeared one afternoon. They must have been returning from some bombing expedition. They had two bombs left, it seems, so they dropped them over the village. Ten people were killed, Pepita's mother among them. It happened three weeks ago."

Pepita was listening quietly. "Sí, padre y madre muerte y Pepe también."

"No," said the garage man, "Pepe will come back. He has just gone for a walk and he will come back."

He told us that she had stopped asking about her mother and only asked for the dog now. He had given her another dog, but she wouldn't take it. She just wanted Pepe.

While the child raised her head, listening with that sad helplessness in her eyes, Lisa clicked her camera.

Then we drove away and promised Pepita that we would look for her puppy.

The car bounced over the ruts in the road. We were silent for a long while. I watched the sun, high in the west. Peasants working in the fields waved to us.

"I wish we could take a rest, both of us," said Lisa, taking my hand suddenly. "Just for a week or two. Where there would be no war. There is a place in the south of France I know, near the Pyrenees. You could go fishing. It almost touches the clouds. There is salmon there. I think there is salmon there. We could rent a place high in the mountains."

I was half-listening to her. "It's the faces of the women and kids. I can understand the faces of the men. Even dead. But there is something in the face of a woman or a child I can't get. They say nothing and seem to expect nothing. Death comes to them in handfuls. I just get a tired feeling inside looking at them. Even the women in the food queues...you want to see them look happy and there is nothing you can do. I have seen enough suffering. It makes me sick."

"I am afraid you have not seen all. This is your first visit to a hospital in Spain, yes?"

"Yes."

"Well then, wait. I am a little used to it. But I remember the first time..."

"It is I who should be telling you...I mean a man should comfort a woman about such things, not a woman a man..."

"Sometimes I can't understand your English," said Lisa. "Maybe, that is because you speak American."

"Canadian."

"It is the same. You say okay the same way as Americans do and you curse the same."

"How far yet, Sanché?"

"Not far." He began to hum *Los Cuatro Generales*. We sang it together.

"It's hard to believe that he's dead," I said.

"Who is dead?" she turned to me quickly.

"Alan...to die at twenty-three. It isn't fair, somehow. You die for a world you hardly know. At fifty. At sixty, perhaps. You've seen the world then, almost all you can of it by that time, or you should have. Then if you die for it, it evens up. But at twenty-three...it just doesn't seem fair, that's all."

She placed her hand in mine again. "You know the answer to that as well as I do. Who has always fought for the world? The men of sixty or the men of twenty? And when the men of twenty become sixty there are more men of twenty to do the fighting. So it has always been."

"Yep. One generation cometh, another passeth away, but the earth abideth for ever."

"But this time it will be a better earth," she said. "It better be. I wonder how it will end for us, for you, for me, for the world, for Spain," she went on slowly. "We have talked a lot to-day. Even Sanché has talked."

"Qué?" asked Sanché, turning his head.

"De nada."

"Whatever will be the end for us, we at least know that by fighting, the world can be made into something better than it is....Good Christ! when I use words like that I want to kick myself. I wish I could make myself clearer."

"I know what you mean," she said.

"Some day I'll say it without words."

"How without words, Kindchen?"

"When what I've tried to say just now becomes so clear to me that I see in front of me like I do that sun, there will be nothing to say. I will take a rifle and fight. It will mean that it has finally become clear to me. And when that happens I won't use so many words."

"It makes me sad when you talk like that," she said, "because it makes me realise that I cannot say you love me and I love you, and that is the most important thing....It makes me see that it isn't."

The sun was just beginning to colour the sky beyond the horizon as we drove up a side road off the main highway at Saelices, through a row of trees, and stopped at the American hospital.

"It is too dark to take pictures, but you will see your friends and we will go."

30

"Madre mia, madre mia, madre mia," a Spanish boy was crying. The room smelled of something I had never smelled before. In another bed lay another Spaniard with no mouth, but he had eyes, and he kept staring in front of him, making sounds through his throat, and spitting.

The doctor was showing Lisa and me through one of the wards. Doug was asleep in a room upstairs.

"What's the smell?" I asked.

"That's the smell of infection," said the doctor. He was tired. He looked at his watch. "Seven o'clock, I'm fagged," he said.

The door of the ward opened, to let in a little old man with a black cap. He went over to the bed where the Spanish boy was crying for his mother and said:

"Sí, sí, chico, sí, sí, shh."

"His father," the doctor said.

"Father?"

"I've seen enough," said Lisa.

"Yes?" The doctor raised his eyebrows.

I stared at the little old man. His clothes hung limply. He stared at his son and kept saying: "Sí, chico, sí, sí." Then he took out a big red handkerchief and blew his nose.

"Madre mia, madre mia, madre mia." It moaned through the ward.

"Comes from this village," said the doctor.

"Will he die?" I asked.

"Oh yes. Bullet in his spine, you know. Paralysis. Can't do a thing for him. He'll die all right. Any minute. His father came from the village. Lucky the boy was sent to this hospital."

"Yeah," I said, "that's luck all right."

"Yes," whispered Lisa.

His face was yellow and his eyes were black and he had probably been the village Don Juan, I thought, and he had said lots of foolish thing to girls, but now he said one thing, and the other soldiers lay quietly and waited for him to die.

The doctor took us from bed to bed and used big words to explain how medical science had advanced since the last war.

"Good God, here's a woman," I said.

"Oh yes, interesting case. Brought here a few weeks ago, when the village was bombarded."

She was asleep and all we could see was her black hair over the pillow. The blanket was down to her waist. One breast showed. It was a nice breast, but there was only one. The doctor explained what happened to a woman when shrapnel hit her on the breast.

She opened her eyes and I felt myself giving her a sickly kind of a smile, but she didn't smile back. She closed her eyes and buried her face in the pillow.

One of the soldiers began to cough and spit up blood and a nurse ran to him and the Spanish boy whimpered for his mother and the doctor shook his head and said: "Some of them call for their mothers and some say 'no pasarán' and some, 'goddamn,' but you get used to it."

"Maybe I can go up and see Doug now," I said.

"We'll try. If he's awake, you can go."

We walked out of the ward.

"Let's get some fresh air," I said to Lisa. She didn't answer, and we both walked out of the door, away from the hospital and sat down on the grass. I had a headache.

"You were right," I said. "You were right about hospitals."

She didn't answer.

"Come, we will see your friend and then go back to Madrid to-night. You must get back by to-morrow—yes?"

"Yes..."

31

"Is there a sun to-day?"

Nurse Helen didn't answer. "He's just awakened," she whispered to us.

"Helen?"

"Yes, Doug."

"Is there a sun to-day?" he asked again.

She bit her lip.

"Why don't I feel it?"

"It's night, Doug," Nurse Helen said.

He tried to grin.

A small light hung from the ceiling. I stared at the white bandage across his eyes, or what had once been his eyes. Below the bandage was a mess of blisters. The lips were swollen and burnt. Doug kept licking them with his tongue.

"Doug, there's someone here to talk to you, a friend of yours."

"Who?"

"Bob Curtis," she said.

Lisa walked to the window. I stared after her.

Doug was quiet. "Bob? You here?"

"Yes, Doug." I walked to his bed.

"I can't shake your hand, Bob, my hands are bandaged. It's good to...I'm glad you came. How are you?"

"Fine," I said. I fumbled in my pocket for a cigarette, placed one in my mouth. I looked at his lips again, and put it back in my pocket.

I looked at the nurse. She motioned for me to say something.

"I saw the guys to-day, Doug. They sent you their regards."

"Thanks. How's the gang?" He kept licking his lips.

"They're swell. A guy by the name of Mickey said he got a few fascists with your machine-gun." I tried to sound cheerful.

"Mickey's a good kid," said Doug.

"Yeah."

"I'll be back soon, Doug," said the nurse.

"Helen?"

"Yes."

"Will you be able to read to me?"

"Of course. As soon as I've finished downstairs."

Lisa pointed her finger at the nurse. She tiptoed out. She pointed downstairs. She would meet me downstairs.

"Helen, let's not read Mark Twain. I don't feel like it now..."

"What would you like me to read?"

"I don't know. Maybe something political. Bob, did you bring any magazines?"

"No."

"Well, anything, I don't care....And Helen?"

"Yes."

"Am I very much of a pest?"

"Darling, you're very much of a fool. You know it gives me a kick to come and read to you." She took out a handkerchief and blew hard. "I'll be back very soon." She walked out with Lisa.

"Bob?"

"Yes, Doug."

"She's wonderful, Helen is. I've never seen her, but she's wonderful to me. How you been?"

"I've been okay, Doug. I'm doing radio work. I——" I pressed my temples. "I've been broadcasting to the States and Canada."

"That's good. How are the guys?"

"They were fine. There was some action this morning. We—they—captured a fascist trench."

"That's swell. I heard Alan and Lucien were wounded. How are they?"

"I don't know..."

I got up from the bed beside him and walked to the window. The room was getting hotter and the smell sharper.

"As long as we're all alive," Doug said, and then, "is Milty still clownin' around?"

"Yes...he's made a radio mike for himself in front of his dug-out. He keeps talking away all day....The guys made a collection and gave me the money to buy you a present. I didn't know what to buy. What would you like me to get you? Is there anything special you'd like?"

"I can't think of anything off-hand...."

"It's okay...we'll think of something. I've got news from home. The C.I.O. won the automobile strike. Recruited about a million new members."

"Gee, that's swell."

I remembered his booming laugh. He kept touching the bandage around his eyes.

"Well," he said quietly, "that's how it is, eh? But I'm not useless. I can still be of use. I can tell the people back home what it's all about. I'm not useless."

"Christ, no!"

"Say, remember the fort? How it stank? It was funny. It stank like hell here, too, for the first week. I didn't know what it was. It was me. My lousy foot was infected and it stank like hell, and I kept squawking about the smell. I said it was worse than the stockyards and here it was me stinking like that."

I didn't know what to say or what to do with myself.

"Alan's dead," I said suddenly. "Lucien's wounded all right, but Alan's dead. He was killed on the twenty-seventh."

A silence. "That's bad. Alan was a good guy." He said it quietly.

"Doug...how about us singing the Abe Lincoln song and the one about religion and the preacher? Eh?"

"Okay..."

"I began to sing the first notes and Doug tried to sing it with me. We stopped half-way. He turned his head to where he thought I was standing. "My lips hurt.... It's so damned dark...but I'm not sorry. See? I did what I wanted to do. So I'll be blind, but I'm not sorry I came."

"I know you're not."

"It's just that it gets so lonely...I get to talking to myself. I must study Braille. Then it'll be better. It's good you came. It's good to talk to someone. I was hoping one of the guys would come. And Helen is so good to me. Her voice is so low and soft. She reads to me every day. She's been reading the Bible to me. There's some swell stuff in the Bible. My mother used to read things to me out of it when I was a kid."

"Maybe you'd like me to read something to you...."

"No, just talk to me. When you see the guys, you tell 'em I'm feeling swell. They know about my eyes, but you tell 'em my morale is high and I'm feelin' great. Don't forget to tell 'em. Tell Harry and Milt that you and I sang songs together and we had a swell time, and that I don't give a damn about my eyes. It'll make 'em feel good."

"I'll tell them."

"How's your hand?" he asked.

"My hand?"

"Yes. It was hurt in Albacete, wasn't it?"

"Yes...it's all better. It's been better a long time. That's how I was transferred to radio work. I stayed over and Motril got a request from Brigade headquarters for a guy to do radio work, so he suggested me and I—well, I accepted."

"I'm glad in a way that you're not fighting," he said.

"Why?"

"Well, I dunno. The six of us. Five of us is enough. I dunno, I just feel that way."

"I don't," I said, "I don't feel that way at all."

He didn't answer.

"They had a Canadian in this room with me. He was a quiet kind of guy. A dum-dum in the arm. Came from Vancouver. I hope they put someone else in the room. It'd be better talkin' to someone. It's not so bad when the sun comes through the window.... and I keep thinking of so many things...sometimes I wish I could stop thinking just for a day or so, to give my head a rest."

I stared at the floor.

> *Religion is somethin' for de soul,*
> *But preacher's belly done get it all,*
> *Preacher's bellee done get it all, dey say—y-i-p...*

"Remember?" he asked.

"Yes."

"Us climbin' the mountains. Laughing. And the fort and the concert. Hmm— everything was so far away—I lie here and think of things I never thought of before. Of my people...of the world...Always I knew there was a difference...me black...others white...but now there's no difference....Maybe it's because I can't see what's black and what's white now...I dunno...but there's no difference.... I think things...things that frighten me because they're so strange...of us, the guys...you know, Bob, the fascists can't win. We've got something inside of us that doesn't live only as long as we live. Even when we die that something lives on and fights for us. Even when I lie here blind as hell, that somethin' in me is fighting. It's with the guy in the trenches. I feel it. Sometimes I talk to the guys. I say, 'You and me, we're fightin' for a new kind of world...where you and me kin sit down and rest after the day's work is done and not worry...' you know what I mean, not worryin'? There'll be no hate, no fight, there'll be peace and quiet...and if I can't see that world it's okay with me. I'll feel it all around me and I'll know that I had somethin' to do with makin' it that way...it'll make up for my not seein' it...see? I know it's a long, long way off, but it's comin'...it'll be here...I know it."

My head was throbbing.

"Bob?"

"Yes."

"Where are you?"

"Here...right here." I walked to the side of the bed.

"Bob, you're going back to Madrid to-night?"

"Yes...I have to be back."

"Helen loves perfume."

"Yes."

"The money the boys raised—is it enough to buy perfume?"

"Yes...more than enough. You can get some wonderful perfume for two hundred pesetas."

"I don't know much about perfume. Just that some stink and some don't smell so bad...and another thing..."

"Yes."

Doug began to chuckle. "Well———" it pained him to laugh—"well, I don't like the perfume she uses now. So you take a whiff when she gets back and be sure not to buy the same thing."

I tried to smile. "Okay, I'll do that."

"Well, have you two settled the international situation?" Helen walked into the room with Lisa. My temples stopped throbbing.

"Doug, I want you to meet a friend of mine, Lisa Kammerer, she's a photographer."

"How do you do?" said Doug. "I'm pleased to meet you."

"Hello," said Lisa.

A silence. "Helen?" said Doug.

"Yes, Doug."

"Helen, please..." His tongue moved over his lips. "I must talk to Bob alone for a minute. Please. Just for a minute."

Helen turned a questioning face towards me. I nodded to her and Lisa.

"All right, dear. I'll go make you some orange-juice." She looked puzzled as she walked out.

"Is she gone?"

"Yes."

"Did you take a sniff?"

"Yeah, sure."

"Now, don't tell her a thing. When can you bring it?"

"Maybe Lisa'll be able to bring it over in a couple of days."

"That's good. I feel good. War or no war, women have got to have their perfume. She loves perfume."

"Okay."

"Bob?"

"Yes."

"Will you write a card?"

"Sure. What'll I write?"

"Just write...well, just write anything, I guess. Write, 'From Doug to Helen.' Christ! think of me buying perfume for a girl."

"What the hell's wrong in that?"

"Nothing, I guess. It seems funny, though. Buying perfume...it seems funny. I never bought perfume for anyone before."

"So you're starting now."

"Maybe...maybe we could write somethin' else."

"Anything you say."

"Well, I don't know. But couldn't we say somethin' like, 'To Helen—Who Brings the Sun to Me Every Day'?"

"Sure, we could write that."

"It's all right, isn't it? I mean, well, it sounds all right, doesn't it?"

"Sure it sounds all right. Sure it does."

Nurse Helen was standing quietly in the doorway, with a glass of orange-juice in her hand when I turned round. Lisa was biting her lip. I looked at Helen and her hand was trembling, so I said good-bye very quickly and Lisa and I told Sanché to drive back like hell.

32

The headlights pierced the blackness of the night. The motor hummed like a vibrato of violins. The white rays of light danced crazily over the road, on the trees, over a stretch of field.

"This was once the hunting-grounds of the royal family," Sanché said. He pressed his foot on the accelerator. "It is good to get into the air again. I do not like the smell of hospitals."

"What time will we be in Madrid?" I asked.

"About two in the morning."

"Can you buy good perfume for two hundred pesetas?"

Lisa was huddled in the far corner of the seat.

"Yes," she said quietly. "I think we can buy good perfume for that amount. If not, we can always add the difference. How fast are you going, Sanché?"

"Sixty-five."

"Go faster. I can still smell it."

"You'll smell it for days yet," I said. "I'll smell it the rest of my life."

"I wanted to put my hand on their foreheads and feel that I could ease their pain," she said. "I wanted to tell the little old man that his son wouldn't die and that I would see to it that he wouldn't. I wanted to tell them that I'd take some of their pain. I wanted to tell them that. And then I wanted to hear planes come and bombs fall, so that the noise could shut out the sounds of their breathing and their coughing and their moaning." She said it quietly, almost in a monotone, and went on: "Seeing so much pain makes one dumb. Pain is wrong. It is an insult against a human being. I hate seeing pain.....Life has become so cheap.... Sanché, tell us, does war raise the dignity of man?"

"Eh?" asked Sanché.

Lisa repeated the question in Spanish.

"Fighting for freedom raises the dignity of man," answered Sanché. "But it is a contradiction, is it not, that modern war has no dignity. Death has no dignity. They do not let you die or suffer in a dignified fashion these days. They have dum-dum bullets and shrapnel. That is not dignified."

"My Sanché has been a philosopher all this time and I did not know it," said Lisa.

"My Lisa has been one too," I said.

We were suddenly shaken out of our seats. The car careened from side to side, shrieking and skidding to a stop. A blow-out! The car turned and tilted to one side, but came to a stop right side up. We were shaken, but not hurt. We found ourselves in a field about five yards from the road. Then we all took deep breaths.

Sanché turned apologetically. "Pardones, camaradas...but we shall have to spend the night here. I have no extra tyre and no tools."

"Smith will raise a howl. I promised to be back in three days."

"Pardones, camaradas," said Sanché again.

"It was not your fault. You did fine," said Lisa.

We opened the door and walked into the field.

"I thought we were dead for a minute," said Lisa. Then shrugging: "So we spend the night here. It is a lovely night. We have two blankets. I have never slept in an open field before."

Sanché said he would much rather sleep in the car. "I will get a lift in the morning and go to the nearest village for tools. I will never be able to get another tyre."

"How the hell does a guy drive a car without any tools?"

"The tools were stolen..."

"Oh, come," said Lisa. "It is a lovely night. We'll forget the war, Spain, everything. Just for one night. It is not such a bad thing to forget everything for one night. Get the blankets. Sanché can sleep here and we will find a place in the field. Ah...." She looked up at the stars.

Sanché made himself comfortable in the back of the car. Lisa and I found a dry spot underneath a tree. I spread the blankets. She lay with her head resting on her hands.

"Recite some poetry," she said.

"Good God, woman, you pick the finest times..."

I sat down beside her.

"Recite something," she said again.

"I was reading Keats a few days ago. Do you like *Ode to a Nightingale*?"

"I love it," she said.

"Picture me reciting—darkling I listen or to cease upon this midnight with no pain or I have been half in love with easeful death...half in love with easeful death. It sickens me."

"All right. Tell me a story."

"About what?"

"Anything nice. A nice story. Make one up."

"Something like the three bears?"

"No."

"Once upon a time..." I began.

"Yes..." said Lisa.

"There was a little boy and a little girl and a little war and..."

"No. Not about war. A little boy and a little girl and..."

"And...it was spring. And there was grass and flowers."

"What was the little girl's name?"

"Teofila."

"And the little boy?"

"Miguel."

"So..."

"So Miguel and Teofila were sure about everything and knew everything and they lived in a city where everybody laughed and danced all the time and life was very simple and things didn't matter more to some people and less to others, so that in the end things didn't really matter at all, because everybody took care of everything there was to be taken care of...Do you like my story?"

"I don't know. Is there more?"

"No."

"When I was a little girl I used to look up and wonder what the lights were. My mother told me they were the eyes of God. The sun was the eye of God by day and the stars were the eyes of God by night. And the moon? The moon was nothing. Just a moon. Listen, do you hear something?"

I listened. "No."

"Listen...come...." She rose and held out her hand.

"What did you hear?" I asked.

"There is a brook somewhere. We shall find it."

I heard it. We walked a little way over thick grass and came to an opening in the trees, where a fast-moving stream flashed silver in the moonlight.

Lisa was as delighted as a child.

"To think that here...but why not? We forget there was beauty here before the war." She sat down a little way, where it was dry.

There were little shafts of moonlight coming through the branches. I listened to the brook making a gurgling sound and took a deep breath. I bent down and smelled the damp earth just where the stream licked it. Lisa pulled at the grass. Her hair fell over her shoulders, catching a streak of moonlight. I walked to where she sat and kissed her hair.

"Thank you," she said. "Sit here. Here. Put your head on my lap. So."

She began to hum the "Song of the Evening Star," from *Tannhäuser*, and caressed the lids of my eyes.

"You know something?" she said, as she finished.

"What?"

"Writers are liars."

"Writers are liars?"

"Yes...I have seen the men...I mean the men fighting in the trenches. They are good human beings, not supermen heroes. They are simple people, like you and I, because you and I are really simple. But the writers make them into stage actors."

"Not all the writers..."

"I know, but so many I have read," she said. "They are good people, your friends, the Spanish soldiers, the people in Madrid."

"What made you think of that suddenly?"

"I don't know...you are good...I love you...you are not a hero...you are not a strong silent man by day and a tender loud lover by night."

"But such men exist and because you happen to love me doesn't mean..."

"There is something good and big in you not wanting to fool yourself and wanting to really find out about yourself and being so afraid that you will weaken in the struggle...."

"But some men have passed that stage. They are already in the struggle and they are not weakening. I haven't come to that yet."

"But you will. And when you do you will be very strong...very strong...and you will never weaken."

"Thanks. You're beginning to make me feel like one of those strong silent men."

"Strong silent men." She said it with a tone of contempt. "Those strong silent men are that way to impress women. They *have* to impress women. I know about them. They are the ones who are afraid and have reason to be afraid. Promise me you will never become a strong silent man."

"I promise. Tell me, has one of these strong silent men bothered you recently?"

She laughed. "No....I remembered a writer I once knew. He was a good man. Honest. Natural. And yet his heroes were all fakes. Take your friends, Harry, Milty, Doug. They are like us. They are human beings."

"Harry said that there are such things as heroes. He meant it in the right way. Not supermen, as you call them, but the boys in the trenches. What he meant is that the process of becoming a hero, what he calls a hero, is the process of forgetting one's self, the process of submerging your ego for something outside yourself, something bigger than yourself. That's the beginning of becoming a hero...."

"But not a superman," said Lisa.

"We're not arguing. We agree....But that's what I have had to learn...first by seeing it. I have seen it. Now...well now, I have to do something about it."

"There is only one thing for you to do right now."

"Yes?"

"Kiss me."

I did.

"Kindchen," she said, "don't you see? You and I have found something. We love each other. I am sure of that now. We have a right to it. How many people find it? Let us keep it as long as we can....Oh, it is good when you kiss me like that and touch me...it is so good....I love you...you are good...good...good...you are wonderful...oh, I love you...oh, love is good...love is so good...."

This Time a Better Earth
PART IV

33

Love is good.
It can make you forget everything. It is like being drunk on good wine. During the day you wait for the night to come and even shelling cannot harm it...very long.

It was true. We had found something. But finding that made me want to find the other thing all the more. Because, in loving, one goes through a process of forgetting about one's self, too. I learned that in Madrid.

But there was something missing. Not in Lisa. In me. And it was missing because I knew that a man must experience more than love to be a man.

"Don't you see," I said to Lisa one day, "that I will never be capable of really loving, of really being sure of anything, until I have fought for the things I believe in?"

And whether she did not see it, or whether she did not want to see it, Lisa answered: "All I know is that it would be wrong for us to break. That is all I know now. Everything in me says, hold this, keep this, keep it for ever. And please do not say you are unhappy, loving me."

These discussions ended with me holding her close to me and telling her I loved her.

And while Lisa and I were loving each other, things were happening, important things.

On April 30th we heard in the press-room that the 15th Brigade had been given leave. The Brigade had been in the trenches on Jarama for seventy-two days. If the Brigade could be spared from the sector it meant two things: there were reserves, and the military situation had improved.

Three days later Lisa and I drove out to Alcalá de Henares, a town not far from Madrid, where the Brigade was on leave. The boys were quartered in an abandoned church. We walked in and saw them packing, ready to leave. Harry and Milty hailed us.

"Where you going?" I asked.

"Back to Jarama," Harry answered.

"But you were just given leave."

"Yes, but this morning we were told we had to rush back to the lines."

"After seventy-two days," groaned Milty. "It's a record. We've been here three lousy days and now back to that lousy sector. I'm getting tired of looking at the same thing day after day."

"That's how it is," said Harry, trying to be cheerful.

"It must be important," said Lisa, "or they wouldn't make you go back so soon. I wonder what it is."

"Well, Martin hinted something. Keep this to yourselves and don't say anything to the reporters, but it looks like the POUM is getting ready for something."

"For what?"

"I don't know exactly," said Harry, "but a couple of POUM battalions have left the Aragon front without orders. Rifles and ammunition have been smuggled into Barcelona. They may try something there. Martin said that the fascists would move simultaneously. So we've got to get back to Jarama."

"Bastards," said Milty.

"If they try anything we'll clean 'em up. But to hell with them. Did you get up to see Doug?"

"Yes. The nurse said his legs are still pretty bad. It'll take some time before he's able to move around. But his morale is swell. He told me to be sure and tell the guys that he was feeling great."

"And his eyes..."

"They're out."

"We thought maybe we heard wrong."

"No. They're out."

"What did you buy him?"

"He wanted me to buy some perfume for his nurse. Lisa bought it and we sent it up with her chauffeur."

"Perfume for his nurse! Just like Doug. We heard about Lucien yesterday from a guy who came from his hospital. Lucien's been made political commissar of the hospital. His arm will take about another month to heal. Well, we have to scram back to Jarama. See you on our next leave. Try to come up again."

"We'll try....I'm sorry you have to go back. I mean, after only three days' rest."

Lisa watched the men form into fours. "I do not feel like taking pictures," she said.

We watched them march through the gates of the town.

34

Back in Madrid, we waited. We didn't have to wait long. A week later came the news that the POUM had attempted to overthrow the Popular Front government in Barcelona. With it came the news of an intensified fascist drive in Asturian and Basque provinces. The communiqués were brief and to the point. After three days of street fighting, the Popular Front government had restored order. The leaders of the POUM were arrested.

"Now the bastards will be dissolved," said Blorio in the press-room. "Franco is going to lose one of his best allies."

Sanché was indignant. "So they are the ones who want the proletarian revolution? Stabbing us in the back! If Caballero does not do something fast he should get to hell out."

"Don't worry," Rosa said, "there will be a clean-up. And how we need a clean-up."

It was the first time I had heard Lisa swear. "The bitches," she said.

In the dying hours of a day in the last week of May came a communiqué announcing that Caballero had resigned and a new Cabinet, with Juan Negrin as Premier, had taken his place.

Blorio rubbed his hands with satisfaction. "Now, it will happen. Now, the government will begin to centralise the army and industry, build reserves, organise the rear. Now, watch...."

In the north the fascists were advancing. The government could not send aid. The northern ports were blockaded. The territory was isolated from the Republic. It looked bad for the Basque and Asturian provinces.

The first sign that the government was building an army of reserves came a few weeks later with the announcement that the 15th Brigade had been given leave. It was in the middle of June.

"I hope this time it will be for a few weeks," said Lisa.

We found the boys a few days later in the town of Albares, about eighty kilometres from Madrid. They were quartered in clean barracks, and this time they knew that "leave" would mean a few good weeks.

We celebrated in the canteen over some whisky. There were six of us: Harry, Milty, Dickson, Lisa, myself and a new guy by the name of Durnor. He was Milty's captain, a nice-looking chap, who had been a student in the University of California before coming to Spain.

"Durnor's got a good voice," said Milty, "and since Doug and Alan don't sing with us any more, Durnor sings."

"To-day I feel like singing," said Durnor.

"Sing 'em the Jarama River Blues," said Milty.

"Fine." Durnor cleared his throat and sang. It was to the tune of the *Red River Valley*. Before long everyone in the canteen was singing.

There's a valley in Spain called Jarama,
It's a place that we all love so well,
For it's there that we wasted our manhood,
And some of our old age as well.

From this valley they say we are going,
But don't hasten to bid us adieu,
For e'en though we make our departure,
We'll be back in an hour or two.

We are proud of the Lincoln Battalion,
And the glorious record it made,
So we ask you to do us one favour,
And take this last word to Brigade:

You would never be happy with strangers,
They would not understand you as we,
So remember the Ja-ra-ma valley,
And the old men who wait patiently.

They sang it a few times. Milty got a little drunk and Durnor just got happy.

"It's a wonderful war...."

Someone started to sing the *Star Spangled Banner*. Everyone joined in.

"It's a wonderful war..." said Durnor.

Lisa and I had to leave and we left them singing the *Star Spangled Banner*.

35

One evening a few days later we were sitting in the press-room listening to the radio.

"Let's get Toledo and hear what Queipo de Llano has to say to-night," said Blorio.

It was time for his scheduled broadcast. His voice came clear. This time he was sober.

"Well, General Miaja," said the fascist general, "what are you waiting for? We know you are preparing something. Come on. What are you waiting for? We are ready for you."

"Does he always make these announcements?" Lisa asked incredulously.

"No. Sometimes he just announces how many Loyalist battalions he has wiped out," said Blorio.

"If he knows something is being prepared, it isn't so good," said Kenneth.

"Makes no difference," said Blorio. "Does he know when we are going to strike and where? That is the important thing. Everyone knows we are preparing something."

"Well, I wish to hell something would happen. I haven't sent a good story for a month," said Powers.

"It'll happen," said Blorio. "Tell your office Miaja has decided to do something, so that there will be some news for the reporters."

"I'm getting fed up with the whole messy business," said Powers. "Sure, you guys are excited. You believe in this goddamned thing. But I don't give a hoot in hell which side wins. And nobody gives a hoot in hell about me. If I send good copy I keep my job. If I don't, I lose it."

"At least he's honest about it," said Blorio. "Our bitten friend, Mr. Wellington, goes around posing as a friend of the government, but every night before going to sleep he prays that Franco will march into Madrid."

"I say there," said Wellington, looking up from a magazine, "were you talking to me?"

"No. I was talking about you," said Blorio.

"Now, don't you think the wine they're serving in the Gran Via is pretty terrible?" said Kenneth, trying to change the subject.

"Yes," went on Blorio, "I said Powers was honest. He doesn't give a damn which side wins and all he's interested in is sending copy to his office."

"Commendable," said Wellington smoothly. "Some reporters forget they are reporters."

"That's right," said Blorio; "they do. And they lie deliberately."

Wellington eased out of it. "So they do. So they do." He walked back to his magazine.

Rosa walked into the press-room and took the situation in at a glance.

"It seems the gentlemen are getting nerves," she said.

"Bah," said Blorio. "I should know when it is a waste of time to talk. Kenneth, let us go to Bob and Lisa's room and have some drinks."

"May we come along?" asked Lisa.

"Eh, yes...yes, of course," said Blorio, smiling.

"That's better," said Lisa, and in a whisper, "how could you let a fool like that get you angry?"

"I am an emotional man," said Blorio.

36

One day the telephone rang and Dickson's voice roared over the phone. "Yeah. Me and Durnor. We had to come in for supplies. We're coming over."

The four of us went to the Gran Via for sherry.

"We're forming a couple of Mackenzie-Papineau companies," said Dickson. "We'll soon have a full-fledged Canadian battalion."

I must have acted jittery.

"What's the matter," asked Dickson, "the shelling getting you?"

"No...."

Lisa looked into her sherry and said nothing.

"I bet Harry's tickled about that Canadian battalion," I said.

"Yeah."

"We're on the agenda for an offensive soon," said Durnor. "This is a nice place. Is this where you eat?"

"Yes," said Lisa, "but the food is very bad."

"How's Feigy and Brown?" I asked.

"Swell. They're both in Albacete. They'll be joining us soon."

"Milty is organising a fiesta for the kids in Albares," said Durnor. "Sometimes he's a crazy bastard. Won't let anyone touch his gun."

Mercédès walked into the cafe.

"Who's that?" asked Dickson.

"That's Mercédès. I think she charges twenty-five pesetas."

"That's cheap enough for me," said Dickson, and turned to Lisa apologetically, "eh..."

"That's all right," said Lisa.

"It's been a long time," said Dickson.

Durnor looked a little embarrassed.

I called Mercédès over and introduced her. A little later she and Dickson went away by themselves.

"Well, I've got to get going," said Durnor. "I didn't think he'd be much help, anyway. I have to see that the truck is ready."

"Give my regards to Milty and Harry...and you can tell them I'll be seeing them soon," I said.

"You and I will have to get away for a rest," said Lisa. "I am worried about you. You are not yourself."

"Don't worry about me. And if I'm not myself, it probably isn't such a bad thing."

37

It was the last week in June. The warm summer days became hotter. One night while coming home from the radio station I counted fifty truckloads of soldiers passing through the city, going northwards towards the Guadarrama mountains.

"That means any day now," I told Lisa.

On July 5th it started. The communiqué from the War Ministry reported that the government troops had swept down from the Guadarrama mountains and stormed Brunete. On July 6th came the report that the government troops had captured Villanueva de la Cañada. A day later Quijorna was reported captured. It was the first successful government offensive since he war began.

"The boys are in this....I must get out there," I said to Lisa.

She didn't say anything.

A week passed. I went to Brigade headquarters to arrange for someone to take over the radio for a couple of days. I met Harvey, the political commissar of the Lincoln Battalion.

"Were our guys in the attack?" I asked.

"In it? And how."

"How does it look?"

"Damned good. But I don't know how much ammunition we have. So far the offensive has gone according to schedule. It's been bloody fighting. Nothing compared to it at Jarama. Jarama was almost a picnic compared to this. But the boys have been splendid."

"Many casualties?"

"Comparatively few so far." He mentioned a few names. I heard him say Dickson.

"Dickson killed?"

"Yes. Damned good man. Led a charge. Was leading one of the Mackenzie-Papineau companies."

"I'd like to go up with you."

"It's all right with me. I'm leaving in ten minutes."

I phoned Lisa.

"No, darling....I have to go. I just have to, that's all. Dickson's dead. I don't know about the others. Harvey just told me. Yes. Tough. Don't worry about me. I'll be back. I love you...good-bye."

38

Dust shimmered over the roads and the fields. Harvey was worried.

"Our boys are tired. The lines are on a hill just below Mosquito Ridge. The fascists have strong machine-gun nests. It's going to be tough to take...half of our officers have been killed or wounded. Tell you what you do. You stay near the propaganda truck when we arrive. It's behind the lines. Then come up when it gets dark and talk to the boys. Tell them what the offensive has meant. It will do them good. They're tired as hell."

Harvey left me at the propaganda truck. Our artillery was blasting at the fascist positions. The shells sang over our heads. I looked around for someone I knew and then decided to crawl along the road and get nearer to the lines.

Whistle of strays. Shriek of shells. Quiet. Noise again. Two men led a mule carrying ammunition towards the lines. They hailed me.

On the left of the dirt road was a small hill. I saw dug-outs. A group of soldiers sat around a telephone. They were doing nothing, just waiting.

Shells were coming fast. I fell flat on my face. Whizzzzz-splushhhhhhhh bang! I got up and ran towards a dug-out.

"Come in quick, you bloody ass," someone said.

I dived in.

Whizzzzz-shplush-shu- shu-shu- bang!

Pieces of shrapnel flew into the dug-out. There was a barrel in one corner and from it extended a rubber-tube. One of the men had the end of the tube in his mouth sucking.

"What the hell are you doing around here?" one of them asked.

"I came up with Harvey." I introduced myself.

"Wilkinson," said the man.

I knew that Wilkinson was the commander of the British Battalion.

"You nearly got killed then," said Wilkinson.

"I know."

"Have some beer." He gave me the tube. "Suck at it. It comes out."

The beer was lukewarm, but I was thirsty.

"We found it in Brunete," one of the others said.

They introduced themselves. Black. Overund. Stowkist. Two Englishmen and a Pole.

"They've got the range, the bastards."

Four shells fell near the dug-out in rapid succession.

"Are the tanks ready?" Wilkinson asked.

Wilkinson was a short, powerfully built man. He scratched his head. "I asked if the tanks were ready?" he shouted.

"I don't know," answered Black. "The telephone lines are still cut."

"Hell," said Wilkinson. "Stinking bloody war. How the hell do they expect me to tell the men to attack without tanks? Try the phone again."

Black held the phone to his mouth. "Hello, headquarters...hello, headquarters...there is a line...Hello, this is Black, Wilkinson's runner."

"Give me the goddamned thing," said Wilkinson.

"Hello. Yes, this is Wilkinson. Yes, I know I'm late. But the tanks haven't arrived yet. I know. I know. It's four o'clock. I have a watch here too. No, he's dead. All my officers are dead. How the hell should I know? I'm not going to order the men over the top without tanks. Not on that hill. It's bloody suicide. I don't give a damn. Well, where are the tanks? You said that four hours ago." He put down the phone and took a deep breath. "Black, get up to the lines and tell whoever is in command to wait for the tanks. Get it? If the tanks don't come they are not to do a thing. Those are my orders. When the tanks come I'll get up and take the boys over myself."

Black got to his feet. A shell exploded in front of the dug-out.

"Wait a couple of minutes," said Wilkinson. "I'm tired. I'm not supposed to be tired, but I'm tired. Harvey is going to be twice as tired. He doesn't know yet. I suppose he knows now. His commander was killed this morning. That means he'll have to take over command. He'll do a good job, too. Not only will he have to worry now about everything he had to worry about before, he'll have the whole stinking job on his hands. Personnel department, medical department, quartermaster's department....I need a good political commissar....I need some tanks...."

"I better go now," said Black.

"Very well. Good luck."

Black walked out of the dug-out. We heard the blast of a shell. Pieces of flesh flew into the dug-out, together with dirt and shrapnel. Wilkinson got up slowly and walked to the entrance. He turned round.

"Overund, get a blanket and cover him up. Drag him away from the entrance. And then you get up to the lines fast and take the same message."

"No," said Overund. I saw him crouch in the corner of the dug-out.

"What! You sonofabitch! Get up there!"

"No," whimpered Overund.

Wilkinson grabbed a blanket and walked out of the dug-out.

"Take it easy there," Stowkist said to Overund.

"I'm not going," said Overund.

Wilkinson came back and stood in front of Overund. "You yellow bastard!"

"Please...I can't help it. I'm going crazy."

"You yellow sonofabitch," he said again.

"He's ill," I said. "I'll go."

"You keep out of this. Stowkist, are you going?"

"Yes," said Stowkist, getting to his feet.

"Got the order straight?"

"Yes."

"Good luck."

Stowkist walked out of the dug-out.

"Now you..." Wilkinson turned to Overund. "Get up and report to the propaganda truck."

Overund didn't move. He began to sob.

Wilkinson began to pound his fist into the palm of his hand. "I said, get up and get to hell out of here! This is what you want, isn't it? I'm telling you to go to the rear. Way in the rear!"

"Comrade," began Overund.

"Don't call me comrade. Get up or I'll pick you up and throw you out."

Overund got to his feet slowly. "I can't help it. I can't help it."

"I know you can't help it. You're afraid you might die. You're afraid you might die....Get out! I get sick looking at you."

Overund walked out of the dug-out holding his head.

"Poor goddamned kid," said Wilkinson quietly, "poor goddamned kid. But what the hell could you say to him? You can't say a thing when they get like that. Poor goddamned kid. He went through the whole business as brave as any of them." He let out a loud sigh. "Where the hell are the tanks? Listen, you can do something besides sitting on your ass. Do you like sitting on your ass? How about going down to the propaganda truck? You'll find a typewriter there. Write out a short piece on the significance of the offensive, for the battalion paper. You can write, can't you? A radio announcer, eh? Well, if you can talk you can write." He stared at me. "You didn't like the way I talked to Overund, did you? Come on. I want to be alone here. Go and write. Don't mind me. If you ask me, I think I'm cracking, myself. You're a good kid. Don't mind what I said. Go ahead and do what I asked you to."

"Are you sure you're all right?" I asked.

"Sure I'm all right!" he shouted. "Can't you see I'm all right? Don't I sound all right? Go over the top without tanks, without artillery, against machine-gun nests. Bloody goddamned suicide. And I've got to tell them to do it. Get to hell out of here and let me alone."

I walked out of the dug-out and made my way down the narrow road. There were a few men sitting around the propaganda truck.

"Did some guy by the name of Overund pass by here?" I asked.

"Overund just got killed," one of the men said. "A shell got the poor bastard on the road. It was Overund, wasn't it?" he said, turning to the man next to him.

"Yes. I saw the guy's face. He must have been on a message for Wilkinson. Somebody should tell Wilkinson that he's dead."

"Where's the typewriter?" I asked.

"There." The man pointed to a group of trees. I walked over. The typewriter was on a box. I heard the drone of planes.

"Scram!" someone shouted.

Bombs started to fall one after the other. The earth shook and I fell to the ground. I lay there waiting. The drone died off. I looked at the typewriter. It was a noiseless typewriter.

That's fine. I'll type softly. I won't make a sound. I won't make a goddamned sound. People are asleep. Overund's dead and Wilkinson's cracking and Harvey will have to take over command and I love Lisa but I won't make a sound with this noiseless typewriter, and I'm going up to the lines to-night to hell with the radio I can only send communiqués and it can wait a day it can wait for ever I'm going up to the lines this time I'm going.

"Are you all right?" A head peered through the trees.

"Yes."

"Geez, take a look at this guy typing away while they were dropping their eggs."

"I'm a brave guy," I muttered to myself.

39

I walked up to the lines. It was dark. A few stars in the sky. Low mumble of men's voices.

"Naturally we had to come back..." someone was saying, "they've got strong machine-gun nests. At least if we'd have had tanks...And I'm so fagged...."

"Anyone around here know where Milty Schwartz is?" I asked.

"Yeah. You'll find him on the hill. Don't get lost. You pass through a dry gulley, then turn to your right."

"Thanks."

"Keep low in the gulley...."

"Okay...."

I came upon Milty sitting behind the parapet on the hill.

"Hello! When'd you get here? Boy, have we been having a picnic! If we thought Jarama was something, then this has been the nuts."

"Where's Harry?"

"Somewhere around."

"He's all right, then?"

"Sure. We attacked this afternoon. It didn't go so hot. Reminded me of Jarama. No artillery. No tanks. The British got it bad. Their commander got killed. They led the attack. It..."

"Wilkinson?"

"Yeah. Know him?"

"I met him this afternoon."

"To-day wasn't so good," said Milty. "The last couple of weeks have been good, though. Our artillery and planes shot the hell out of 'em. But we ain't got enough planes and now their planes are blasting the hell out of us. I never saw so many planes in all my life. But we advanced. Boy, you shoulda seen us taking that town with Canada attached to it."

"Villanueva de la Cañada?"

"Yeah...sixteen hours of fighting. The Moors tried to pull a fast one. They came out with a white flag and had some women and kids walking in front of them. When we came close they began throwing hand-grenades. We fixed the bastards later for that trick. Dickson got killed. Martin, our commander, was wounded. Then Oliver, the negro comrade, took over and he got killed this morning. Now Harvey's commanding us."

Someone sat down beside us. It was Harry.

"Surprise finding you here," he said.

"I wanted to come up. After I heard about the offensive I wanted to get up here....It's been some day. It's hellish about Wilkinson. I was in his dug-out this afternoon. I met four men there, and three of them are dead already."

"Who? Do we know them?" Milty asked.

"One was named Black, the other Overund."

"Don't know them."

"Did Lisa come up with you?" Harry asked.

"No. I came up alone this time."

"They'll have to give the guys a rest," said Harry. "It's too much for them. Three weeks without a stop. The bastards are going to counter-attack soon and the boys will be dead on their feet. Some of the kids have fallen asleep over their rifles."

"Yeah, and we haven't eaten for two days," said Milty.

"That's because we advanced too fast. The kitchen didn't keep up with us. We'll get our rations to-morrow."

"Maybe you've got a cigarette?" Milty asked.

"You know damned well I haven't got a cigarette," said Harry.

"You?" he turned to me.

"No. I'm sorry."

"When are you going back?" Harry asked.

"I'm going to stay over to-night...."

"Boy, swell. You can sleep in our dug-out," said Milty.

"Fine. It'll be nice, the three of us together," said Harry.

"Give me a gun now," I said. "At least let me feel that I might be of some use around here."

Milty got up and came back with a rifle. "Can you handle a gun?"

"Yes...." I held it and saw Harry grinning up at me. "You look like a real soldier now," he said. "I'll see you guys later. I've got to get back to my gun. I'm in the Mackenzie-Papineau company now, did you know?"

"No...."

"Best company in the battalion," said Harry.

"Yeah...." said Milty.

Harry went off. "See you later."

"Hello," someone else said. It was Durnor. "I thought I heard voices. I was down in the gully trying to get a drink from that leaky water-pipe. What's news from Madrid?"

"They're excited as hell about the offensive."

"When you go back tell them we're tired," said Durnor.

"Say, Durnor, you know we have no water for Mother Bloor," said Milty.

"When did you water her last?"

"Yesterday."

"Well, that's enough water. For Christ's sake, you worry more about that gun than yourself."

"Well, the sun made it too hot to-day. If there's going to be any action to-night it won't be good for it." Milty peeked through the parapet. "Gee, it's quiet."

"Too quiet," I said.

"Funny how when it's quiet a guy gets the jitters and when there's noise a guy gets the jitters. Seems a guy's always getting the jitters. Say, you know what's funny?"

"No. What?"

"Remember in the movies when a guy gets hit and he bends over first and then he looks at the sky and then he takes time to turn around and then he flops...?"

We waited.

"Well, it's funny, because that's just what happens."

"It's very funny," said Durnor.

"When this thing is all over and if I get home, I'm going to run a chicken farm," went on Milty.

"Chicken farms smell bad," said Durnor.

"Smell bad?" There won't be a smell on earth that'll bother me after this," said Milty. He yawned. "I'm sleepy. Come on, Bob, let's go into the dug-out and wait for Harry."

"Sweet dreams," said Durnor.

We were in the dug-out five minutes when we heard the thunder of a shell. Then machine-gun firing.

"Come on, looks like an attack."

We ran to the trench.

"Got your gun?"

"Yes."

Durnor was giving orders. "Good. I wondered when the hell you'd get here. Get your gun in position. Bob? Got a gun? Okay, get over there and start shooting. Got bullets? Here's a strapful."

I put my gun through the parapet and took aim. I pulled the trigger and the gun kicked against my shoulder.

"Moors!" Milty shouted.

"Okay now, kid," said Durnor, "wait till they come close and then give it to them. Take your aim and in short spurts."

Tata-tat-tata-tat-tata-tat came from the machine-gun.

Durnor poked his head above the parapet. "Hey, Mike, better get some more ammunition...." I heard him groan. "Oh, hell...hell...hell..." He stumbled backwards toward me. I held out my arm to stop him from falling. He clutched at his stomach. I placed his head on my knee. "Stay...shoot...your gun..." Durnor said.

"They're running back," shouted Milty. "They're running back!"

"Good old Milty...you *can* say No Pasarán...thought was a lie...I'm glad...not sorry...not...not...no..." I couldn't hear him. He was trying to say something. Then his head fell on my arm. Blood trickled out of his mouth.

"They're running back, the bastards....Good old Mother Bloor....What a gun! What'd I tell you?" Milty turned from the gun.

"Christ! Dead?"

"Yes."

"Goddamn it!" He turned to his gun and pressed the trigger and his body shook violently as the shots crackled into no-man's-land.

Later we buried Durnor behind the lines, and at the foot of his grave we planted a cross and on it we wrote Durnor's full name:

ALVIN DURNOR. AMERICAN. KILLED IN ACTION. BRUNETE FRONT.

40

The sun was fading over the sierras. From our hotel room we could hear the rumble of trucks below and the clang of trams. The wind ruffled the curtains and the window-shade kept rustling. I pulled at the string of the shade and it flew upwards.

"That noise makes me nervous....Have you got a cigarette?" I asked.

"What is the matter? Something has happened. Tell me."

"I need a cigarette."

"I have one. We'll break it in two." She broke it and we both puffed away. I stared out of the window.

"We've never gone to see the zoo," I said.

"Tell me...you do not love me any more?"

I turned quickly. "God, no...it isn't that. It's just that I needed a cigarette."

"Soon we will have all the cigarettes we want."

"Ricardo get a new batch?"

"No."

"Then how?"

"I have fine news..." she began.

I threw the butt out of the window and walked to the bed. "No," I said, "you listen first. I've made up my mind. I'm going to ask for a transfer."

She looked at my face and I saw her lower lip tremble.

"All right," she said softly. "If you think it is right."

"You know it's right."

She ran her hand through her hair. "I had fine news for us. I wanted to tell you yesterday, but you have been so strange since you came back from the front. You have been so strange to me. I was so happy about it...my editor has given me a leave of absence." She crushed her cigarette.

I was silent.

"I thought you would ask for leave and we would have a real honeymoon. We would go to Paris..."

I couldn't bear looking at her face.

"Do you love me?" she asked suddenly.

"You know I love you."

"Then ask for leave. Only for two weeks...just for two weeks...in Paris...then you will have time to think and not do anything on the spur of the moment."

"Time to think? Darling! How can you..."

"We will go to a beach and swim and lie in the sun. You have never seen me in a bathing-suit. I look very beautiful. You should see. Oh, darling..." She held me tightly. "It is not fair...it is not fair...if you go into the trenches I will...I do not know what I am saying. Hold me...."

I rubbed my chin on her head. "I'll ask for a two-week leave. We'll have our honeymoon."

She was crying.

"Don't cry. Please don't cry. You should be happy about this."

"I am happy about it," she said between sobs, "I am-very-happy. But something is cutting me here." She pressed her hand over her heart.

"We'll be all right. I'll see you when I get leave."

"Do not talk! Just hold me...you must ask for leave on Monday. I told my editor I would get more action pictures. To-morrow we will go to the front. Let us try to leave Monday. Ask if you can go to Paris. We can live in my apartment. We will not stay in Paris long. We will go to the country. We will be so happy in the country...."

"Yes," I said.

"Shh, do not talk. Let me talk. You do not talk...but we will win, Kindchen, we will win....I do not want to cry....I do *so* not want to cry....I love you." She dried her eyes and tried to smile at me. "I will get the front passes in the morning. I will not wake you. I will phone you from the War Ministry....I will write my mother to come to Paris. I want her to see you. She will love you. We will have a real honeymoon."

"We'll get married," I said.

"Yes...yes...in a church, yes? My mother will be happy."

"In a church."

"Hold me tight...." She began to whisper in German. "Tight. Tight. Like you would never let me go....I wish time would stand still....I hate them! I hate them! They are killing everything for us."

"They're trying to. But they won't."

41

Next morning I found a note beside the pillow.

I will phone you. I love you. You are beautiful when you sleep. L.

I looked at the calendar. Sunday, July 25th. The morning papers lay on my bed and I read that yesterday Brunete had been entered twice by the fascists and they had been driven out twice by the government troops. There had been heavy fighting.

The telephone rang. "Lisa? Coming right over."

The street car was crowded. A heated discussion was taking place.

"Brunete's retaken."

"No, it isn't."

"It is."

"It isn't."

"Aw, what does it matter if it is? We've taken Quijorna, Villanueva de la Cañada and Villanueva del Pardillo. That's our new army. I tell you we'll soon sweep the bastards into the sea."

"Not if they keep on sending more Italian troops."

"Italian troops? Did you ever hear of a place called Guadalajara?"

I got off. Lisa was waiting beside the car. She wore khaki overalls and her blonde hair was flying. I told her about the discussion on the street car. She smiled. She said nothing about yesterday's discussion.

Sanché said that he knew exactly where the action was taking place. He would take us right to the lines outside Brunete. Sanché could speak American by now, not English. Okay was the word he knew.

The sun became stronger and the car became hotter.

"Let's sing," said Lisa.

"Okay," said Sanché.

We sang French songs, English songs, American songs, German songs, and Spanish songs until we got tired of singing.

Lisa held up her hands and yawned happily. "To-morrow we make preparations to leave for Paris. I must get some good action pictures. If they are still fighting near Brunete it will be my chance to get some." Then turning to me: "I am sorry about last night."

I kissed her.

Sanché began to describe how the fields around Brunete stank from the dead. Both of us had been in Brunete, so we knew how it stank. But Sanché wanted to make it more elaborate. He not only described the stink, but the guts, the smashed heads of men.

Everything was quiet. The sun was strong. There was hardly any traffic on the road. We passed Villanueva de la Cañada and saw the sanitary corps stationed along the road. Blood-streaked stretchers were lying in the ditches, waiting.

"Where is the Lincoln Battalion?" she asked me.

"There, to the left of Brunete." I pointed.

We stopped. Division headquarters. We walked through a rolling wheat-field. Everything was strangely quiet.

The general somehow wasn't glad to see us. "Of all days to come," he groaned. "You must go back immediately. Go back. Go right back."

"What! I am going to Paris to-morrow. This is my last chance to get some action pictures. I must stay. Please let me stay," she pleaded.

"No," yelled the general. "Take her away, someone. Go away immediately. I tell you I cannot be responsible for you. Who let you come? Go away. In five minutes there will be hell."

"Come," I said.

"You can go. I'm staying here."

"But the general says..."

"To hell with the general."

The general meanwhile had gone into his dug-out, so he didn't hear her.

"Please come," I said; "this is no place for you."

"This is *exactly* the place for me."

"Well, okay, okay. I think you're crazy. You and your action pictures. I shouldn't have let you come. But let's get away from the general. There are some dug-outs on the little hill there."

We snuggled into a dug-out big enough for my feet.

We heard the drone of planes. Twelve of them. You could see the tiny pursuit planes flying around them like flies.

The drone became louder, louder, louder, and they came so slowly. You felt they would stop in mid-air. But they didn't stop. They turned and swung towards us. Then thunder. Then black clouds—about a hundred yards in front of us. Again thunder. Again. Again.

Lisa was busy taking pictures.

I was trying to see what I could use to make the hole larger.

Thunder! A shower of earth.

"Put your head down!" she shouted.

"Where'll I put it? I can't put it into my chest."

"Put it down. Put it down."

"Are you all right?"

"Who, me?" she asked. "Sure. You?"

"Sure." We smiled at each other. She bent towards me swiftly and kissed my cheek.

The air cleared. The stuttering drone became dimmer. Heads began to appear out of dug-outs. Soldiers grinned. Some looked pale and didn't grin.

"Why don't you go?" I said. "I can take the pictures and meet you in El Escorial."

"Now please do not be a pest," she answered.

A drone. A soft hum. Just imagination. It becomes louder. Twenty planes come out of the sky.

The planes came for one hour in relays. They bombed the government lines, and while they were bombing, the fascist shells were coming. There were no government planes. It was about one o'clock when they started. Lisa asked the time. Two o'clock. Suddenly quiet.

We looked ludicrous in that hole in the ground. My knees and head showed above the ground while Lisa somehow managed to get her feet underneath mine.

"If they come again you'd better watch your head," she said; "shrapnel, you know."

"I know. But you're taking pictures and your head is above the ground."

"Yes. But I must take pictures and you don't have to."

Again we heard the drone.

"Look, they're not bombers."

Nine Caproni biplanes flying low swung towards the road which stretched behind us. Lisa clicked her Leica. Her film camera lay in its leather case beside the unfinished dug-out. The first plane swung on its side, swung low, and then we heard the tat-tata-tat-tata of machine-gun fire. The second plane did the same. The third, the fourth. All nine of them and then the first began again. Then twelve bombers came and bombed the lines. Then the shells came, and for thirty minutes there was black hell.

"It must end some time," I said.

Lisa didn't answer. She took pictures of the black earth and the smoke which came from the bombs and she took pictures of the dust and white smoke which came from the shells. She took picture after picture and I sat there crouching. Suddenly she said: "Put your head down."

The planes swung toward us. They saw us. They must have seen her camera flashing in the sun. There was a machine-gun in the next dug-out. They must have seen that too. Men crawled about when they should have been lying quiet. The first plane turned on its side and dived gently toward us. The earth in front of the hole began to rise in short spurts.

Tata-tat-tata-tat. Tata-tat-tata-tat. Tata-tat-tata-tat.

Lisa got a picture of the earth jumping in spurts. Then she took pictures of the planes as they came down toward us.

"Damn it, the roll is finished." To place another roll would mean raising her body. There were no anti-aircraft guns in this sector. I saw men shooting at the planes with their rifles.

Tata-tat-tata-tat. Monotonous, nerve-racking drone. I grabbed the camera lying beside us and placed it on Lisa's head to protect her from the machine-gun bullets.

"You fool," she said. "It will break the camera."

"Shut up now or I'll break your head."

Then the bombers came again. This time thirty of them. We counted. Clouds of black smoke rose in front of us. Then we heard a terrific noise of machine-gun fire. On the hill in front of us we saw men coming. They were coming all along the lines.

"We're retreating," I said.

The bombers saw the lines crumble and they went to town. Then came the strafing. The shells weren't hitting their mark, but the bombing and strafing were enough. We saw men fly into the air. Lisa put another roll into her camera. She clicked it. I didn't know what was more maddening then, the planes or the camera.

One section of the lines was orderly and the retreat went comparatively well. But a retreat is a retreat, and there was confusion. Men got panicky and ran anywhere as long as they ran. In front of us a few soldiers took positions with guns and dared anyone to pass them. This stopped a panic. Lisa forgot about her camera and was yelling at the top of her lungs for them to stop and re-form their lines.

I picked up a rifle which had been thrown away and jumped out of the dugout. I was only conscious of one thing—the lines must re-form.

She was up beside me and took my arm.

"Get back there! You'll get hurt," I shouted.

"Don't be silly."

Her hand trembled as she took a cigarette from her case and lit it.

"Where'd you get them?" I asked.

"At the War Ministry. I didn't tell you because I was saving them. I only have three. We would have smoked them all in the car." She offered me one, but my mouth was too dry, and I didn't like those Spanish cigarettes.

It was quiet. The planes had done their job and were gone. It was very quiet. The retreating troops re-formed their lines a little beyond the hill. Here and there a figure moved. A cool breeze came down from the Guadarrama. The wheat swayed gently. Behind the hill little puffs of white clouds could be seen. There was not even a rifle-shot. The Spanish countryside looked peaceful. I looked at the sky and it was peaceful too.

I gave the rifle to a passing soldier, who took it without a word.

We saw the division doctor, a Scotsman, coming towards us. He looked worn out. All his equipment was lost, he told us. Many of his comrades had been killed.

We began to walk through the fields towards Villanueva de la Cañada. The lines were now between the two towns. The fascists obviously had had superiority in the air that day, but they couldn't follow up the retreat. On the road there were many dead. Men groaned and begged for *agua* (water). Some were silent. By this time Lisa had no more film.

The planes came again. We flung ourselves beneath an overturned truck. But the planes passed over. They weren't looking for us.

We got into Villanueva de la Cañada, and it stank. Two men were sitting beside a wounded comrade under cover of a hut's remaining wall. They saw the doctor's arm-band.

"Please come. He is badly hurt. Please look at him," one of them said.

The doctor was tired. "I've got nothing. Nothing. No bandages. Nothing. What can I do? He will have to wait for an ambulance."

"Please look at him."

The doctor went over to the man and lifted the blanket covering his legs. The legs looked as if they had gone through a meat-grinder. The man made no sound. His eyes were on the doctor's face. Lisa said something about hoping that some day she'd be able to take a different kind of picture. I said nothing.

A tank passed. We stopped it, put the wounded man on, jumped on ourselves and started. The planes came again. There were four tanks behind us. Clumsy-looking animals. The planes dove. Tata-tat-tata-tat.

Silly getting killed now after what we've been through.

"Bah, they can't hit a thing," said Lisa.

They didn't hit any of the tanks. The tank was hot. It snorted and wheezed and made lots of noise and swung from side to side. We held on tightly. The white house beyond Villanueva de la Cañada served as a dressing-station. We took the wounded man off the tank. The doctor got a car and rushed away to get ambulances. The wounded were dragging themselves or being carried to the dressing-station. A few tanks stopped. It was silly. A marvellous target for planes.

"Got the camera?" she asked.

"Yes."

A large black touring car came down the road. We stopped it and asked for a lift as far as El Escorial. Sanché had probably gone there when the retreat started and was waiting for us.

"Sure, get on," the chauffeur said.

We jumped on the running-board.

"Lisa, you go on the other side."

"Why? It is big enough. We can both stay here."

She put her cameras on the front seat of the car. There were three wounded men inside. Salud. Salud.

She took a deep breath. "Boy—that was a day. I feel good. The lines re-formed and I feel good. And I got the best pictures of my life. To-night we will have a farewell party in Madrid. And then, next week—Paris." She held back her hand for me to take. She squeezed my hand. "Think you will have time to ask for leave to-night?"

"I don't know."

There was some confusion ahead of us. A tank was jerking ahead in spurts, swerving from side to side on the road, out of control. Our car swung to the left. "Hold on," she laughed gaily, "you don't want to fall off now and break your leg."

I saw it. Just the side of the tank. Then I was on the road. Then I knew that both my legs were off. Then I knew they weren't. Then I saw blood on my right leg and the pants torn on my left. There was no pain.

"Lisa!"

Two soldiers ran toward me and pulled me into a ditch.

"Dónde está mujer! mujer! mujer!"

Then I saw her face—just her face. The rest of her body was hidden by the car. She was screaming. I saw men bending over her. Her eyes looked at me and asked me to help her, but I could not move. There was no pain, but I could not move. The tank was quiet now. It had swung round and now it was quiet. The young Spanish driver looked at us. He was frightened.

Then the planes came. The man beside me dropped. The other pulled me into a ditch. Everyone ran for the fields.

"Lisa! Where are you? Lisa!"

The planes went away.

"Dónde está muchacha? Where is the girl?"

"She's been put into an ambulance," someone answered.

"Are you sure? Es verdad?"

"Sí, sí."

"And her camera, where is her camera?"

"I don't know," the Spanish boy answered.

Someone brought me a brown cloth belt. It was crumpled and the wooden buckle was broken into little pieces.

"It is hers," he said.

"Where is the car?" I asked.

"Yo no sé."

Then someone brought me her purse. The handle was all twisted.

Then I began to feel the pain. "*Agua* (water). I want water."

But no one had water.

They put me on a stretcher and placed me in the back of a Ford camion. There was no water.

We stopped at a dressing-station. A German doctor was in charge. He was alone. His two assistants had been killed by bombs.

"Did you see a young woman, a small, pretty girl with blonde hair?"

"There was no girl. I did not see a girl."

They gave me water.

The camion started. I looked at my watch. It was six-thirty. I put it to my ear, but it did not tick. It had stopped.

"Six-thirty. That's when we were hit."

"What?" said the man lying beside me.

"Nada. Cómo está?"

"Just a machine-gun bullet in the thigh," he said.

It was growing dark. I still held the belt in my hand. It was becoming wet from sweat. Then I fainted.

I came to. The man lying beside me was slapping me.

"Cómo está ahora?" he asked.

"Bueno," I answered weakly.

The road was bad and every jolt of the camion was like a knife through my foot. Then came the American hospital at El Escorial. I asked if they had seen a young woman, a...

"Yes. Lisa Kammerer. Yes. She's here. Are you Mr. Curtis? She asked about you. She was brought here some time ago."

"How is she?"

"She's all right."

"Can I see her?"

"No. She's just had an operation. You cannot see her."

They injected anti-tetanus into my arm and marked a cross on my forehead.

"Will I be able to see her in the morning?"

"Yes."

"How is she?"

The nurse smiled. "I told you she was all right. She's suffering from shock. Her side was hurt pretty badly, but she'll be fine and dandy in the morning."

"She needed an operation?"

"Naturally. Why do you think we gave her one?"

"I don't know."

Dr. Wellbridge came over to my stretcher.

"How do you feel?"

"Good. Can I see Lisa?"

"No. I'm afraid not. She's suffering from shock. It would be bad if you saw her. I will tell her you are here. She's been asking about you continually."

"But she and I—I—she's my wife."

"Sorry. You cannot possibly see her until morning."

"Couldn't I just look at her?"

"Sorry. No."

The wounded men lay on the floor of the hospital on stretchers. All the beds were occupied. The ambulances kept on unloading.

The pain became worse.

Dr. Wellbridge gave me a shot.

"There, now you'll go to sleep."

"Does she say anything?"

"She asked for her camera. She asked me to ask you whether you would mind wheeling her around during your honeymoon. You'll both see each other in the morning. Better rest now."

My watch still showed six-thirty. I asked the time. Three-thirty a.m. I couldn't sleep.

A nurse came over. "What's that?" she asked.

"It's her belt."

"Oh."

All night the wounded came. The doctors worked smoothly, swiftly. Here—this one. Clothes cut off. Fracture? Abdomen? Bring him to the theatre. Take this one first. This one. Dead? Take him away. This one. No, the other. All through the night.

A Spanish boy lay beside me moaning. A nurse gave him a shot and he became quiet.

"What time is it?"

"Five o'clock. Why don't you sleep?"

"I can't sleep. Can I see her now?"

"No."

Well, I would see her soon, joke about the fact that we had to be hit by a tank after missing all the bombs and bullets in the world, and she would probably raise a fuss about losing her camera.

At five-thirty Dr. Wellbridge came to my stretcher. "Well, everything looks much better. Frankly, we were worried. She was badly shocked and her side terribly battered. She may never walk straight again. We just gave her a transfusion and she said: 'Whee, I feel good.' She asked about her camera again, and I told her it was lost. All she said was 'C'est la guerre.' She's really a remarkable woman. She also told me to tell you not to flirt with the nurses. She said something about Paris."

"Can I see her now?"

"For God's sake, man, not now. She must sleep now. If she sleeps everything will be all right. She's badly shocked. You'll see her later. It's for her good. You must have patience."

I drank some coffee. The head nurse had not slept all night. Neither had Dr. Wellbridge or the other doctors. They were sleepy. Wellbridge passed me, smiled and went upstairs. I saw a nurse follow him.

"I'll try to sleep now," I said to myself. "My feet don't pain."

The morphine made me feel dull and shapeless.

Wellbridge came toward me.

"I'm afraid I have bad news for you."

I waited.

"Lisa just died."

"Give me a cigarette."

Wellbridge lit his cigarette. He turned and came back with a needle.

"No. I don't need it. For Christ's sake, I don't need it. When I need it I'll ask for it. I feel no pain."

"Give me your arm. You're going to need it."

He jabbed it into my arm.

"Hell!"

I wanted to ask if he were sure she was dead, but I didn't. I wanted to go to sleep and forget a lot of things, but I couldn't. A nurse came over and told the doctor about another case.

"Would you like to be taken into my room?" he asked.

"Please, if you can."

The anti-aircraft began firing away and the shutters rattled.

Wellbridge came back.

"You'll never know how sorry I am that I didn't let you see her. But I didn't know. I really thought she would recover."

"Oh, hell, that's all right."

Wellbridge stood in front of me and turned his face. "If you want——" he paused—"if you want to, you can see her now. But it isn't good to see someone dead whom you've loved."

"Hell, I don't want to see her now."

But I did. I didn't believe she was dead. They brought me upstairs on a stretcher and I looked at her and her face was not quite the same.

Then they carried me down and I kept slipping on the stretcher, and the boys carrying me told me to hold on or I would fall.

Someone gave me an American cigarette. The smoke curled gracefully. Then the nurse brought me Lisa's cigarette-case. There was one cigarette left. I put out the American cigarette and smoked the one in Lisa's case. It was a Spanish cigarette, and I never liked Spanish cigarettes. The doctor asked me what I wanted to do with her body, and I wanted to tell him to go to hell, but he meant well and I asked if he could arrange to ship it to Paris. He said he would.

Then the nurse came over, and she said she was sorry.

42

"Sure that your foot is okay?"

"It's perfect."

"What's the rush about getting into the lines? You should take a few more weeks to recuperate."

"I've been recuperating for a very long time now," I said.

Harry rubbed his chin.

"Let's see you walk," he said.

"Don't be a fool. The damned foot is all right. Look." I walked a few steps.

"Looks all right," said Harry.

"It *is* all right."

"Bob?"

He looked up from his desk. "I'm not talking like a captain now. But are you sure about this...you're sure that it isn't because of Lisa...?"

"It isn't Lisa...I made up my mind before that. I told her I was going to the front. We planned to go away for two weeks, a sort of honeymoon, and then I was to come back....Well, we had all the honeymoon we could get, I guess....We...she...but that's not the reason I asked for a transfer....It was all settled before she...before she died."

"Okay...." He got up from the desk. "We'll go to the lines. Lucien is back with us. Got back yesterday. Fit as a fiddle. C'est la guerre, says Lucien. We'll put you into Milty's company. You know he's a sergeant now, don't you?"

"Hell, no. I hadn't heard. One of the guys in the hospital told me that you'd been promoted to captain, but I didn't know about Milty."

"Yep, Sergeant Milty Schwartz. I think he's giving a bunch of rookies the lowdown on machine-guns now. He'll be tickled to see you."

Harry put his hand on my shoulder and we walked along the streets of Quinto to the lines outside the town.

In a field near the outskirts of the town Sergeant Milton Schwartz was giving a lecture.

"Listen to him," grinned Harry. "He's been reading a lot lately and his English is improving."

"There are thirteen parts to a Russian Maxim," Milty was saying. "And it can be entirely dismantled by hand. I'll dismantle it for you later. There are no screws or bolts. You push these pins out with a cartridge. A German Maxim has twenty-one parts and needs tools to dismantle it.

"This machine-gun," continued Sergeant Milty Schwartz, like a college professor, "is gas-operated. Do you know what gas-operated means? You don't. Now see this. This is called the safety-lock. You push this up and then you press the trigger. The bullet is caught by the tea-cups, and when it is fired out of the barrel it releases gas. This gas enters a cylinder that pushes the barrel back and turns the loading mechanism, pulls out the empty shell and grabs another bullet all in one operation. This gun will shoot five hundred and fifty bullets to the minute. Our cartridge-belts only have two hundred and fifty bullets, so you'll have to take my word for it. Now come here and look. See, that's the water jacket. It holds about eight and three-quarter quarts of water. If the gun isn't watered, then the barrel will warp and the steel will get so hot that it'll explode. Now, there are lighter guns. There are air-cooled Maxims that only weigh thirty-three pounds. The Hotchkiss is also air-cooled. But an air-cooled gun is inferior in firing power. A water-cooled gun like Mother Bloor suffers in manœuvera—manœuverability." Milty took a deep breath and went on: "In comparison to an air-cooled gun, but it shoots faster. You got to take care of your guns the same way a mother takes care of a baby. You got to keep it clean. You got to see that it's watered. Now, any questions?"

"Yeah," one of them said. "When the hell are you going to stop talking and let us handle the damned thing?"

"Oh, a wise guy, eh?" said Milty. "A wise guy. First, this is no damned thing, and second, I'll talk till I'm sure I've knocked some brains into some of you guys. A lot of you guys still think you've come to a picnic. Well, let me tell you..."

"Cut it...we get our political education from the political commissars," one of them said.

"Looks like we're going to have trouble," said Milty, grinning.

He turned.

"Bob!"

"Hello, Sergeant."

"He's joining your company," said Harry.

"Honest?"

"Honest."

"Wheee...gentlemen, you are dismissed. We shall gather here to-morrow at the same time."

Milty ran to me. "Honest?"

"Honest."

"Get Lucien. Where's Lucien? Lucien!"

"What the hell is the matter?" Lucien called from a dug-out.

"Bob's back!"

"Salud there!" Lucien yelled.

"Salud yourself!"

Lucien came toward us. We looked at each other and grinned.

"How's the wound?" I asked.

"All wounds get better in time," said Lucien. "How's yours?"

"Likewise."

"We'll all share the same dug-out," said Milty, "and I'll teach you how to shoot a gun good."

"Swell," I said.

Arm in arm we walked toward the trenches. The sun was high in the sky.

THE END

Explanatory Notes

The explanatory notes for This Time a Better Earth chiefly emphasize and clarify three aspects of the book: instances of non-English-language text, place names and general but important references to biblical, historical, literary, biographical and other cultural material. I have not provided notes on topics, events or people when they are addressed at some length in the Introduction.

Words or phrases have not been translated when an English-language translation or meaning has been given within the text. When words or phrases have been translated they are followed, within square brackets, by an indication of the language that appears in the text. Translations are my own and they reflect a desire to represent the diversity of language usage in the text through three major modes of translation: (1) direct and literal translation; (2) translations of literary and figural language; and (3) translations of recorded speech from characters who do not have a comprehensive grasp of the language.

I have attempted to identify three levels of the political geography of present-day Spain when giving notes on place names: municipal, provincial and the autonomous community. Spain is made up of seventeen autonomous communities and two autonomous cities. Provinces are divisions within autonomous communities. Municipalities are divisions within provinces.

Although Allan makes the claim that his characters are fictitious (other than a select list of Spanish leaders, generals or civil personages), it is clear that some of his characters are close approximations of real historical figures. I have resisted the temptation to be overzealous in my speculation about possible links between characters and real people within these notes. I have no doubt that with a greater degree of historical and military knowledge than I possess, speculations about characters resembling historical figures could turn into reasonable correspondences. Although I have provided a few notes on dates, I strongly encourage the reader to consult a good chronology of events of the Spanish Civil War. I have found the chronology published in Madrid 1937: Letters of the Abraham Lincoln Brigade from the Spanish Civil War (edited by Cary Nelson and Jefferson Henricks) to be useful.

164   This Time a Better Earth

Each entry signals a page reference followed by a line reference; for example, "51.3" refers to page fifty-one, and the third line of text from the top of the page. Generally, the first instance of text requiring reference is given a note while subsequent instances are left unexplained.

ABBREVIATIONS

OED   *The Oxford English Dictionary*

KJV   *The Bible, King James Version*

PART I

3.1–5 *Abe Lincoln* by Earl Robinson and Alfred Hayes: I have retained the copyright notice of the first edition for contextual explanation: Earl Robinson (1910–1991) was a Seattle-born musician. Alfred Hayes (1911–1985) was a British-born writer. They are best known for their composition of "Joe Hill" ("I dreamt I saw Joe Hill last night"), which was recorded by Paul Robeson, Pete Seeger and Joan Baez, among others.

3.4–5 Joseph Seligman: Listed as Joseph Selligman, Jr. on the "Roll Call of American Volunteers in the Spanish Civil War" (held in the Abraham Lincoln Brigade Archives at Tamiment Library of New York University).

5.3 Largo Caballero: (1869–1946) Spanish Socialist leader and prime minister (1936–1937). He was ousted as prime minister. He fled to France in 1939. After spending most of World War II imprisoned in a Nazi concentration camp, he died in Paris.

5.3 Juan Negrin: (1891–1956) Spanish Socialist leader and prime minister (1937–1939). A professor of physiology at the University of Madrid, he was active in the Socialist Party and was elected to the Cortes in 1931. He fled Spain to France and then to England. He died in Paris.

5.4 José Miaja: (1878–1958) Republican Army officer (general). After being named commander of the Junta de Defensa (Defence Council) for Madrid in November 1936, Miaja resisted the Nationalist siege for twenty-nine months.

5.4 Francisco Franco: (1892–1975) Spanish general and fascist dictator. Franco participated in the July 1936 coup d'état against the elected Popular Front government. After the failed coup had evolved into the Spanish Civil War, Franco emerged as leader of the Nationalists who fought against the government. With the help of Mussolini and Hitler, Franco defeated the government forces and assumed authoritarian control of Spain until his death.

5.4–5 **Queipo de Llano:** (1875–1951) Spanish Army officer who fought for the Nationalists during the Spanish Civil War. In July 1936 he led Nationalist forces in the capture of Seville and then became commander-in-chief of the Southern Army.

5.5 **Colonel Gonzales:** (1909–1983) Republican military commander. Valentín González was known as El Campesino ("The Peasant" [*trans. from Spanish*]). He worked as a miner and was a member of the Communist Party. He established one of the first militia units to counter Franco's Nationalist Army. In 1978 he returned from exile in the Soviet Union and France to live in Spain. He died in Madrid.

5.6 **Colonel Enrique Lister:** (1907–1995) Spanish communist leader and Republican general. He led the 5th Regiment, which he had organized as a militia, in the defence of Madrid in 1936. He then commanded the 11th Division at Guadalajara.

5.6–7 **Dolores Ibarruri [Gómez] (La Pasionaria):** (1895–1989) Spanish communist leader. Secretary general of the Communist Party of Spain (PCE) (1944–1960), President of the PCE (1960–1989), and a member of the Spanish national assembly (Cortes) (1936 and 1977–1979). Her orations against the fascists earned her the name La Pasionaria ("The Passion Flower" [*trans. from Spanish*]).

7.5 **Pyrenees:** A mountain range in southwest Europe that forms a natural border between France and Spain.

9.28 **Abraham Lincoln Battalion:** The Abraham Lincoln Battalion consisted of volunteers from the United States and Canada who served in the Spanish Civil War in the International Brigades. They fought for Spanish Republican forces against Franco and the Spanish Nationalists in the XV International Brigade. American volunteers mostly joined two battalions (the Lincoln Battalion and the Washington Battalion), but volunteers from the United States also served with the Canadian Mackenzie-Papineau Battalion, the Regiment de Tren (transport), and the John Brown Anti-Aircraft Battery. The International Brigades were withdrawn in 1938.

10.15–17 **Religion is somethin' for the soul:** "Preacher's Belly" was published in Lawrence Gellert's *Negro Songs of Protest* (New York: American Music League, 1936).

10.22 **National Guard:** The National Guard of the United States is a reserve military force.

11.19 **non-intervention patrols:** Patrols of the border between France and Spain were administered by the Non-Intervention Committee (1936–1939). The committee was established to prevent volunteers and supplies from reaching either side of the conflict. The committee emerged out of the Non-Intervention Agreement that was proposed in early August 1936 by the governments of Léon Blum (1872–1950) in France and Neville Chamberlain (1869–1940) in Great Britain.

11.22 **Alouette:** A popular Canadian children's song about plucking a skylark's feathers.

11.38 **Viva Norteamericanos:** Long live the North Americans [*trans. from Spanish*]. A common slogan that celebrated the international volunteers that came from North America.

12.32–12 **No Pasarán:** They shall not pass [*trans. from Spanish*]. Rallying cry of the Loyalists in the Spanish Civil War made famous by Dolores Ibárruri in her "No Pasarán" radio broadcast of 18 July 1936.

12.37 **Marx:** Karl Marx (1818–1883). A philosopher, political economist, historian, sociologist, humanist, political theorist and revolutionary credited as the founder of communism.

12.37 **Lincoln:** Abraham Lincoln (1809–1865). The sixteenth president of the United States. He was an abolitionist who led his country through the American Civil War.

12.37 **Browder:** Earl Russell Browder (1891–1973). General secretary of the American Communist Party from 1930 to 1944.

15.1 **C'est la guerre:** That's war or Such is war [*trans. from French*].

15.18 **Catalonia:** An autonomous community in the northeast part of Spain.

15.24 **Barcelona:** Both a province as well as the capital city of Catalonia.

15.29 **Madrid:** An autonomous community, a province, as well as the capital city of Spain. Madrid is located in central Spain.

16.1 **cojones para tu:** Balls for you [*trans. from Spanish*]. In this case, "cojones para tu" would be like saying "balls to you!" or "go fuck yourself," though it should be "cojones para TI." It is probable that the narrative is presenting a situation in which Alan's grasp on Spanish is less than perfect. Therefore, the "tu" has been retained in the current edition.

16.14 what England will do: See note on non-intervention patrols, above (11.19).

17.5 Moor: Originally used to describe a native or inhabitant of ancient Mauretania, a region of North Africa corresponding to parts of present-day Morocco and Algeria. The word later became associated with members of a Muslim people of mixed Berber and Arab descent inhabiting northwestern Africa.

17.19 Arabella: The *Arabella* carried John Winthrop, who wrote *A Modell of Christian Charity*, from England to Massachusetts in the spring of 1630.

17.20 Mayflower: The *Mayflower* was the ship that transported the English "Pilgrims" from Southampton, England to Plymouth, Massachusetts in 1620.

17.31 Berengaria: Launched in May 1912, the German ship was originally named *Imperator*. She was renamed *Berengaria* in February 1921 after being acquired by the Cunard Line.

18.32 Albacete: A city in southeastern Spain. It is the capital of the province of Albacete in the autonomous community of Castilla-La Mancha. The city was the headquarters and training camp of the International Brigades during the Civil War.

20.16–18 Now, ole Abe Lincoln: See note on *Abe Lincoln*, above (3.1–5).

20.20 Is it true what they say: "Is it true what they say about Dixie" was written by Irving Caesar (1895–1996), Sammy Lerner (1903–1989) and Gerald Marks (1900–1997). The Mills Brothers, Al Jolson and Dean Martin recorded it, among others.

20.24–27 In the days of yore: A version of "The Maple Leaf For Ever," a patriotic Canadian song composed by Alexander Muir in October 1867, the year of Confederation.

21.1–7 O Canada, our home, our native land: "O Canada" was composed by Calixa Lavallée and the lyrics were written, in French, by Sir Adolphe-Basile Routhier in 1880. An English text, written by Robert Stanley Weir, has multiple versions. "O Canada" was not Canada's official national anthem until 1980.

21.9–15 Rubáiyát: Although a Rubáiyát (or Ruba'iyat) is a collection of Ruba'i (in Persian poetry, a quatrain), the poetry of Omar Khayyam (1048–1123), published as *The Rubaiyat of Omar Khayyam*, is the best known of the genre. The first English translation appeared in 1859.

21.17 The quality of mercy is not strained: Spoken by Portia in Shakespeare's *The Merchant of Venice* (4.1.181–183).

168   This Time a Better Earth

21.20–21 My heart aches and a drowsy numbness: From John Keats's 1819 poem "Ode to a Nightingale." John Keats (1795–1821) was a British Romantic poet. See lines 1–4:

> My heart aches, and a drowsy numbness pains
>   My sense, as though of hemlock I had drunk,
> Or emptied some dull opiate to the drains
>   One minute past, and Lethe-wards had sunk: (1–4).

21.22 Bottom: A character in Shakespeare's *A Midsummer Night's Dream*.

21.23 the raging locks and shivering shocks: Spoken by Bottom in *A Midsummer Night's Dream* (1.2.27–30).

22.25 Valencia: A coastal city in Spain (east of Madrid, south of Barcelona). It is the capital of the province of Valencia in the Valencian autonomous community. During the Spanish Civil War the capital of the Republic was moved from Madrid to Valencia.

23.10 Prensa department: Press department [*trans. from Spanish*].

23.17 Salud: literally means "health" and used as a common greeting [*trans. from Spanish*].

24.18–19 People's Front of Spain: The People's Front or Popular Front was a name given to coalitions between parties on the left, be they workers' parties or liberal capitalist parties. The Communist International adopted the Popular Front policy in 1935.

24.24 those eventful November days: The Nationalist army arrived on the outskirts of Madrid on the first of the month, and what has come to be known as "The Battle of Madrid" began. The International Brigades arrived shortly thereafter and helped hold off the Nationalists.

24.29 tomb of fascism: "Madrid will be the tomb of fascism" was a popular antifascist slogan that represented the hope that the rise of fascism in Europe and around the world would be stopped with the defeat of fascism in Spain.

24.34 People's Army of Republican Spain: The army of Spain's Popular Front government.

25.12 *Die Moorsoldaten*, the *Peat Bog Soldiers*: A protest song that is sung in many languages, it became a popular anthem for antifascists in the Spanish Civil War and later on for the resistance movement during the Second World War. It was written and performed by socialist and communist internees in a Nazi concentration camp in 1933.

27.17 Ach, ist gut: Oh, it is good [*trans. from German*].

27.20 International: The "Internationale" is the anthem of international socialism. Eugène Edine Pottier (1816–1887) wrote the original lyrics (in French) in 1871. Pierre Chretien De Geyter (1848–1932) composed the music in 1888. While there are many different versions of the lyrics in many different languages that do not correspond, the musical composition is seldom changed.

27.25–36 The following translations from each language are not literal translations. They attempt to represent the highly figurative enunciations of socialist struggle:

> Arise ye prisoners of starvation
> Debout les forçats de la faim—Arise, convicts of hunger [*trans. from French*]
> Das Recht wie Glut im Kraterherde—Justice [glows] like embers in the crater of a volcano [*trans. from German*]
> Il tracollo non è lontan—The collapse is not far [*trans. from Italian*]
> Sterft gij oude wormen en gedachten—Die ye old worms and thoughts [*trans. from Dutch*]
> Snart verden Grundvold sig forrykker—Soon the foundation of the world is upset [*trans. from Danish*]
> Boz to jest nasz ostatni—This fight is our last [*trans. from Polish*]
> We have been naught, we shall be all!
> 'Tis the final conflict.
> Let each stand in his place,
> The International
> Unites the Human Race.

28.15–18 Hold the Fort: The original song was written by the American evangelist Philip P. Bliss (1838–1876). There are many versions but the most notable adaptations are those of the British Transport Workers toward the end of the nineteenth century and the On-to-Ottawa trekkers of 1935.

28.23 Viva Brigada Inernationale! Viva Democracia!: Long live the International Brigades! Long live Democracy! [*trans. from Spanish*].

29.3 Romeo and Juliet: An early tragedy by Shakespeare.

29.6 Moro!: Moor! [*trans. from Spanish*].

29.18 El no Moro, pero camarada negro, camarada Norteamericano: Not a Moor, but a Black comrade, a North American comrade [*trans. from Spanish*].

29.27 Mira!: Look! [*trans. from Spanish*].

29.33 "fathista" and "no patharan": "fascist" and "no pasaran." The prose attempts to represent the "lisp" in the peninsular or regional pronunciation of the Spanish language.

31.24 sea blockade: See note on non-intervention patrols, above (11.19).

31.29 C.I.O. and the Labour Party: The Congress of Industrial Organizations, or CIO, was a group of unions that organized workers in the United States and Canada from 1935 to 1955. The American Labor Party was founded in New York in 1936 by labour leaders and liberals. They supported Franklin Delano Roosevelt's New Deal. The party was dissolved in 1956.

31.34–35 merci beau-coups: Thank you very much [trans. from French].

31.37 Light Cavalry: *Leichte Kavallerie* (Light Cavalry) is an operetta in three acts by Franz von Suppé (1819–1895). It was first performed 21 March 1866 in Vienna.

32.4 O night of nights: Unknown song.

32.6 Bury the Dead: A play by Irwin Shaw (1913–1984). The play was first produced in 1936 and is set in the "second year of war that is to begin tomorrow." It is an antiwar play in which six soldiers who were killed on the battlefield refuse to be buried.

32.6 Waiting for Lefty: A play by Clifford Odets (1906–1963). The play was first produced in 1935 and is set in a union meeting wherein union members debate a strike. It is based on a 1934 taxi strike in New York.

32.7 people's theatre in Canada: For detailed information on Canadian theatre in the 1930s see Alan Filewod's "Performance and Memory in the Party: Dismembering the Workers' Theatre Movement" (*Essays on Canadian Writing* 80 [Fall 2003]: 59–77).

32.8 Mais non, il est nécessaire d'avoir un gouvernment très fort: But no, it is necessary to have a strong government [trans. from French].

33.6 Scottish Ambulance Corps: The Scottish Ambulance Unit Committee was formed in 1936 by Sir Daniel Stevenson, politician and chancellor of Glasgow University.

33.7 Málaga was captured by the Italians a week ago: Málaga is a port city in the province of Málaga in the autonomous community of Andalusia. Málaga was the site of "The Battle of Málaga" (3 February–8 February 1937).

33.13 Socorro Rojo: The Socorro Rojo Internacional was the Spanish affiliate of the International Red Aid, which was an international social and medical service organization connected to the Communist International.

33.28 Anarchists: Although there are many versions, anarchism is basically a political philosophy that calls for abolition of the state and centralized institutions.

33.28 Poumists: POUM (Partido Obrero de Unificación Marxista [*trans. from Spanish*]; Partit Obrer d'Unificació Marxista [*trans. from Catalan*]) Workers' Party of Marxist Unity or Workers' Marxist Unification Party. The POUM was an anti-Stalinist Spanish communist party that was formed in 1935 by Andreu Nin (1892–1937) and Joaquín Maurín (1896–1973).

34.8 Prime Minister: Arthur Neville Chamberlain (1869–1940). A British Conservative politician and prime minister of the United Kingdom from 1937 to 1940.

34.13 Jarama front: Jarama is a river in central Spain, east of Madrid. It was the site of the "Battle of Jarama" (6 February– 27 February 1937).

36.15 puttees: A puttee is a "long strip of cloth or leather wound spirally round the leg from the ankle to the knee and worn by soldiers, walkers, etc., for protection and support in rough terrain" (OED).

39.21 castanets: A castanet is an "instrument consisting of a small concave shell of ivory or hard wood, used by the Spaniards, Moors, and others, to produce a rattling sound as an accompaniment to dancing; a pair of them, fastened to the thumb, are held in the palm of the hand, and struck with the middle finger" (OED).

39.23–32 the moon shines bright: Spoken by Lorenzo in Shakespeare's *The Merchant of Venice* (5.1.1–6).

40.1 Oh swear not by the moon: Spoken by Juliet in Shakespeare's *Romeo and Juliet* (2.1.151).

40.1–2 blessed, blessed night! I am afeard: Spoken by Romeo in Shakespeare's *Romeo and Juliet* (2.1.181).

41.5 alcalde: mayor [*trans. from Spanish*].

41.21 O comfort-killing night: From Shakespeare's 1594 narrative poem "The Rape of Lucrece" (764–765).

46.13 refugio: shelter or safe place [*trans. from Spanish*].

50.12 kaker: shithead [*trans. from Yiddish*]. The term "alter kaker" literally means "old shit" and would be the coarse version of "old geezer" in English.

51.9 Modesto: Juan Modesto Guilloto León (1906–1968). Spanish Communist leader and Republican general.

51.10 Aragon front: Aragon is an autonomous community in northeastern Spain, west of Catalonia.

51.12–13 political commissars: A commissar is "a representative appointed by a Soviet, a government, or the Communist party to be responsible for political indoctrination and organization, esp. in military units" (OED).

53.31 West Point: The United States Military Academy.

54.21–22 Salvo Conducto: Safe Passage [*trans. from Spanish*]. A document or permit that provides safe passage in times of war.

54.23 Ah, Internationale, bueno, adelante camarada: Ah, an International, well, go ahead comrade [*trans. from Spanish*].

55.3 Un petit, petit peu: A little, little bit [*trans. from French*].

55.4 Moi aussi: Me too [*trans. from French*].

55.6 No, maintenant je vais à Madrid pour travailler, eh, well, la radio: No, now I go to Madrid to work in radio [*trans. from French*].

55.7 Ah, muy bueno, pour Norte Amérique: Ah, very good, for North America [*trans. from Spanish*].

55.8 Oui: Yes [*trans. from French*].

55.10 Ruso?: Russian? [*trans. from Spanish*].

55.32 Flamenco: A Spanish "style of singing or dancing; a song or dance in this style" (OED).

56.14 Dónde el frente Jarama?: Where is the Jarama front? [*trans. from Spanish*].

56.25–34 Los cuatro generales: A popular song of the Spanish Civil War based on a Spanish folk song, "Los cuatro muleros."

> *Los cuatro generales* [The four generals]
> *Los cuatro generales* [The four generals]
> *Los cuatro generales, mamita mia,* [The four generals, my mother]
> *Que se han alzado* [They have rebelled]
> *Que se han alzado.* [They have rebelled.]

Quieren pasar los Moros, [The Moors want to pass,]
Quieren pasar los Moros, [The Moors want to pass,]
Quieren pasar los Moros, mamita mia, [The Moors want to pass, my mother]
No pasa nadie, [Nobody passes,]
No pasa nadie. [Nobody passes.] [trans. from Spanish].

56.35 Telefonica: Telephone building in Madrid, built in 1929, that stands 88 m in height.

57.7 Velásquez Street: Calle de Velázquez is a street in central Madrid where the International Brigades building was located (63 Calle de Velázquez).

57.15 Vas ist das?: What is this? [trans. from German]. The prose, with a "V" instead of "W," attempts to represent a German accent.

57.34 Brigade paper: The Brigade paper was called *Volunteer for Liberty*.

57.37 Hôtel Nacional: A hotel in central Madrid, originally built in 1924.

58.26–27 just like your Broadway it was, the Gran Via: The Gran Via is a large street in Madrid built between 1904 and 1929. It was a showcase of early twentieth-century architecture. The Gran Via was also a large hotel across from the Telefónica building.

58.30 Mucho calor: Very hot [trans. from Spanish].

PART II

61.10 allo, allo, esta estacíon: hello, hello, this is station [trans. from Spanish].

61.10 Station E.A.R.: The radio station from which the Loyalists broadcast was EAQ Madrid. For the transcript of a broadcast given by Norman Bethune see: *Listen in: This is station EAQ, Madrid Spain*. (Toronto: Committee to Aid Spanish Democracy, [1937?]).

61.12 Claro?: Clear? [trans. from Spanish].

61.16 Himno de Riego: El Himno de Riego (Hymn of Riego [trans. from Spanish]) dates from the Trienio liberal, a period of liberal rule from 1820–1823 and is named in honour of Colonel Rafael del Riego (1785–1823), a Spanish general and revolutionary. The song became the national anthem of the Republic.

61.19 Sí, hombre: yes, man [trans. from Spanish].

61.19 Madrileños: people of Madrid [trans. from Spanish].

61.21 Alcala: Calle de Alcalá, one of the main streets of Madrid that heads in an easterly direction from the Puerta del Sol. See note on Puerta del Sol, below (67.9).

62.1 señores y señoritas: gentlemen and ladies [*trans. from Spanish*].

62.13 café con leche: coffee with milk [*trans. from Spanish*]. Similar to the French café au lait.

62.26 Cómo está?: How are you? [*trans. from Spanish*].

62.32 Juanita Crawford in a sensacionale, excepcionale cinema: Joan Crawford in a sensational, exceptional film [*trans. from Spanish*]. Joan Crawford (1905–1977) was one of the most prominent stars in Hollywood during the 1930s.

63.26 February twenty-seventh: The Abraham Lincoln Battalion fought in the "Battle of Jarama" and on the 27th they were ordered to carry out a suicide attack. The attack was ordered by Colonel Vladimir Copic (1891–1939). Robert Merriman (1908–1938), Lincoln Battalion commander, protested but was forced to follow orders. He led the attack.

64.11 Esta la guerra: That is war [*trans. from Spanish*].

64.26 "Salud, hombre, cómo está?" And he would answer: "Bueno, y tu?" and you would answer back: "Muy bueno,": "Hey, man, how are you?" And he would answer: "Well, and you?" and you would answer back: "Very well," [*trans. from Spanish*].

65.5 L'Humanité: The daily newspaper of the French Communist Party (PCF).

65.9–10 Guadalajara Province: Guadalajara is a province as well as a city in the autonomous community of Castilla-La Mancha northeast of Madrid.

66.9 The agency men, Powers and Alexanders: "Agency men" refers to journalists who are hired by an organization "that collects news items and distributes them to subscribing newspapers, broadcasters, etc." (OED).

66.21 Buenos días: Good day [*trans. from Spanish*].

67.6 hydrophobia: Hydrophobia is a "symptom of rabies or canine madness when transmitted to man, consisting in an aversion to water or other liquids, and difficulty in swallowing them" (OED).

67.9 Puerta del Sol: Gate of the Sun [*trans. from Spanish*]. The Puerta del Sol is a busy square in the heart of Madrid that serves as the symbolic centre of Spain and is the basis of numbering in the Spanish road system.

67.12 Entrez: Enter [*trans. from French*].

67.24 Fifth Column: The term "fifth column" was coined by the Nationalist General Emilio Mola (1887–1937) in a 1936 radio address to suggest that he had a group of supporters within Madrid in addition to his army of four columns stationed outside the city. The term has the pejorative connotation of treason. It was also the title of Ernest Hemingway's only full-length play, first published in 1938.

67.29 University City: A hillside suburb of Madrid that houses the University of Madrid. The Republican and Nationalist forces entered into a stalemate from early November 1936 until it was taken by the Nationalists, allowing them to take Madrid and end the war on 31 March 1939.

68.6 Alto!: Halt! [*trans. from Spanish*].

68.12 Yo Norteamericano. Camarada, camarada: I'm North American. Comrade, comrade [*trans. from Spanish*].

68.15 Anti-fascista: Antifascist [*trans. from Spanish*].

68.19 Qué pasa, hombre? . . . Por qué?: What's the matter, man? . . . Why? [*trans. from Spanish*].

68.25 loco Norteamericano: crazy North American [*trans. from Spanish*].

68.31–32 Dónde Hôtel Nacional, camarada, por favor, muchas gracias?: Where is the Hôtel Nacional, comrade, please, thank you very much? [*trans. from Spanish*].

69.24 English Tories and the democracies of the world: see note on non-intervention patrols, above (11.19).

69.27 Ethiopia: The Second Italo-Ethiopian War was an imperialist attack by the Kingdom of Italy (Regno d'Italia) on Ethiopia, also known as Abyssinia, which started in October 1935 and ended in May 1936.

70.4 Mais oui: But yes [*trans. from French*].

70.6–7 Parlez-vous français, peut-être?: Do you speak French, perhaps? [*trans. from French*].

70.8 Non. Mon français est très mal. Allemand et anglais: No, my French is very bad. German and English [*trans. from French*].

70.25 The Florida: A hotel in Madrid on the Plaza Cayou. The hotel is a recurrent setting in Ernest Hemingway's *The Fifth Column and Four Stories of the Spanish Civil War* (New York: Charles Scribner's Sons, 1969).

70.27 The Palace: A hotel in Madrid that was built in 1912 at the direction of King Alfonso XIII.

71.2 Figueras: A town in the province of Girona in the northeast of Catalonia. It was the Spanish destination of international volunteers who crossed the Pyrenees from France on foot. It was also the birthplace of the painter Salvador Dalí (1904–1989).

77.7 Brihuega: A town in the province of Guadalajara. It was the place where Italian forces were defeated in the "Battle of Guadalajara" (8–23 March 1937).

78.35 Diez centimos: Ten cents [*trans. from Spanish*].

79.2 Victoria á Guadalajara!: Victory at Guadalajara! [*trans. from Spanish*].

79.16–17 Pardones, pardones: Pardon, pardon [*trans. from Spanish*]. This is anglicized speech. The correct usage in the Spanish language is "Perdón, perdón."

79.22 Neptune: In Roman mythology Neptune is the god of the sea and corresponds to the Greek Poseidon.

79.25 Muchas obuses ahora: Many shells now [*trans. from Spanish*].

79.29 The Cuatro Caminos: A district outside Madrid's city centre located at a junction of four big streets.

80.1 Chatos! Chatos! Nuestra! Nuestra!: Snub-nosed [Russian planes]! Snub-nosed [Russian planes]! [they're] ours! [they're] ours! [*trans. from Spanish*].

80.8 Guapa!: Beautiful! [*trans. from Spanish*].

80.8 Gracias: Thank you [*trans. from Spanish*].

80.11 camion: A truck or wagon.

80.14–15 Charlot Chaplin in Modernos Tiempos: Charlie Chaplin in *Modern Times* [*trans. from Spanish*]. A silent film (1936) that features Chaplin's iconic Little Tramp character.

81.10 Perros!: Dogs! [*trans. from Spanish*].

82.10–11 Cabinet changes: In May of 1937 a crisis forced Caballero's resignation, and Juan Negrin became prime minister of the Republic. See note on Caballero (5.3) and on Negrin (5.3), above.

83.13 Keats: John Keats. See note on "Ode to a Nightingale," above (21.20–21).

86.11 Gorki: Aleksey Maksimovich Peshkov (1868–1936). Better known as Maxim Gorky. A Russian writer and dramatist.

Explanatory Notes   177

86.11 Dostoievsky: Fyodor Mikhaylovich Dostoyevsky (1821–1881). A Russian writer, essayist and philosopher who wrote *Crime and Punishment* (1866) and *The Brothers Karamazov* (1881).

86.11 Tolstoi: Lev Nikolayevich Tolstoy (1828–1910). Better known as Leo Tolstoy. A Russian writer who wrote *War and Peace* (1869) and *Anna Karenina* (1877).

86.11 Turgenev: Ivan Sergeyevich Turgenev (1818–1883). A Russian novelist and dramatist who wrote *Fathers and Sons* (1862).

86.11 Chekov: Anton Pavlovich Chekhov (1860–1904). A Russian short-story writer, dramatist and physician who wrote *The Seagull* (1896), *Uncle Vanya* (1899-1900), *Three Sisters* (1901) and *The Cherry Orchard* (1904).

86.11 Pushkin: Alexander Sergeevich Pushkin (1799–1837). A Russian poet and dramatist.

86.15 Lenin: Vladimir Ilich Lenin (1870–1924). Originally Vladimir Ilich Ulyanov, Lenin was a Russian Marxist philosopher and politician who led the Bolshevik Revolution of 1917.

86.15 Engels: Friedrich Engels (1820–1895). A German revolutionary, social theorist and author who co-founded, with Karl Marx, modern socialism.

86.15 Stalin: Joseph Stalin (1879–1953). Originally Iosif Vissarionovich Dzhugashvili, Stalin was a Soviet politician and dictator who consolidated power after Lenin's death.

89.3 Kindchen: A diminutive of the German noun "Kind" or "child," also used as an endearment (for both Singular and Plural).

95.6 Morata de Tajuna: An area within the Madrid province, near the Jarama Front.

PART III

97.11 Intendencia: Supply and command office [*trans. from Spanish*].

98.28 Duke of Alba: The "Casa Alba" (House of Alba) is an aristocratic family of Spain. The ancestry can be traced back to when the first "Alba" was made Lord of the City of Alba de Tormes in 1429.

100.3 Suicide Hill/Pingarron Hill: During the "Battle of Jarama" the British Battalion took up position on this hill amid severe casualties. See note on Jarama, above (34.13).

100.25 Bango: colloquial use of bang, as in thoroughly, completely or exactly (OED).

102.7 Soviet Maxim: A descendent of the first self-powered machine gun, invented in 1884 by Sir Hiram Maxim (1840–1916).

102.23 Murcia: Both a city and an autonomous community located in southeastern Spain. An autonomous community of the region of Murcia that consists of a single province.

102.24 Saelices: A small town located in the Cuenca province in the autonomous community of Castilla-La Mancha in central Spain.

103.32 The Ladies' Home Journal: Originally The Ladies Home Journal and Practical Housekeeper, the magazine began publication in 1883. It became one of the leading popular magazines of the twentieth century.

104.28 William Lyon Mackenzie: (1795–1861) Canadian journalist, insurgent leader and champion of democratic government. Mackenzie led a group of insurgents in an attempt to seize Toronto in 1837. The naming of the battalion came exactly one hundred years after Mackenzie and Papineau fought for democracy.

104.28–29 Louis Joseph Papineau: (1786–1871) French Canadian political leader and insurgent. His critiques of the treatment of French Canadians by British colonial policy led to a rebellion in 1837.

104.31 George Washington: (1732–1799) Washington led the American army to victory over Great Britain in the American Revolutionary War (1775–1783), which led to his serving as the first president of the United States of America.

106.4 Garibaldi Battalion: A group of mostly Italian volunteers who fought in the XII International Brigade. The Battalion was named after Giuseppe Garibaldi (1807–1882), an Italian patriot and soldier of the Risorgimento (a nineteenth-century movement for Italian unification).

106.4 La Pasionara Battalion: A Battalion in the Spanish 66th Brigade.

106.5 Thaelmann: The Thaelmann Battalion was predominantly German, named after German communist leader Ernst Thälmann (1886–1944).

106.5–6 English and Franco-Belge Battalions: The English battalion was better known as the British Battalion though it was formally named the Saklatvala

Battalion after Shapurji Saklatvala (1874–1936), a communist member of Parliament in the United Kingdom. The Franco-Belge Battalion was officially known as the 6th February Battalion.

109.25 Tory: A nickname for a person affiliated with conservative politics or the Conservative Party of the United Kingdom.

109.34 Kipling: Joseph Rudyard Kipling (1865–1936). An English author of fiction and poetry who wrote *The Jungle Book* (1894).

110.8 no, gracias; no, por Brigada Internacionale: no, thank you; no, for the International Brigade [*trans. from Spanish*].

114.4 Schweine!: Pigs! [*trans. from German*].

116.2 Irish Company: A group of Irish volunteers, unhappy to serve in the British Battalion under former members of the British army, fought with the Lincoln Battalion.

118.7 blighty: Blighty is a slang word for a wound that is severe enough to warrant being sent home.

118.9 Malo?: Bad? [*trans. from Spanish*].

118.10 No, de nada: No, it's nothing [*trans. from Spanish*].

118.32 Perales: Perales de Tajuña is a village in the province and autonomous community of Madrid.

119.22 Tarancón: A small town located in the Cuenca province in the autonomous Community of Castilla-La Mancha in central Spain.

119.38 Listers: Troops who fought under he command of Enrique Lister. See note on Colonel Enrique Lister, above (5.6).

120.35 Qué pasa, muchacha?: What's wrong, little girl? [*trans. from Spanish*].

121.1 Pepita: A "pepita" is either a pip, kernel or seed; a nugget; or, the diminutive form of the female given name, Josefa or Josie [*trans. from Spanish*].

121.2 Mi perro: My dog [*trans. from Spanish*].

121.10 Sí, padre y madre muerte y Pepe también: Yes, father and mother died and Pepe too [*trans. from Spanish*].

122.5 Los Cuatro Generales: See note on *Los cuatro generales*, above (56.25–34).

122.16–17 One generation cometh, another passeth away, but the earth abideth for ever: Cf. Ecclesiastes 1:4: "One generation passeth away, and another generation cometh: but the earth abideth for ever" (KJV). Although the placement of "cometh" and "passeth away" in the present text varies from KJV, I have retained Bob's reversal. The KJV passage is reproduced as an epigraph on the title page of both editions and the epigraph of each edition uses "forever" instead of "for ever."

123.2 Madre mia, madre mia, madre mia: My mother, my mother, my mother [trans. from Spanish].

123.19 Sí, sí, chico, sí, sí, shh: Yes, yes, boy, yes, yes, shh [trans. from Spanish].

123.30 Don Juan: Don Juan refers to a fabled Spanish nobleman and lover who was first dramatized by Tirso de Molina, also known as Gabriel Téllez (1571?–1648), in his *El burlador de Sevilla y convidado de piedra* (*The Trickster of Seville and the Stone Guest* [trans. from Spanish]) in 1630. Don Juan has had many incarnations, and his invocation is usually suggestive of a rake, libertine or womanizer.

125.21 Mark Twain: Mark Twain was the pen name of Samuel Langhorne Clemens (1835–1910), an American writer. He is the author of *Adventures of Huckleberry Finn* (1884).

131.21 Ode to a Nightingale: See note on "Ode to a Nightingale," above (21.20–21).

132.28 "Song of the Evening Star," from Tannhäuser: *Tannhäuser und der Sängerkrieg auf Wartburg* (*Tannhäuser and the Singing Contest at Wartburg* [trans. from German]) is an opera by Richard Wagner (1813–1883) that was first performed in 1845. "O du mein holder Abendstern" ("Song of the Evening Star" [trans. from German]) is sung by Wolfram (baritone) and comprises the second scene of the third act.

PART IV

135.28 Alcalá de Henares: A town situated to the east of the city of Madrid, on the Henares River in the autonomous community of Madrid. Alcalá de Henares is the birthplace of Miguel de Cervantes (1547–1616), author of *Don Quixote* (1605).

137.3 POUM had attempted to overthrow the Popular Front government in Barcelona: The news accounts about what was happening in Barcelona were often contradictory. Indeed, the series of events that took place in Barcelona during May 1937 are perennially debated. Allan, a member of the Communist Party of Canada, makes his allegiance apparent.

Explanatory Notes   181

137.4–5 Asturian and Basque provinces: The Principality of Asturias is an autonomous community in the North of Spain. The term "Basque provinces" could refer to both the autonomous community of the Basque Country as well as the larger cultural region that spans the northern border between Spain and France. The "Basque provinces" is the site of the bombing of Guernica, the notorious massacre of civilians by the German Luftwaffe "Condor Legion" and the Italian Aviazione Legionaria. The massacre was memorialized by Pablo Picasso (1881–1973) with his painting *Guernica* (1937).

137.29 Albares: A town located in the Guadalajara province.

138.1 Jarama River Blues: Allan is most likely referring to the song that came to be known as "There's a Valley in Spain called Jarama" or simply known as "Jarama Valley," which was set to the tune of "Red River Valley." See note on "Red River Valley," below (138.2–3). The earliest known version of "Jarama Valley" was written by Alex McDade (1905–1937), a Scottish volunteer in the XV International Brigade. The song has been recorded by Woody Guthrie and Pete Seeger, among others.

138.2–3 Red River Valley: A common folk or country song that is thought to have originated in Canada or the northern United States in the late nineteenth century. The song has been recorded by Carl T. Sprague and Woody Guthrie, among others.

138.24 Star Spangled Banner: "The Star-Spangled Banner" became the national anthem of the United States of America in 1931. The music was written c.1760s by John Stafford Smith (1750–1836), a British composer. The lyrics come from a poem written in 1814 by Francis Scott Key (1779–1843).

138.28 Toledo: Both a city and a province in central Spain. The city is the capital of the autonomous community of Castilla-La Mancha.

141.11 July 5th: The 15th Brigade reached the Brunete front lines on 5 July 1937.

141.13 Brunete: A town west of the city of Madrid within the autonomous community of Madrid. It was also the site of the "Battle of Brunete" (approx. 6–26 July 1937).

141.14 Villanueva de la Cañada: A town just north of Brunete.

141.14 Quijorna: A town just northwest of Brunete.

142.6 Mosquito Ridge: A piece of high ground that was tactically important in the "Battle of Brunete."

151.12 Villanueva del Pardillo: A town just northeast of Villanueva de la Cañada.

152.4 general: Allan names the general as "General Walter" in his unpublished typescript, "That Day in Spain" (TAF, box 32, file 30). General Walter was the Polish Karol Świerczewski (1897–1947), a general in the service of the Soviet Union and Republican Spain.

153.1 El Escorial: A monastery and palace, built between 1563 and 1584, on a southeastern slope of the Sierra de Guadarrama, northwest of Madrid.

153.17 Caproni biplanes: Caproni was an Italian aircraft manufacturer. A biplane is an "aeroplane having two 'planes' or main supporting surfaces, one above the other" (OED). The model to which Allan makes reference is most likely the Caproni Ca.100 Caproncino. The Italian Air Force used it in the 1930s as its standard training aircraft.

156.16 Dónde está mujer! mujer! mujer!: Where is the woman! the woman! the woman! [*trans. from Spanish*].

156.36 Yo no sé: I do not know [*trans. from Spanish*].

160.34 Quinto: A town located in Aragón, between Madrid and Barcelona.

161.21 Hotchkiss: Hotchkiss refers to "certain firearms invented by [Benjamin] Hotchkiss or manufactured by the company he established, esp. a carriage-mounted cannon with a set of revolving barrels, and also machine-guns developed by his successors" (OED).

Textual Notes

These notes are divided into three sections: VARIANTS, EMENDATIONS and HYPHENATED LINE ENDINGS. The copy text for this critical edition and basis for the collation in these notes is the British edition (UK) of *This Time a Better Earth*, published in London by William Heinemann Ltd. in 1939. An American edition (AM) was published in the same year by William Morrow & Co. Each entry in the notes signals a page reference followed by a line reference; for example, "51.3" refers to page fifty-one, and the third line of text from the top of the page.

The VARIANTS section accounts for textual variations between the British and American editions. Each entry records the text of the British edition (UK) before the square bracket ( ]) and the text of the American edition (AM) after the square bracket. Three types of variants are so ubiquitous that they do not appear in the TEXTUAL NOTES. In the following instances the text of the UK edition has been maintained. (1) British spelling of the UK edition has been maintained throughout the current edition. For example: "ou" instead of "o" or "u" as in "colour" and "moustache"; "s" instead of "z" or "c" as in "dramatise" and "practising"; "ll" instead of "l" as in "travelled"; and, "re" instead of "er" as in "centre." (2) While the current edition maintains the UK edition's use of the Spanish spelling of "comandante," the AM edition uses the Portuguese "commandante." (3) The dated hyphenated forms of "to-morrow," and "to-day" and "to-night" have been retained from the UK edition without acknowledgement of their modernized form in the AM edition. Variations in diacritical marks (such as the acute accent, the grave accent, the circumflex and the tilde) have been noted in the first instance and left unstated in subsequent instances.

Because relatively few emendations were made to the copy text of the current edition, a separate list of EMENDATIONS follows the VARIANTS section. These EMENDATIONS represent the editor's own incursions into the text. The editorial incursions deal mostly with diacritical marks, spelling of words in languages other than the English language, and accidentals. In some cases these emendations also list variants between the UK and AM editions. Finally, a list of HYPHENATED LINE ENDINGS is provided to signal the lines in either the UK edition or the AM edition that end with hyphens and have no precedent within the texts to signal a change in hyphenation.

LIST OF VARIANTS
PART I

5.1–7 ital.] no ital.
7.20 bull-fights] bull fights
6.4 say:] say,
7.30 What] what
9.33 coal-miner] coal miner
9.39 Daddy] daddy
10.5 negro] Negro
10.5 stock-yard] stockyard
10.8 stock-yards] stockyards
10.9 south-west] southwest
10.23 himself,] himself
10.35 with:] with,
11.1 razor-blade] razor blade
11.2 for ever] forever
11.3 joke] joke,
12.8 man,] man
12.14 gas-masks,] gas-masks
12.24 ceiling,] ceiling
12.27 water-pipe] water pipe
12.27 grape-vine] grape vine
12.28 taps] faucets
13.18 windows,] windows
13.23 armpits] arm-pits
13.24 wash-rooms] washrooms
14.2 said:] said,
14.3 prize-fighters] prize fighters
14.13 taps] faucets
14.14 tap] faucet
14.20 boys] boy
14.25 washed,] washed
15.3 mess-hall] mess hall
15.16 ploughed] plowed
15.20 Harry,] Harry
16.16 Fascists] fascists
16.37 wash-rooms] washrooms
17.3 Jesus!] Jesus,

17.22 Only] Only,
17.29 circus-barker] circus barker
17.32 remember] remember,
18.11 left-turned] left turned
18.11 right-turned] right turned
18.21 for ever] forever
18.35 post-cards] postcards
18.36 writing-paper] writing paper
18.38 been,] been
19.4 post-cards] postcards
19.11 glue,] glue
19.11 half-way] half way
19.14 pipe-smoking] pipe smoking
19.20 poison-gas] poison gas
19.20 eau-de-Cologne] Eau de Cologne
19.37 situation, if] situation. If
19.37 away,] away
20.15 Sandbags] Sand-bags
20.17 Oh,] Oh
21.1 Canada,] Canada
21.1 home,] home
21.9 Rubáiyát] Rubaiyat
22.9 got] gotten
23.8 off-hand] offhand
23.14 off-hand] offhand
23.19 good-bye] goodbye
24.1 gone?] gone.
24.3 mess-hall] mess hall
24.10 cigarette-smoke] cigarette smoke
24.16 throat,] throat
25.2 till] until
25.15 inside,] inside
25.16 quality,] quality
25.17 *Ins Moor, ins Moor*] *Ins moor, ins moor*
25.19 noise,] noise
25.28 again,] again
27.19 calm,] calm
27.20 it,] it
27.28 *Il tracollo non è*] *Il traccolo non r*

186 This Time a Better Earth

28.4 still hissed in the pipe and trickled out of the taps,] pipe still hissed and trickled out of the faucets
28.8 anæmic] anemic
28.8 bugle-call] bugle call
28.9 taps] faucets
28.11 ploughed] plowed
28.20 half-mile] half mile
28.21 Suddenly,] Suddenly
28.25 Sí, sí] Si, si
28.29 times,] times
28.32 place,] place
29.12 negro] Negro
29.15 negro] Negro
29.18 negro] Negro
29.30 negro] Negro
30.13 mayor (*alcalde*) of] mayor, *alcalde*, of
30.23 roared] roared,
30.27 orange-blossoms] orange blossoms
30.31 blue,] blue
30.31 on to] onto
31.16 guns?] guns,
31.36 half-closed] half closed
31.39 train-wheels] train wheels
32.4 *nights,*] *nights*
32.9 *trenches,*] *trenches*
32.17 barrack,] barrack
32.27 Otherwise,] Otherwise
32.32 Qué] Que
33.19 Alan,] Alan
33.29 other's] others'
33.35 all,] all
33.35 Harry,] Harry
34.12 Battalion,] Battalion yesterday,
34.19 packet] package
34.23 packet] package
34.35 him,] him
35.20 here,] here
35.22 here,] here
35.27 Valencia,] Valencia

Textual Notes

36.1 market-square] market square
36.7 hair-cut] haircut
36.15 puttees,] puttees
36.17 puttees,] puttees
36.21 hair-cut] haircut
36.23 hair-cut] haircut
36.26 that,] that
36.35 brothel] whorehouse
36.35 government-inspected] government inspected
36.37 government-inspected] government inspected
37.3 brothels] whorehouses
37.4 been] gone
37.4 brothels] whorehouses
37.11 apartment-house] apartment house
37.18 of] to
37.19 brothel] whorehouse
37.20 María] Maria
37.34 barracks,] barracks
37.35 Fine, fine!] Fine, fine,
38.1 Spain,] Spain
38.1 role] rôle
38.14 duty,] duty
38.18 news-reel] newsreel
38.23 sent to] sent up to
38.29 truck-drivers] truck drivers
38.31 truck-drivers] truck drivers
38.37 'Moro!'] Moro!
38.37 faster,] faster
39.5 war!] war.
39.16 rest-home] rest home
39.20 hair,] hair
39.30 Troilus, methinks,] Troilus methinks
40.1 Oh,] Oh
40.7 air-raid] air raid
40.17 voice:] voice,
40.27 One! Two! Three! Four!] One. Two. Three. Four.
40.30 courtesy] kertesy
40.31 half-past] half past
40.33 up!] up,

41.14 then,] then
41.20 hurt!] hurt.
41.21 comfort-killing] comfort killing
41.21 Alan,] Alan
41.22 jaw-bones] jaw bones
41.34 said:] said,
41.35 said:] said,
42.1   clap-trap] clap clap
42.5   all's well,] all's well;
42.7   baby-carriage] baby carriage
42.13 sound] sounds
43.5   round] around
43.16 grey] gray
44.12 packet] package
44.12 round] around
44.12 packet] package
45.10 debris] débris
45.13 drunk] pissed
45.21 brothel] whorehouse
47.6   Ouch!] Ouch,
47.10 Oh,] Oh
47.15 Madrid,] Madrid
47.23 scratch,] scratch
48.7   help,] help
48.17 Twenty-one!] Twenty-one.
48.17 Twenty-one!] Twenty-one.
48.35 happen,] happen
49.14 To-morrow,] Tomorrow
49.34 me,] me
50.1   gone,] gone
50.10 bad,] bad
50.20 writing-pad] writing pad
50.32 good-bye] goodbye
51.6   talking,] talking
51.11 there,] there
51.21 lousy,] lousy
51.28 good,] good
51.31 and,] and
51.31 necessary,] necessary

52.8 casualty-list] casualty list
52.13 this,] this
52.19 market-square] market square
52.30 casualty-list] casualty list
52.32 Hell,] Hell
53.23 else,] else
53.36 got] gotten
54.7 sleep,] sleep
54.31 excitedly:] excitedly,
55.9 round] around
55.10 Ruso?] Rusio?
55.18 round] around
55.24 "No, gracias,"] no, gracias,
55.25 wine-pouch] wine pouch
55.30 bus-driver] bus driver
55.34 French,] French
55.35 folk-song] folk song
55.35 bus-driver] bus driver
55.36–37 bus-driver] bus driver
55.38 Olé!] Olé.
56.1 *bus-driver*] *bus driver*
56.6 *bus-driver*] *bus driver*
56.27 *mia,*] *mia*
56.30 *Moros,*] *moros,*
56.31 *Moros,*] *moros,*
56.32 *Moros,*] *moros,*
56.32 *mia,*] *mia*
56.33 *nadie,*] *nadie*
56.35 *Mira!*] *Mira.*
57.6 apartment-houses] apartment houses
57.7 Velásquez] Velasquez
57.8 good-bye] good bye
57.24 scarcity,] scarcity
57.28 change,] change
57.37 Hôtel] Hotel
58.4 long, long] long long
58.16 José] Jose
58.16 Gonzales,] Gonzales
58.25 But,] But

58.35 and,] and
58.35 anyhow,] anyhow
59.4   rot] crap
59.5   guts] crap
59.6   God!] God
59.7   God!] God,

PART II

61.8   city,] city
61.10 *estación*] *stacion*
61.11 wave-lengths] wave lengths
61.14 ear-phones] earphones
61.21 Sí,] Si
61.28 *obuses*—pardon] *obuses*, pardon
62.1   say,] say
62.1   señoritas,] señoritas
62.14 No,] No
62.18 News-boys] Newsboys
62.20 Mira!] Mira,
62.21 shell-holes] shell holes
62.23 it,] it
62.37 press-room] press room
63.21 here] there
63.28 casualty-lists] casualty lists
63.30 some] *some*
64.13 Hello,] Hello
64.13 Hello,] Hello
64.14 wave-length] wave length
64.15 p.m.] P.M.
64.15 p.m.] P.M.
64.23 packet] package
64.26 answer:] answer,
64.27 back:] back,
64.32 packet] package
64.36 profit,] profit
65.1   Everyone] every one
65.1–2 cigarettes,] cigarettes

Textual Notes 191

65.3 packet] package
65.4 reporters:] reporters,
65.7 press-room] press room
65.7 week-end] week end
65.25 walked from] walked in from
65.32 me:] me,
65.33 steam-roller] steam roller
66.2 press-room] press room
66.6 press-room] press room
66.16 mostly] mostly,
66.18 Mercédès] Mercedes
66.16 prostitute] whore
66.33–34 half-pound] half pound
66.36 He-he!] He-he,
67.10 pitch-dark] pitch dark
67.10 shell-holes] shell holes
67.25 Ah——] Ah—
67.27 me] me,
67.33 but] but,
67.36 *anything,*] *anything*
68.4 machine-gun fire] machine-gunfire
68.4–5 City,] City
68.6 night:] night,
68.14 bayonet-point] bayonet point
68.19 Por qué] Porque
68.20 round] around
68.20 bayonet-point] bayonet point
68.27 rifle-shot] rifle shot
68.31 Nacional,] Nacional
68.31 camarada,] camarada
68.34 block,] block
68.36 round] around
69.5 said] said,
69.14 ill,] ill
69.23 press-room] press room
69.28 some] *some*
69.34 press-room] press room
70.2 press-room] press room
70.2 asked,] asked

70.3 Press] press
70.7 peut-être] peut-etre
70.14 press-room] press room
70.39 her:] her,
71.14 kerb] curb
71.33 sure.] sure,
72.6 press-card] press card
72.14 ask,] ask
72.24 bona fide] bonafide
72.27 tap] faucet
72.28 Ice-cold] Ice cold
72.34 hotel——] hotel—
73.10 too——] too—
73.14 me,] me
74.2 shh!] shh,
74.3 So——] So—
74.5 God!] God,
74.7 another,] another
74.9 happen——] happen—
74.18 cheerful,] cheerful
74.22 whispered:] whispered,
74.36 Left-wing] left-wing
75.7 good-bye] goodbye
75.11 please?] please.
75.21 hotel,] hotel
75.39 night-pass] night pass
76.21 cheekbone] cheek bone
76.25 said:] said,
77.9 Good-bye] Goodbye
77.9 up,] up
77.17 dressing-gown] dressing gown
77.18 shouted:] shouted,
77.29 course,] course
78.4–32 *ital.*] no ital.
78.4 *Hello, Guys*] Hello guys
78.11 *much,*] much
78.14 *rotten*] crappy
78.15 *why,*] why
78.16 *business,*] business

Textual Notes 193

78.20 *arrive,*] arrive
78.32 *Bob.*] Bob
78.37 pedlar] peddler
79.1 the news-boys] newsboys
79.2 Victoria á] Victoria a
79.6 stop] stop,
79.9 her:] her,
79.8 said] said,
79.33 working-class] working class
79.34 crowded,] crowded
79.34 usual,] usual
79.37 sandbags] sand-bags
80.7 said] said,
80.16 pedlar] peddler
80.28 again,] again
80.29 street,] street
80.30 could,] could
80.35 whining:] whining,
80.37 came,] came
80.2 Sí,] Si
81.4 happened,] happened
81.5 whimpering:] whimpering
81.17 street-cleaners] street cleaners
81.24 press-room] press room
81.28 nerves!] nerves.
81.29 press-room] press room
82.1 casualty-list] casualty list
82.10 Cabinet] cabinet
82.24 over—] over,
82.25 Madrid,] Madrid
82.27 anywhere,] anywhere
82.20 last long] last very long
83.23 God!] God,
83.34 saying:] saying,
85.26 came,] came
85.30 too,] too
85.33 But——] But—
85.37 fruit-stores] fruit stores
85.38 archæologist] archaeologist

86.2   bus-boy] bus boy
86.5   vacuum-cleaners] vacuum cleaners
86.24   thing,] thing
87.2   salesman,] salesman
87.25   then,] then
87.29   photographer,] photographer
87.37   then:] then,
88.8   diarrhœa] diarrhea
88.9   diarrhœa] diarrhea
88.11   press-room] press room
88.18   English,] English
88.19   men,] men
89.3   Kindchen] kindchen
90.8   day,] day
90.27   me,] me
91.7   Alcalá] Alcala
91.19   negro] Negro
91.23   negro] Negro
92.5   kerb] curb
92.15   kerb] curb
92.31   coughed,] coughed
93.3   down-town] downtown
93.20   reporters,] reporters
93.22   open,] open
93.36   began:] began,
94.1   cannot,] cannot
94.16   But,] But
94.17   course,] course
94.23   galley-proof] galley proof
95.7   writing-pad] writing pad
95.11   packets] packages

PART III

97.4   smelly,] smelly
98.2   ammunition-truck] ammunition truck
98.10   light,] light
98.19   there,] there

Textual Notes 195

98.28 Alba,] Alba
99.14 Christ!] Christ,
99.35 morning,] morning
99.39 hilly,] hilly
100.20 weeks,] weeks
100.37 But,] But
101.6 sandbags] sand-bags
101.15 grape-vines] grape vines
101.21 sandbags] sand-bags
101.26 rifle-shot] rifle shot
101.27 pot-shots] pot shots
101.34 Ouch!] Ouch.
102.6 And,] And
102.7 calmer:] calmer—
102.14 Christ!] Christ,
151.17 sandbags] sand-bags
102.25 sandbags] sand-bags
102.31 Dickson,] Dickson
102.38 no-man's-land] No Man's Land
103.18 towel-rack] towel rack
104.1 skull:] skull,
104.9 'hero'] hero
104.9 'fool'] fool
104.11 die,] die
104.20 speech,] speech
104.22 on.] on,
104.30 Milty.] Milty,
104.33 laughed:] laughed,
105.2 years,] years
105.15 rifle-shot] rifle shot
105.24 Eddy] Edy
105.33 sign:] sign,
105.38 song——] song—
105.39 shell-hole] shell hole
106.3 Brigade:] Brigade.
106.7 understood,] understood
106.18 loud-speaker] loud speaker
107.20 there,] there
107.33 waist.] waist,

107.39 asked,] asked
108.18 out,] out
108.19 again,] again
108.20 dinner-suit] dinner suit
108.22 the——] the—
108.24 dinner-suit] dinner suit
108.27 half-grunted] half grunted
108.28 Christ!] Christ,
108.31 Lisa:] Lisa,
109.2   blankly.] blankly,
109.3   shouting:] shouting,
109.9   Oscar——] Oscar—
109.12 then:] then,
109.25 Imperialist,] Imperialist
109.27 interests,] interests
109.31–32 Majesty's Cavalry,] Majesty's Royal Cavalry
109.35 economy,] economy
109.36 finally] finally,
110.7   him,] him
110.8   said, 'no, gracias; no, por Brigada Internacionale,'] said no gracias no, por Brigada Internacionale,
110.12 nerves,] nerves
110.16–17 no-man's-land] No Man's Land
110.18 between,] between
110.25 it,] it
110.27 now,] now
110.27 work,] work
110.27 this,] this
110.28 appreciated?),] appreciated?)
110.31 no-man's-land] No Man's Land
110.32 spot,] spot
110.36 unfinished,] unfinished
111.1   "Not] Not
111.5   "Not] Not
111.9   "Not] Not
111.10 apart,] apart
111.11 day,] day
111.12 heart.] heart
111.14 from."] from.

111.15 then:] then,
111.14 suddenly,] suddenly
111.26 dress-suit,] dress suit
111.30 it] It
112.13 Later,] Later
112.21 said,] said
113.14 field-hospital] field hospital
113.15 half-way] half way
113.15 First-aid] First aid
113.21 "strays."] strays.
113.31 Get the] Get me the
114.31 Machine-gun fire] Machine-gunfire
114.38 stop,] stop
115.10 half-dozen] half dozen
115.19 crack-shots] crack shots
115.25 well built] well-built
115.28 then:] then,
115.28 Boys!] Boy!
115.33 How do you do] How-do-you-do
116.24 rifle-shot] rifle shot
117.9 time,] time
117.15 Well,] Well
117.15 Mickey—] Mickey,
117.15 Chicago—] Chicago,
117.35 good-bye] goodbye
117.39 school-teacher] school teacher
117.5 field-hospital] field hospital
117.10 No, de] No. De
117.25–26 on to] onto
118.26 highway,] highway
118.29 tyres] tires
118.31 mule-carts] mule carts
119.4 Kindchen] kindchin
119.5 you—] you,
119.17 bull-fighter,] bull-fighter
119.22 petrol] gas
119.22 Tarancón] Tarancon
119.29–30 sergeant!] sergeant.
119.31 Anarchist,] Anarchist

120.2 Sanché] Pedro
120.5 under-estimate] underestimate
120.6 fight,] fight
120.7 involved,] involved
120.9 Front,] Front
120.21 accelerated] stepped on the gas
120.21 round] around
120.21 shot:] shot,
120.24 petrol-station] gas station
120.28 station-house] station house
120.29 centimo,] centimo
120.30 crying,] crying
121.7 left,] left
121.10 también] tambien
121.14 dog,] dog
121.20 sun,] sun
121.26 half-listening] half listening
121.38 Maybe,] Maybe
122.11 fair,] fair
122.17 for ever] forever
122.19 us,] us
122.23 fighting,] fighting
122.28 Kindchen] kindchen
123.4 eyes,] eyes
123.11 opened,] opened
123.12 said:] said,
123.13 *indent* "Sí, sí, chico, sí, sí, shh."] "Si, si, chico, si, si ,shh."
123.31 thing,] thing
123.35 ago,] ago
124.7 said:] said,
124.12 answer,] answer
124.18 to-morrow—yes] tomorrow, yes
125.25 Well,] Well
125.35 I——] I—
125.38 We—they—captured] We—they captured
126.11 off-hand] offhand
126.19 no!] no.
126.32 half-way] half way
127.14 work,] work

Textual Notes 199

127.24 so,] so
127.26 soul,] soul
127.27 all,] all
127.28 all,] all
127.37 know,] know
128.12 Yes.] Yes?
128.25 Well――] Well―
129.1 orange-juice] orange juice
129.17 Christ!] Christ,
129.19 funny,] funny
129.29 doorway,] doorway
129.29–30 orange-juice] orange juice
129.30 round] around
129.31 good-bye] goodbye
130.2 accelerator] gas
130.17 fall,] fall
130.19 on:] on,
130.31 side,] side
130.32 blow-out!] blow-out.
130.33 side,] side
130.33 shaken,] shaken
130.36 tyre] tire
131.2 shrugging:] shrugging,
131.7 tyre] tire
132.4 others,] others
132.5 all,] all
132.18 trees,] trees
132.21 little way,] little away
132.25 shoulders,] shoulders
132.30 said,] said
133.20 fakes. Take] fakes. All supermen. All great ones with the women....Take

PART IV

135.9 Because,] Because
135.17 answered:] answered,
135.18 for ever] forever
135.19 unhappy,] unhappy

135.24 30th] 30th,
135.24 press-room] press room
136.29 nurse!] nurse.
137.8 press-room] press room
137.17 Cabinet,] cabinet
137.18 Premier,] premier
137.30 barracks,] barracks
137.32 us:] us.
137.34 chap,] chap
137.37 any more] anymore
137.11 *two.*] *two,*
138.23 war...] war....
138.26 press-room] press room
139.13–14 something,] something
139.19 friend,] friend
139.19 Wellington,] Wellington
139.18 government,] government
139.32 walked] went
139.34 press-room] press room
140.33 help,] help
141.3 myself,] myself
141.8 city,] city
142.3 good-bye] goodbye
142.25 dug-out. There was a barrel] dug-out. There was a blast of heat. *paragraph break* Four men we sitting in the dug-out. There was a barrel
142.26 rubber-tube] rubber tube
142.27 mouth] mouth,
142.35 lukewarm,] lukewarm
143.11–12 Hello, headquarters...hello, headquarters] Hello headquarters... hello headquarters
143.12 line...] line....
143.25 tired,] tired
144.19 said,] said
144.28 poor] poor,
145.24 *for ever*] *forever*
146.5 picnic!] picnic.
146.9 right,] right
146.17 good,] good
146.26 negro] Negro

146.32 there,] there
147.25 gully] gulley
147.25 water-pipe] water pipe
147.29 Say,] Say
147.38 Say,] Say
148.6   home,] home
148.28 Hey,] Hey
149.2   no-man's-land] No Man's Land
149.3   lines,] lines
149.9   window-shade] window shade
149.29 yesterday,] yesterday
150.6   bathing-suit] bathing suit
150.21 Kindchen] kindchen
150.23 eyes] eyes,
151.29 me:] me,
151.8   Brunete,] Brunete
151.34 stink,] stink
152.2   wheat-field] wheat field
152.15 dug-out,] dug-out
152.35 Who,] Who
153.5   lines,] lines
153.20 machine-gun fire] machine-gunfire
153.22 came,] came
153.24 some time] sometime
153.28 said:] said,
154.1   Monotonous,] Monotonous
154.7–8 machine-gun fire] machine-gunfire
154.17 *is*] is
154.29 one,] one
154.30 dry,] dry
154.35 rifle-shot] rifle shot
154.37 soldier,] soldier
155.4   *agua* (water)] *agua*, water
155.8   Cañada,] Cañada
155.10 arm-band] armband
155.16 meat-grinder] meat grinder
155.20–21 Clumsy-looking] Clumsy looking
155.22 Silly getting killed now after what we've been through.] "Silly getting killed now after what we've been through."

155.26 dressing-station] dressing station
155.29 dressing-station] dressing station
155.37 running-board] running board
156.36 sé] se
156.38 *Agua* (water).] *Agua.* Water.
157.3 dressing-station] dressing station
157.5 small,] small
157.8 ear,] ear
157.17 Cómo está] Como esta
158.16 a.m.] A.M.
158.34 Well,] Well
158.37 again,] again
159.21 dead,] dead
159.22 things,] things
159.30 Oh,] Oh
159.31 want——] want—
159.37 stretcher,] stretcher
160.2 cigarette-case] cigarette case
160.3-4 cigarette,] cigarette
160.5 body,] body
160.5 hell,] hell
160.7 over,] over
160.23 honeymoon,] honeymoon
160.30 Hell,] Hell
160.31 captain,] captain
161.9 Schwartz,] Schwartz
161.11 safety-lock] safety lock
161.12 tea-cups,] teacups
161.16 cartridge-belts] cartridge belts
161.22-23 manœuvera—manœuverability] maneuvera—maneuverability
161.23 on:] on,
161.29 First,] First

EMENDATIONS

3.2 34 and 35] 32 and 33 UK; 37 and 38 AM
3.4 164 and 165] 158 UK; and 188 AM
12.32 Pasarán] Pasaran UK; Pasaran AM

12.38 Pasarán] Pasaran UK; Pasaran AM
13.10 PASARÁN] PASARAN UK; PASARAN AM
16.1 tu,'"] tu'," UK; tu,'" AM
19.9 cigarette paper] cigarette-paper UK; cigarette paper AM
24.27 Pasarán] Pasaran UK; Pasaran AM
27.12 Pasarán] Pasaran UK; Pasaran AM
27.29 gedachten] dedachten UK; dedachten AM
27.30 Grundvold] Grunvold UK; Grunvold AM
31.34 accepted] acepted UK; accepted AM
38.36 Doug.] Doug." UK; Doug. AM
54.30 Pasarán] Pasaran UK; Pasaran AM
55.9 turned] tnrned, UK; turned AM
56.14 Dónde] Donde UK; Donde AM
61.21 Madrileños] Madrilenos UK; Madrilenos AM
62.1 yes.] yes, UK; yes. AM
62.26 Cómo está] Como esta UK; Como esta AM
63.1 Cómo está] Como esta UK; Como esta AM
64.26 cómo está] como esta UK; como esta AM
66.21 Buenos días] Buenas dias UK; Buenas dias AM
67.9 Puerta] Puerto UK; Puerto AM
68.19 qué] que UK; que AM
68.31 Dónde] Donde UK; Donde AM
75.9 harmless."] harmless.". UK; harmless." AM
81.28 to-day] today UK; today AM
90.32 mean] meant UK; mean AM
93.26 Madrileños] Madrilenos UK; Madrilenos AM
110.9–10 peasant."] peasant. UK; peasant." AM
111.12 image] innings UK; image AM [grammatically plausible but unlikely]
118.15 We] we UK; we AM
123.19 saying: "Sí, chico, sí, sí."] saying: Sí, chico, sí, sí." UK; saying, "Si, chico, si, si." AM
124.7 pasarán] pasaran UK; pasaran AM
124.8 some, 'goddamn,'] some, goddamn,' UK; some, 'goddamn' AM
128.37 please...] please.. UK; please... AM
141.11 July 5th] July 15th UK; July 5th AM
148.33 Pasarán] Pasaran UK; Pasaran AM
156.16 Dónde está] Donde esta UK; Donde esta AM
156.26 Dónde está] Donde esta UK; Donde esta AM

HYPHENATED LINE ENDINGS

11.19 non-intervention—UK, AM
14.34 cement-like—UK, AM
21.21 Lethe-wards—UK, AM
31.35 beau-coups—UK, AM
35.32 white-washed—UK, AM
36.11 window-pane—UK, AM
40.18 spot-lights—UK, AM
57.8–9 motherly-looking—UK, AM
65.38 north-west—UK, AM
66.25 blonde-streaked—UK, AM
80.21 taste-less—UK, AM
104.23–24 unseeing] unseeing UK; un-seeing AM
109.33 downfall] downfall UK; down-fall AM
120.25–26 under-nourished] under-nourished UK; undernourished AM

CANADIAN LITERATURE COLLECTION /
COLLECTION DE LITTÉRATURE CANADIENNE

Series Editor: Dean Irvine

The Canadian Literature Collection / Collection de littérature canadienne (CLC) is a series of nineteenth- to mid-twentieth-century literary texts produced in critical editions. All texts selected for the series were either out of print or previously unpublished. Each text appears in a print edition with a basic apparatus (critical introduction, explanatory notes, textual notes, and statement of editorial principles) together with an expanded web-based apparatus (which may include alternate versions, previous editions, correspondence, photographs, source materials, and other related texts by the author).

Previous titles in this collection

Patrick A. McCarthy (editor), Chris Ackerley (notes), and Vik Doyen (foreword), *In Ballast to the White Sea* by Malcolm Lowry, 2014

Ruth Panofsky (editor), *The Collected Poems of Miriam Waddington*, 2014

Michael A. Peterman (editor), *Flora Lyndsay; or, Passages in an Eventful Life* by Susanna Moodie, 2014

Vik Doyen (editor), Miguel Mota (introduction), and Chris Ackerley (notes), *Swinging the Maelstrom* by Malcolm Lowry, 2013

Alan Filewod (editor), *Eight Men Speak* by Oscar Ryan et al., 2013

Gregory Betts (editor), *The Wrong World—Selected Stories and Essays* by Bertram Brooker, 2009

Neil Querengesser and Jean Horton (editors), *Dry Water* by Robert J.C. Stead, 2008

Colin Hill (editor), *Waste Heritage* by Irene Baird, 2007